A Model Wife

Maggie Christensen

Cover and interior design: J D Smith Design
Editing: John Hudspith Editing Services

Dedication

As always, to Jim, my own soulmate

Also by Maggie Christensen

Oregon Coast Series
The Sand Dollar
The Dreamcatcher
Madeline House

Champagne for Breakfast

Sydney books
Band of Gold
Broken Threads
Isobel's Promise

Scottish books
The Good Sister
Isobel's Promise

Check out the last page of this book to see how to get
a free download of one of my books.

One

'Welcome to Sydney's Golden Couple!'

Amid tumultuous applause, the MC gestured to Celia and Bill to move forward.

Celia's face ached from the forced smile that had been there ever since she entered the room. She looked down at her immaculate white suit, the red silk shirt peeping out from the collar, the matching red high heels she wished she hadn't chosen to wear, and just wanted this whole damned thing to be over.

Tonight, the room at Sydney's Darling Harbour was filled with a mixture of Sydney glitterati and Bill's old football mates and supporters – people who'd come to celebrate the launch of his memoir: *Bill Ramsay – A Footy Legend*. Even the Premier of New South Wales was there, an unexpected tribute to the man she'd married over twenty-five years ago, the man she couldn't wait to be rid of.

When she'd agreed to be part of this media circus, Celia had known it wouldn't be easy, but nothing had prepared her for the upsurge of media interest. Bill Ramsay had been a force to be reckoned with during his long football career, and her own fame as a model had added to his reputation.

Over the years, both of their careers had faded into obscurity, and Bill had become a spent force, a bloated drunk and a bully who'd do anything to get his own way. The man she'd once loved and admired, had turned into someone she despised. But now, it seemed, Bill's star was again on the rise, and she was being caught up in his surge of popularity.

'Thank you, friends.'

Celia's eyes glazed over as Bill recounted his former exploits on the field. As if in a dream, she heard the raucous laughter as he retold one of his favourite tales of how he'd single-handedly won the shield for his team year after year, and the applause to his oft-repeated account of how he'd been lauded as the player of the year more than any other before or since.

She'd heard it all before – many times. And her pride in being there as his companion, then partner, then wife, had faded long ago along with any respect she'd had for him.

Celia was brought back to the present by Bill's grip tightening on her arm. She raised her eyes to see him nodding towards her.

'Now, my wife would like to say something.' His smile was almost a leer.

Celia flinched. This hadn't been part of the deal.

When she walked out almost two years earlier, tired of his bullying, she'd been a wreck. But, thanks to Bel, a good friend, and Bob, her solicitor, Celia was now part-owner of an upmarket boutique in the classy Sydney suburb of Mosman and was renting a beautiful apartment with views of Middle Harbour.

But her life had only changed for the better at a cost. The price of her new-found independence was now being exacted. At Bob's urging, and in return for a down payment of the divorce settlement, she'd agreed to be part of this promotion.

And, although she'd agreed to accompany Bill to these events, it had never been suggested she'd speak. *How could she? What could she say? How could she pretend to have any feelings left for the man who'd treated her so badly, for the man who'd disowned his two daughters – one because she formed a lesbian relationship, and the other who had the misfortune to become pregnant at seventeen?*

Celia looked out into the crowd. They were waiting for her to begin.

*

'Hello again.'

Celia looked up, puzzled, and met a pair of amused blue eyes. She took a gulp from the champagne glass someone had thrust into her hand as she stood on the edge of the crowd, trembling with relief. Unwilling to mingle with the throng who all seemed to want to congratulate Bill and be part of his new-found fame, Celia had been wondering how soon she could leave. The only people she knew here were Bill's friends. They were the last people she wanted to talk to, and she had no inclination to start a conversation with strangers and pretend she was still Bill's wife.

'I thought you did very well. You spoke off the cuff, but not from the heart, I think.'

How little he knew.

Celia racked her brains. The face was vaguely familiar, but she was sure she didn't know him. She'd have remembered this tall, broad-shouldered man in his forties, blond hair falling over his face in a way that made her want to push it back. *Where had that thought come from?*

'It must have been a couple of years ago. Marcus King. Ring a bell?' the man asked.

'Marcus?' Celia hesitated. 'Oh, Jan Turnbull's brother-in-law?' *Was he a friend of Marcus?*

Was it Celia's imagination, or did he take a step back at the sound of Jan's name?

'You're a friend of Jan's? That figures.'

What did he mean by that?

He was speaking again, 'You ran out on me last time,' he said, his eyes twinkling. 'I don't believe your husband was with you on that occasion. Bill Ramsay's wife? I should have known a classy lady like you would be spoken for. You were Celia Lang back in the day, weren't you? Before you became part of Bill's charade. Pity our paths didn't cross before…'

But Celia had had enough. It was bad enough she'd had to pretend to be the dutiful wife, she didn't need this charmer trying to chat her up. She was no twenty-year-old looking for an affair. She was forty-five with two grown-up daughters. She was a grandmother. She was trying to extricate herself from a marriage gone sour. The last thing she needed in her life right now was another man, even – or especially – one who looked like a Greek god.

With a tight smile, she handed him her now empty glass. She then turned on her heel and left, her heels making no noise, sinking into the soft carpet as she hurried along the corridor and down the wide staircase.

Once outside the Convention Centre, Celia walked towards the water and stood for a few moments, allowing the breeze to calm her down. She remembered him now. Johnno was his name. She'd managed to avoid him at the barbecue, leaving when she'd seen him heading her way. The shadow of a smile flickered on her lips as she recalled her initial impression of him – sex on a stick. And a charmer to boot. But he could take his charming self somewhere else. Celia tossed back her short blonde hair, letting it fall back into its habitual chin-length bob.

It was a beautiful Sydney evening. The moonlight shone on the water. Several dinner cruise ships were rocking on their berths as they awaited their passengers for the evening. Darling Harbour was bustling with tourists, and Celia began to feel part of the lively crowd. She suddenly felt hungry. She'd been too nervous to eat much for breakfast or lunch and had refused all of the canapes offered at the launch, while managing to drink two glasses of champagne in quick succession.

Noticing she was outside a Thai restaurant, Celia was drawn in by the spicy aromas. Once seated, with a view of the harbour, she took time to study the menu before deciding on a prawn salad dish with an accompaniment of green tea.

Celia began to relax. Until now, she hadn't realised how tense she had been ever since she awoke that morning. She thought back to the start of the day.

When her eyes flew open, she was almost blinded by the bright sunlight streaming in through the venetian drapes.

It was today!

After almost two years of living in limbo, today was the launch of her soon-to-be-ex-husband's memoir. She flinched at the thought of his face adorning the covers of piles of hardback copies of the book, which were, even now, being displayed in bookstores across the country.

She lay still for a moment, dreading the day ahead, then slid out of bed and headed for the shower. But, this morning, even a hot shower failed to bring its customary feeling of well-being and, as she dressed carefully, her hands shook. She was so edgy, it took much longer than usual to apply her make-up – to become the Celia who was ready to face the day. Throughout her modelling career, the other girls had always joked that she could beat them hands-down when it came to putting those final touches to her persona. Not today.

But the fiasco with Bill had begun, and it would soon be over. She'd pretend to be the model wife for a bit longer. She just had to try to maintain her courage and she'd get through it.

'Madam?'

Celia looked up to see a waiter gazing at her with concern, her meal and tea on a tray.

'Thanks,' she said, pulling herself together.

Two

It was almost eight o'clock by the time Celia was driving across the bridge, and she didn't feel like being on her own. Instead of heading for home, she turned off and made her way down the winding road towards the house where her two daughters lived along with Hannah's partner, Ingrid, and Celia's two grandchildren.

'It's only me,' Celia called, pushing open the front door of the Federation house. As soon as she walked in, a small figure wearing blue pyjamas featuring a large lion's head came rushing to greet her, almost knocking her over in his enthusiasm.

'Grandma!' little Simon yelled as she picked him up and enveloped him in a hug. 'I'm in my Larry the Lion PJ's and we're making chocolate brownies and Mia has chocolate all over her face.'

'So I see,' Celia laughed. 'And you're not doing too badly yourself.' She took out a tissue to wipe his mouth. 'Is there any chocolate left for the brownies?'

'Yes. Aunty Han has put them in to cook. Come and see.' He wriggled, slid down, grabbed Celia's hand and dragged her through the house into the kitchen where her older daughter was attempting to remove chocolate from the face and hands of the small red-haired child sitting in a high chair. The little girl gurgled and attempted to wave her arms in the air at the sight of Celia.

Hannah looked up at Celia's arrival, and blew her hair out of her eyes. 'Hi, Mum. How did it go? Let me just get this one cleaned up and I'll make some tea. Have you eaten?'

'Yes, I had a bite before I left Darling Harbour. I'll make it. I'm glad today's over, though it's just the beginning.' Celia grimaced as she filled the electric jug and took a couple of mugs from the cupboard. 'Juice for these two?'

'Water,' Hannah replied. 'They've had quite enough sugar today already.' She swiped the facecloth across the little girl's face and gave her a kiss. 'There, that'll do for now. The rest will have to wait for your bath.'

She joined Celia at the table. 'I'm a bit behind tonight. She's usually in the bath by now, but we started cooking and…' She raised her hands in the air.

Celia smiled. It was good to see Hannah like this. She'd played the role of a professional woman for many years before she and her partner had decided to have a child. Now Hannah, the child's mother, worked part time from home while Ingrid was the main breadwinner.

'Where are the others?'

'Ingrid's working late. And Chloe's out with a *friend*.' She paused as if to let her words sink in.

'Friend as in boyfriend?'

'Yes. She met this guy when she was in the park with Si. So he knows she has a child. They kept in touch, met up a few times and she's gone to a movie with him. He seems a decent sort.'

'Mmm.' Celia wasn't sure how she felt about this piece of news. She knew Chloe would find someone one day, but already?

'Now,' said Hannah, 'how was it really? Did Dad behave?'

Celia sighed and wrapped her hands around her mug. 'Your dad was as he always is – full of himself. And the audience loved him. I'm sure the book will do well. I suppose that's one thing to be grateful for. But he made me speak too. It was awful. I've never been good at speaking in public.'

'You're not regretting your agreement?'

'No, but…' Celia wasn't sure what she meant. She'd gone into this deal with her eyes open. When she left Bill almost two years earlier, she'd had nothing. She found a temporary job in an upmarket boutique, and the owner had offered her a place to stay for a time. Celia had been in limbo, but had felt free. For the first time in her life, she'd been able to make her own decisions. But she wasn't free, was she? Not until this travesty was all over. Then she could file for divorce and end the pretence.

When she'd decided to make the separation legal and pursue a divorce, Celia had met an impasse. Bill was going to write his memoir, and a bitter ex-wife wasn't part of his plan. With the help of a friendly solicitor, Celia had reached an agreement that she participate in all the media circus surrounding the book in return for a hefty payout. It was an offer she couldn't refuse.

And now she was caught up in fulfilling her part of the agreement. She wasn't looking forward to the next few weeks.

'So, he's had the launch. What's next?'

Celia took a gulp of the lemongrass and ginger tea before replying. She put down her mug and, tapping her fingers, enumerated the events. 'On Monday there's an interview on *Sunrise*, so I have to be at the Martin Place studio bright and early, then on Wednesday there's a radio interview with Kyle and Jackie O on *FM Breakfast*, then a tour of Sydney bookshops starting with Dymocks in the city. I'm glad I have Val to help in the shop or I don't know what I'd do.'

'Wow! So you get to meet Kochy and Sam *and* Kyle and Jackie?' she said, referring to the program hosts. 'That should be exciting. Will *you* be interviewed too?'

Celia recoiled. 'Oh, I hope not! They're not interested in me. I'm just there for window-dressing, or that's what your dad's publicist said. Today was a bit of a surprise. I'm just the wife, after all.'

'Don't put yourself down. You were Celia Lang – top model – long before you and Dad got together. You were on the covers of all the glossies. I've seen your scrapbook. Why shouldn't they be interested in you? I presume you're in the book?'

'That was all a long time ago – another lifetime. I suppose I'm in the book. I haven't read it.'

'Don't you want to?'

'No!' Celia spoke decisively. 'I lived through it – that was quite sufficient. And I'm sure he's glossed over his shortcomings and exaggerated his successes. Your dad's always been good at that. There were some good years in the beginning and when you two were little.' Her eyes took on a faraway look. Then she blinked as if to dismiss the memories. 'But he changed, I changed. And I'm grateful I came to my senses in time.'

'It was hard,' Hannah bit her lip, her eyes filling with tears. 'When he wouldn't… And now there's Mia.' She gazed fondly at her daughter.

'He's missing so much.' Celia's eyes moved from her granddaughter to little Simon, playing happily with a pile of Lego on a mat in the corner. 'I'm glad I stopped listening to him and started to have opinions of my own.'

When Hannah had revealed her flatmate was also her partner, Bill had ranted and raved to such an extent that the pair left Sydney for London where they'd remained for several years.

At that time, Celia had been so under Bill's thumb, she accepted his dictum to have nothing to do with her daughter, though it had hurt her dreadfully. But the crunch had come when Chloe revealed she was pregnant at seventeen, only weeks after her boyfriend, Simon, had been killed in a surfing accident. Celia was now ashamed that she'd stood by when he'd thrown Chloe out of the house.

Fortunately, Simon's mother had taken her in, and now Jan Turnbull was one of Celia's best friends. But it hadn't been easy. It had taken Simon's birth for Celia to ignore Bill's edict and to restore a relationship with her daughters, and another year or more for her to actually leave her bullying husband.

There was the sound of the front door opening, and a young woman with short brown curls and an open smile appeared in the doorway. 'Hello, Celia. Didn't expect to see you here tonight. Did the launch go well?'

'Hi Ingrid. I've just been telling Hannah about it. It all went well, thank you. But I should go.' She rose.

'Don't go on my account.'

'No, no. You guys have things to do, and I need to rest. It's been a long day.' Celia picked up her bag. 'Thanks for the tea and for listening, Han.'

Celia bent over to give Mia a kiss on the forehead and leant down to ruffle Si's hair. The little boy was so intent on the truck he was building that he barely noticed.

'Mum's on *Sunrise* on Monday,' Hannah told Ingrid as Celia straightened up. 'We'll record it, Mum. And we can all watch together. Why don't you come to dinner? We should be home.' She raised her eyebrows at Ingrid who nodded.

'I'm not sure it'll be worth watching,' Celia replied. 'But dinner sounds good. Thanks, girls.'

'I'll see you out.' Hannah handed Mia to her partner and followed Celia to the door.

'If it all gets too much, you can always refuse – say you've had enough,' Hannah said as she hugged her mum.

'It'll be fine. And it's not forever. I have to remember that. See you on Monday.'

But as Celia drove the short distance home, she wondered how she was going to survive the next few weeks; how she was going to manage to put on a brave face; how she was going to pretend to be Bill's loving wife. If today was anything to go by, he was going to make the most of her pretend devotion – milk it for all it was worth.

She couldn't wait for it all to be over, for the day she could file for divorce, for the time when she no longer needed to call herself Mrs Celia Ramsay.

*

John Henderson, known to his friends as Johnno, took a sip of malt whisky and flicked through the book on his coffee table, wondering why he'd bought it. He'd attended Bill Ramsay's book launch on a whim. Never much of a fan, he'd almost thrown the invitation in the garbage, but something had held him back and, as it was a lovely evening, he'd walked down to Darling Harbour and across the bridge to the Convention Centre.

It had been a pretty boring event. All the usual suspects were there – former footy players, figures from the entertainment and media industries, a few politicians including the current premier, and… Bill's wife. That's when it all became more interesting. Johnno recognised the former model as the woman he'd seen briefly at a barbecue a few years earlier. She'd sparked his interest then, but they hadn't had a chance to talk. He hadn't known then she was Bruiser Ramsay's wife, and she certainly hadn't seemed married.

What did he mean by that? Johnno took another sip of the tawny liquid, relishing the sharp tang on the back of his throat.

He gazed out through the wall of glass, reflecting on his unerring taste in purchasing this high-level apartment with its extensive views of Sydney Harbour. But, despite his love of this place, there was a niggle of something he didn't recognise. Was it discontent? What did he have to be discontented about? He had everything a young man-about-town could want. Maybe that was the problem. He wasn't as young as he used to be.

He rubbed his chin, leant his head against the back of the black leather sofa and gazed around the room, his eyes roaming over the corner bar, the wall-mounted widescreen television and the barely noticeable state-of-the-art sound system. Those items, along with the sofa on which he was sitting and the round glass-topped coffee table, were the only furnishings. It was a perfect bachelor pad, designed to deter any home-making aspirations held by the young women he brought back here on a regular basis – though that hadn't been happening quite as frequently in recent times.

Face it, Johnno, he told himself, your days as a playboy and player are numbered. The big five-o is looming closer. He sighed and walked over to the bar to refill his glass, before stepping out onto the balcony with its superb view. From here, he could look straight across to the Convention Centre where he'd attended the launch earlier in the evening, where…

Damn the woman! He couldn't get her out of his mind. He remembered her from her modelling days. She hadn't changed much – a little older, but still a svelte blonde elegant woman. She'd been way out of his league back then – beautiful and intelligent, and running with the elite. When he'd returned from a stint in the UK and started dating models, she'd vanished from the scene.

But Johnno didn't do married women. His one foray into the realm of married women had been a disaster – his one and only rejection, and it had hurt. No matter how much he'd tried to pretend indifference, it had hurt when Jan Turnbull ran out on him. And he'd vowed never again.

Since then, he'd stuck with airheads – young women who were grateful to be seen with him, to be taken to the expensive restaurants he liked to frequent, be noticed at big charity events, get their names in the society pages and mix with the high end of town. All without any need for commitment. They came and went with such regularity, Johnno was ashamed to admit he was sometimes hard-pressed to remember their names.

But recently, he'd noticed a hankering for something different – something more. He'd discovered he was mixing with a much younger crowd – men as well as women. All his old mates were married or in long-term relationships. Many had kids. That he could do without. It was enough he had a couple of nephews. His brother had done his bit in perpetuating the family name.

But, he thought, someone to come home to, someone non-judgemental, someone who loved him. He shrivelled inside as the L word invaded his consciousness. Love was something he'd eschewed, considering it led to what he'd always believed to be the equivalent of a prison sentence.

He thrust a hand through his hair. What was he thinking? More importantly, what had led his thoughts in this direction? His eyes fell again on the book on the coffee table, lying open at an old photograph of the Ramsay couple in their heyday – when they'd been called Sydney's Golden Couple. He'd been back in Brisbane that year and had missed all the hype. When he'd returned to Sydney a few years later, the social scene had changed, and they weren't in his orbit.

He peered at the photo again. The younger Celia, although blonde where the other was dark, bore a strong resemblance to Siri Lake, a model he'd known for years. She'd become too fond of him, and he'd run a mile. But maybe now...

Johnno picked up his phone.

Three

Johnno cursed as he pulled on his spandex shorts and snug-fitting short-sleeved top. He threw a sweater round his shoulders. It was cool now, but it would be warm once they were on the water. His head was pounding. The last thing he felt like doing this morning was rowing. But he couldn't let Marcus down. They'd been rowing on Middle Harbour every Sunday morning since his mate returned to Sydney.

The fact he'd drunk too much last night was his own fault – the malt whisky on top of the champagne had taken its toll. He had to admit he wasn't as young as he used to be, and these were the times it showed.

It was still dark when Johnno drove his yellow Saab across the Harbour Bridge, but as he reached Spit Bridge over Middle Harbour the sky began to lighten – a hint of the sunrise glowing pink and golden on the horizon. His mood began to lift. What the hell! He knew he'd enjoy it once he got there. There was nothing quite like the feeling of the scull scudding across the glassy water in the early morning light.

He'd been a fool to call Siri last night, only to hear her reluctant voice tell him she was married. Shit! Even Siri had been caught up in a conventional partnership. But what had he expected? That she'd always be available – ready to come running when he called?

He drove down into the car park, seeing Marcus climbing down from his grey four-wheel drive.

'Hi!' Marcus greeted him.

'On your own this morning?' Johnno asked, as the pair walked over to the boathouse and proceeded to carry out one of the double sculls.

'Yeah. Jon has a school thing, and Anna decided to finish some marking then drop him off. She'll join us for breakfast.'

'Right.' Johnno wasn't sure he could face breakfast.

'You look a bit under the weather, mate. Heavy night?' Marcus didn't wait for a reply, but continued, 'Time you slowed down. You're not getting any younger. Don't know how you keep up with all those young things. May be time to think of settling down – finding yourself a good woman.'

This was so close to Johnno's own thinking, he chose not to reply, but he did think it was a bit rich of Marcus to start handing out advice. His mate had played around for a few years himself when they'd both been younger. Then Marcus had married, gone off to the States, had a family, divorced and was now... happily married again.

'Like you?' he joked.

'There's not another like Anna. But, yes. There must be someone out there who'd take pity on an old guy like you.' Marcus was grinning as they lowered the scull into the water and climbed in, locking the oars in place.

'Ha!' replied Johnno, before the two set off, moving across the water in silence, all of their breath reserved for the task at hand.

It wasn't till they returned to the shore that Marcus took up the conversation again. 'So, who was it last night?'

'No one,' Johnno replied shortly. 'I managed to wipe myself out all by myself. But you may be right. I'm getting too old for this sort of thing. Maybe I *should* take a leaf out of your book. But who'd have me?'

Marcus was saved from replying by the arrival of two families, the teenage boys rushing into the boathouse despite warnings to go slowly from their parents.

'See you at the Echo,' Marcus called as he fired up his big beast, referring to Echo on the Marino which was their go-to restaurant every Sunday.

'I...' Johnno began, but it was too late. With a wave of his hand, Marcus was off, and it was left to Johnno to follow unless he wanted to get into a complicated explanation afterwards.

But he was beginning to experience some hunger pangs. The fresh air had done its usual good job of clearing his head and settling his stomach. The only challenge was the conversation Marcus had started.

*

Anna was already seated at a window table when the two men arrived at the restaurant.

'I ordered,' she said. 'The mushroom dish for me and the Big Breakfast for you two. Right? With lashings of coffee.'

'Good thinking.' Marcus said, rubbing his hands together and throwing a glance towards Johnno. 'A good fry-up will get you going – fix that hangover.'

'Mmm.' Johnno wasn't so sure, but the lashings of coffee sounded good.

'So, what have you been up to, Johnno?' Anna asked, once their coffees arrived.

Johnno took a long gulp of sustaining caffeine before replying. 'I went to a book launch last night.'

'Oh?' Anna raised her eyebrows. 'Whose?'

'An old footy player has written his memoir. Remember Bruiser Ramsay, Marcus? We played against him way back when…'

'Bruiser Ramsay? My God. Is he still around? I'd heard…'

'At the Convention Centre. He and his wife…'

'Wait a minute,' Anna interrupted. 'Are you talking about Bill Ramsay? The guy who played…'

'That's the one. Can't be two of them. He…'

'And his wife? Did you say his wife?'

They were interrupted by a waitress delivering breakfast and asking if they wanted more coffee.

'Please,' said Johnno, draining his cup. The others nodded.

Anna seemed to be thinking. She forked up a piece of mushroom and avocado before speaking. 'Celia. I've met her. Lovely lady. You have too, Marcus. She was at one of our barbecues. She's little Simon's other grandmother. She… she left him. I'm sure of that. But…' She paused as if trying to remember something. 'Got it!' She waved her fork in the air. 'There was some sort of agreement. I think Bob arranged it.'

Johnno was puzzled. *An agreement? And what did Anna's brother have to do with it?*

'I don't think...' Marcus said. 'It's not our business.'

'Oh, but it's interesting. Celia took Jan's place at that boutique in Mosman, then she bought into it when the owner moved overseas – Scotland, I think. From what Jan told me, she – Celia – had to make some sort of a deal that she'd show up for the book stuff in return for... something or other. Money, I expect. It's always about money, isn't it?'

Johnno saw her eyes dart across the table at the two men – Marcus seemingly as puzzled as he was.

'So,' he said, a jolt of something like excitement rushing through his body, 'they're not together?'

'No. Definitely not. Why?' Anna eyed him speculatively. 'Are you interested?'

Johnno felt his stomach lurch, whether from the thought of Celia or the plateful of saturated fats sitting in front of him, he wasn't sure. So, Celia Ramsay had left her husband and was appearing with him in public out of some misplaced sense of loyalty or for some agreed-upon recompense? Did that change anything? When he'd met Anna's sister, Jan, she'd left her husband too, and look what that had led to.

'Interested? Me? You must be joking. Hardly my scene,' Johnno said, before making a start on his breakfast.

Four

'How was it?' Val asked, as Celia pushed open the door at Isabella.

Before Celia could reply a customer walked in behind her, and she gratefully scurried through to the office at the back of the shop and turned on the electric jug.

What had she expected? She wasn't sure, but the interview at the *Sunrise* studios had exceeded anything she could have imagined. The interviewers were great – very professional and quite as wonderful as she'd anticipated. It had been a thrill to meet her heroes face-to-face.

But Bill! Celia pressed a fist to her mouth remembering his sycophantic ramblings, his hand on her knee, his clear insinuation that they were still *Sydney's Golden Couple*, and his leering grin when he thought the cameras were off him. She felt dirty – soiled – to have been part of his gloating presentation of himself as an aging hero who was still one of the beautiful people. Who was he kidding? Had he looked in a mirror recently? And to have him smirking about their *wonderful marriage* and *beautiful children*. She'd felt like throwing up or throwing something at him – impossible when he was gripping her hand so tightly she couldn't escape.

Celia was sipping a cup of camomile tea, hands wrapped around the cup, her eyes half-closed, when Val popped her head in.

'Sorry it took so long. She was one of those customers who couldn't make up her mind. She tried on half the shop, then walked out with nothing.' She paused, seeming to notice Celia's drawn face. 'Was it that bad?'

'No, not really.' Celia roused herself, put down the cup and pushed back a stray strand of hair. She should really get it cut, she thought. She'd had this style for what seemed like forever. 'Kochy and Sam were wonderful. It was magic to see them, to be in the same room with them. They're so warm and friendly – and professional. But…'

'Bill,' Val guessed.

Although her assistant had never met her husband, she was familiar with what Celia had suffered at his hands and had often made clear her opinion of the agreement Celia had made.

'Yes.' Celia sighed. 'Up to his usual tricks. He seems determined to portray us as a loving couple.'

'Wasn't that the deal?'

'I suppose so. But, when I agreed to be available for the publicity, I didn't expect to have to put up with the snide comments, the hand on my knee, the arm snaking around my shoulders, the kiss on the cheek. To think I once loved that guy.' She shivered. 'Now all I can see is a gross, bloated bully of a man, trying to relive his youth for the media circus his publicity agent has provided. At least this morning's over.'

'What's next?'

'The radio station on Thursday, then the tour of Sydney bookshops. Thank goodness Bob managed to get me out of the regional tour. I don't think I could have survived that. And there are fewer bookshops than there used to be. I used to regret that; right now, I'm glad.'

'Bob – he's your solicitor?'

'Yes.' Celia's face relaxed into a smile. 'And little Mia's dad. I told you about that, didn't I? He was the sperm donor for Han and Ingrid. Mia is Han's daughter and they're planning another child with Ingrid carrying the baby next time.'

'And the father?'

'Bob again. It means they're both related to Chloe's Simon, too.' Seeing Val's puzzled expression, she added, 'Bob's little Simon's…' she thought for a moment, 'great-uncle, I suppose. Si's dad was Bob's nephew. We're a bit of a weird mob, aren't we?' She laughed, then became more serious. 'The girls want to get married, but it seems the government won't debate a same-sex marriage bill. It looks like it's going to go to some sort of referendum, and Han's worried about all the vitriol that might unleash.'

'Surely not!'

'I hope you're right. They've been through enough with Bill's prejudice.'

'And he still hasn't recognised your granddaughter?'

'He hasn't met either of his grandchildren – considers them both to be bastards and beyond the pale.'

Val's lips tightened, and Celia was glad, not for the first time, that she'd decided to employ her as an assistant when she'd bought over the shop from Bel eighteen months earlier. It had been a bit of a gamble, taking on her formal modelling colleague. But she'd been heartened by the fact Bel had taken a gamble on her, and she'd taken to it like a duck to water. The same could be said for Val.

Unlike Celia, Val's marriage had been a happy one, ending only with the death of her daredevil husband in a seaplane accident when he was touring the Whitsundays. When they'd reconnected at a fashion show, soon after Bel returned to Scotland, Val was in despair and sorely needing something to occupy her. Isabella had proved to be the answer for her, just as it had been for Celia.

'You're sure you still want to do this?' Val asked, pouring herself a cup of tea with one eye on the shop door.

'No, not at all.' Celia was trembling. 'But I must. It's only because of the deal with Bill that I have all this.' She lifted her head and straightened her shoulders. 'Sorry I gave way for a moment. It won't happen again. I promise. Now, fill me in on what's been happening while I was gone.'

*

'Mum!' Hannah gave Celia a warm hug as soon as she entered the kitchen which was filled with the enticing aroma of a spicy curry. 'We're more organised tonight. Chloe came home early and bathed the kids. She's putting them down now, so if you want to see them awake you'd better hurry. I'll have a glass of wine waiting for you.'

Celia went into the bedroom where both of her grandchildren were lying in bed, and Chloe was reading from a well-worn copy of *Are You My Mother?* It had been a favourite with the girls and now, it seemed, was a favourite with the next generation.

Chloe stopped reading and glanced up at Celia.

'Hello, both of you,' Celia said, kissing the children on the forehead. 'Enjoying the story?'

'Mia has two mothers, and I only have one,' said Simon, as if bemoaning his fate. 'I don't have a daddy either.'

Chloe made a face at Celia. 'We were talking families in pre-school today. It became a bit awkward. Si told everyone his cousin had two mothers, and there was a bit of a fuss from one of the mums who was helping out.' She put a finger in the book to keep her place, rose, and hugged Celia. 'I can only see things getting worse as this debate continues. Some are even comparing children like Mia to the stolen generation.'

'What? That's ridiculous. There's no comparison. The Aboriginal children were taken away from their parents, whereas this little cherub is living with two loving parents.'

'I know. That's...' But Chloe was interrupted by her son grabbing for the book. 'Sorry, I'd better finish this. Catch up later.'

Celia walked slowly back through the house, devastated by Chloe's revelation. She knew Hannah and Ingrid had expected some degree of bitterness. But this! To take it out on the children! And in their pre-school! At least Mia was too young to be troubled by it. But Si would require some explanation. How could someone his tender age be expected to understand the bigotry of grown-ups?

She sighed. And it wasn't going to go away. The sooner the government made a decision the better. Hannah and Ingrid were a lovely couple. They had a relationship which engendered trust and respect – a better relationship than the one she'd had with Bill for all those years.

'What's wrong, Mum?' Hannah asked, handing Celia a large glass of red wine.

Celia took a gulp before replying, letting the smooth liquid linger for a moment on her tongue before sliding down her throat. 'Chloe...' She used her glass to gesture to the room she'd just left. 'Si...' Her voice broke.

'Oh, Chloe's told you about what happened at the pre-school today. Well, it was to be expected, though I wish Si hadn't been there to hear it. Hopefully, he didn't understand the slight. He's just feeling somewhat deprived that he only has Chloe. It's making her feel sad too, I guess. That may be why...' She buttoned her lip.

'Why?'

'It's for her to say. Now, Ingrid should be back soon, and we can eat.' Hannah turned away, ostensibly to check the stove, and Celia knew she wouldn't get any more out of her on the subject. She'd have to wait till her younger daughter appeared.

'What's this news I haven't been told, Chloe?' Celia asked, when they were all seated with steaming bowls of eggplant curry and all the accompaniments.

Chloe blushed.

Uh-oh, Celia thought. *This is something more than a cinema date with a guy she met in the park.*

She saw Chloe turn even redder and take a deep breath. 'I've met someone.' There was silence, as everyone stopped eating and seemed to be awaiting Celia's response.

When none came, Chloe continued, talking hurriedly. 'Owen. He's nice. You'd like him. He's very different from Simon. He's interning with a local IT company. He gets on well with little Si and...'

Celia tried to take all this in. 'And?' she asked, when Chloe stopped to draw breath.

'And he wants us to move in together.' Chloe picked up her glass and almost choked as she swallowed quickly.

Celia saw Hannah and Ingrid look at each other across the table. There was a deathly hush.

'I knew it would be like this.' Chloe's pretty mouth took on an unattractive pout. *Just like it had when she was Si's age.*

Celia knew this had to be handled carefully.

'It's a big step,' she said slowly after a long pause. 'Are you sure it's the right thing for you... and Si?'

'I haven't said yes,' Chloe said, becoming angry. 'But I'm considering it. It's going to become crowded here when these two – she nodded towards Hannah and Ingrid – have another baby.'

'But that's no reason...'

'You don't...'

Celia and Hannah spoke at once, then Ingrid said in a calm voice, 'It's okay, Chloe. No one's upset with you. And you must do what's best for you and your little one. We only have your good at heart and don't want you to make a mistake. You haven't known Owen very long, and we've barely met him. Your mum didn't know anything about him till now. You must understand it's a shock.'

'And we're in no rush to have our next one.' Hannah reached over to take Ingrid's hand. 'Ideally, we'd like to be married first, but if that's not to be… Anyway, it takes nine months to cook a baby. You should know that. And a lot can happen in nine months. There's no need to rush into something that…'

'I knew you'd all be like this!' Chloe snapped.

'Calm down, Chloe,' Celia said, stretching an arm around her daughter's shoulder, and feeling her tremble. 'Your news has come as a bit of a surprise, that's all. Han and Ingrid knew about this Owen, but I hadn't heard of him till now. How long have you known him?'

Chloe turned to her mother, her eyes beginning to fill with tears. 'We've been seeing each other for six months, but I knew Owen before that. He was two years above us at school. Our paths never crossed there. He was one of what we called the nerdy ones.' She gave a small watery smile. 'But he's not really like that. He's kind and gentle and… he loves me and Si.'

Celia began to understand. Chloe had put on a brave face despite all that had happened to her – her father's disapproval, her early pregnancy, becoming a single mother, giving up her uni place. She'd seemed to cope amazingly well, choosing to study online for a Certificate in Childcare and finding a job at the same pre-school Si was enrolled in. She was planning to continue her studies and complete the degree she'd intended to do when she left school. What would happen to those plans now?

'I'd love to meet him,' Celia forced a smile. 'Maybe a Sunday lunch?'

Chloe appeared mollified. 'Okay,' she said mulishly. 'I'll ask him, but no interrogating him, right?'

'Of course not.'

The rest of the meal passed without further dispute. As soon as it was over, the girls cleared the table and stacked the dishwasher.

'Now,' Hannah said, 'we can watch the TV star.'

The four women settled themselves in the living room, Celia sitting between Hannah and Chloe, while Ingrid dropped to the floor, resting her back against Hannah's legs. 'Ready?' she asked, her finger poised to turn on the recording.

'Can't wait,' Hannah said.

'Didn't you watch it live?' Celia asked.

'What? With Mia? You must be joking. I wanted to share it with all of you anyway.'

Ingrid pressed *play* and the programme began. Celia and Bill's spot was towards the end of the morning show, so she fast-forwarded until Chloe called, 'Stop!'

Celia watched half-amused, half-embarrassed. There she was sitting beside Bill, a smile on her face and looking for all the world as if she was thrilled to be there.

'You look great, Mum.' Hannah squeezed her arm. 'But look at Dad. My God, he's gone to seed. He looks...'

'Shh.' Chloe put a finger to her lips. 'I want to hear.'

The program continued, Celia cringing once again as she listened to Bill's bluff responses and exaggerated reminiscences, seeing herself as others would – a glamourous empty-headed former model. Was that how she appeared to the world? She began to shudder just as the interview came to an end and the credits started to roll.

'Are you okay, Mum?' Hannah asked. 'You're shivering.'

'Fine. How do I seem to you? I mean, on the program. How do I come across?'

'As our mum,' Chloe said with a frown.

'No, to...' How could she explain?

'I know what you mean.' Ingrid twisted round to look at Celia. 'You want to know how it would look to a stranger.' She thought for a moment. 'You look very elegant. But then, you always do. You look... distant – as if you're there, but not there – if you know what I mean. Your body is there but your mind is far away.'

'That's about right.' Celia laughed.

'But, Dad!' Hannah almost exploded. 'What planet is he on? He's acting as if...'

'He's God's gift to women,' Chloe concluded. 'Really, Mum. How could you bear it?'

Celia felt her cheeks burn as both her daughters regarded her with alarm – and they hadn't been able to see Bill's hand on her knee. It was Ingrid who came to her rescue.

'Your mum is doing what she has to. It'll be over soon, then she can get on with her life – we can all get on with our lives.'

Celia threw her a grateful glance, then the full import of Ingrid's words hit home.

'Your lives? You mean…?'

'People know who we are,' Chloe said gently. 'Owen asked about Dad when the book was first advertised. And,' she picked on an invisible thread on her jeans, 'the other staff at the pre-school were talking about it today. It seems he was pretty well-known. They wanted to know if I was going to cash in on his new-found fame.'

'How…?'

'*Daughters of famous footy star speak up. My life as Bill Ramsay's daughter.* Can't you see the headlines? *The Woman's Weekly* or *New Idea* would lap it up. Hell, you could give an interview too – *Married to a Footy Legend.* Wouldn't Dad just love it?' Chloe sniggered.

'Don't.' Hannah began to laugh too, sobering up at Celia's horrified expression.

'Only joking. We don't mean it, Mum. But, you have to admit, it would deflate his ego to reveal the real story.'

'It's not something to joke about. I have no intention of staying in the limelight any longer than necessary. And I guess I should go home and let you guys get to bed.'

They all rose and accompanied Celia to the door, promising to listen to the radio interview on Thursday, despite Celia's protestations that she wouldn't be saying anything.

As she drove home, Celia reflected on the girls' reactions to the media attention, then her mind moved to Chloe. Had she been too harsh on her daughter? Simon had been dead for almost four years. She had every right to move on with her life. But it was the secrecy that rankled. *Were her daughters beginning to see her as an irrelevance? Were they trying to protect her? From what?* She sighed as she drove into the underground car park and took the lift up to her third-floor unit. Once there, she could close the door on the world and enjoy her own private space.

Five

Celia shrugged off Bill's arm as they walked out of the radio station in North Ryde. She pressed the control to unlock her car, thankful the interview was over. The hosts had been great, and it had been interesting to see the inside of a radio studio, but Bill's continual presence and his inevitable closeness had been difficult to tolerate. She'd managed to avoid participating in the interview by a judicious shake of the head when Kyle glanced towards her with raised eyebrows, but hadn't been able to avoid Bill's hand reaching towards her.

Now it was over, and Celia could feel a few drops of rain falling. She looked up into a grey sky. There was a storm brewing, and she wanted to get down the highway and back to the shop before it struck.

'How about some breakfast? We had an early start.'

Celia cringed. There was no *we*. She had no idea what sort of early start Bill had. She'd risen at the same time as always and performed her customary yoga poses. She'd eaten a healthy breakfast of muesli and yoghurt and enjoyed her first coffee of the day on the balcony with its northerly aspect and peaceful distant views of Middle Harbour.

All of this had helped promote the calm mindset that had helped Celia make it through the morning. She'd been managing reasonably well till the door closed behind them, and Bill's arm tried to snake around her shoulders.

'I need to go.' Celia started to walk away, only to be pulled back towards Bill.

'Don't be like that, sweetie. You can surely take a bit longer. There's

GG Espresso just up the road. We can at least get a coffee there. These interviews give me an appetite. Couldn't eat much for breakfast.'

Celia gazed at him in amazement. Did he really think she'd be prepared to sit down for coffee with him – after all they'd been through? And what was all that about not eating breakfast? She'd never known Bill to leave home without eating a large breakfast. But she'd been preparing it for him, she reminded herself. Was he letting things slide, now he was on his own, or could he be suffering from nerves about these interviews? Surely not!

'Sorry, you'll have to go there on your own. I need to…' Celia managed to extricate herself and reached the car just as the rain began to fall in earnest.

Just two more weeks, she told herself as the car sped down Epping Road, the windscreen wipers moving back and forth in time to her thoughts.

'Busy morning?' Celia shook the water from her umbrella as she hurried through the shop to the back office.

'So-so. I expect the rain will keep everyone home now. We can get on with sorting the new range. I started pricing them. There are some lovely pieces. I'll have to keep a grip on myself or my wages will be spent before pay day.'

'Thanks. Be with you in a jiffy.' Celia dropped her umbrella into the waste basket, her bag to the floor and checked herself in the mirror before joining Val in the store. Lucky Val! Unlike Celia, her assistant wasn't short of cash and could easily afford to kit herself out with new outfits each season. Maybe once this circus was over, once she could finally divorce Bill, then she'd feel she had enough to be able to relax and spend money without worrying about how she'd pay the next bill.

The deal with Bill had provided her with enough to buy into Isabella and pay for the deposit on her unit, but that was all, and money was still tight.

Celia gave a tight-lipped smile at the woman in the mirror, patted her hair into place and went to join Val.

The two women had just finished with the last garment and were about to make some tea when the door opened, and a large woman breezed in carrying a dripping umbrella.

'Heather, how lovely to see you,' Celia smiled as she greeted the woman who had become a valued friend. She'd been a customer of Isabella long before Celia's time and proved a loyal and trusted friend to the previous owner. 'Have you come to check out the new range or to join us in a cup of tea?'

But Heather didn't return Celia's smile.

'Have you seen today's paper?'

'Not today's. No.'

Celia had been avoiding the newspapers, reluctant to see their reports of Bill's book launch and her own presence at his side.

'Can I talk with you privately, Celia?' Heather propped her umbrella in a corner.

Surprised, Celia excused herself to Val and led the older woman into the back shop where she filled and switched on the electric jug.

'Sit down, Heather,' she said to the woman who was still standing in the middle of the small room. 'What's the matter?' she asked, noting the pallor on Heather's face. 'Are you feeling okay? Are you sick again?' She was aware the other woman suffered from emphysema and worried she might be experiencing a relapse, after an unexpected, but welcome, remission.

'No, it's not me. It's...' Heather sat down and took a folded newspaper from her capacious bag. 'It's your...' She coughed. 'It's Bill Ramsay. On the front page.'

'The book, you mean? I'm trying not to see all that. I think you know I agreed to be part of it on sufferance, but I don't need it being thrust in my face.' Celia busied herself with preparing three mugs and opening a box of teabags. 'You like peppermint, don't you?'

Heather didn't reply but began to open out the paper. 'You should see this. It's not about the book, though I suppose it's all the attendant publicity that prompted it.'

Curious, Celia took the paper and, with a startled glance at Heather, read the headline.

Model Accuses Footy Hero

She gasped and squeezed her eyes shut. But, when she opened them again, it was still there. Her eyes skimmed down the page seeing the photos of Bill and Eva Barton who'd been one of the most photographed models back when she and Bill were in the limelight – just after Celia had retired from her own modelling career.

Celia tossed the paper down on the desk. She couldn't bear to read it. She'd known about Bill's infidelities, put up with them. She'd been aware of the string of models, friends, wives of friends, mothers of their children's friends, he'd pursued over the years. She'd managed to ignore them, hold her head high, remain his wife. And, as the years went on and he was no longer the handsome, popular darling of the media, they'd seemed to drift away.

But all of these instances – the ones she'd been aware of – had been consensual. He'd been an attractive man, charming. *She'd* fallen for him. But this! Celia picked up the paper again, scanned the article and threw it down. This was an allegation of sexual abuse – of non-consensual sexual advances. Surely Bill hadn't needed to, had been more circumspect, more respectful, more sensitive than to…? Her stomach clenched. She felt sick. She sat down with a thump and covered her face with her hands.

'I thought you should know,' Heather said gently. 'The media… they may come wanting a statement.'

Celia looked up, her eyes widening with fear. Was there no end to the agony this man was to put her through?

Her phone rang. She checked the number, then, with a 'Sorry' to Heather, pressed to accept the call.

'Bob!'

'You've seen it?' The break in her voice must have given her away.

'Just now.' Celia's heart was racing. 'What does it mean, Bob?'

'I'm not sure at this stage. They must be pretty sure of their facts to publish. Was there any indication?'

'No!' Celia shook her head, even though she knew Bob couldn't see her. 'He always had one woman or another on the side. I knew that. But they were glad to be there, to be seen with the big man he was back then.' She paused, remembering the humiliation she'd experienced for years, the snide comments, the veiled looks. No more!

'The media? Do you think they'll…?'

'Come after you? It's a possibility. As far as they're concerned you're still his wife – being seen together at the launch, on *Sunrise* and…' Bob hesitated. 'The book signings are next week, aren't they?'

'Yes. Do I still need to be there? I did agree.' Celia felt her stomach roil at the thought of being part of the media frenzy the article was bound to provoke. She didn't think she could face it. It had been bad enough before, but this was something else altogether.

There was silence at the other end of the phone. Celia moved her mobile from one hand to the other. Heather gestured to the door and half-rose, but Celia shook her head just as Bob began to speak again.

'Let me talk with Bill's solicitor. See his take on it. It may all blow over.'

Blow over? A front page story? Bruiser Ramsay guilty of sexual assault? Not likely. But Celia bit her tongue and listened.

'The first signing at Dymocks, George Street isn't till next Wednesday, is it?' Celia heard Bob tapping on his computer. 'Then there are a few more later in the week and the week after. Best we try to get you out of those, I think.'

Celia let out the breath she'd been holding. 'I don't really need to be there. It was just for window dressing, his publicist said. To show solidarity.' But even as she spoke, Celia realised her presence might be needed even more now. She thought of pictures of Members of Parliament standing on their doorsteps, wives loyally beside them, as they refuted rumours of misconduct. She couldn't be expected to do that, could she?

Bob was speaking again. 'Right. I probably need to speak with her too. Maybe we can manufacture a sudden illness,' he chuckled. 'Don't worry, I'll see what I can do and get back to you as soon as I can. Meantime...'

'I keep a low profile and hope the paparazzi don't find me?'

'You've got it.'

'But if they do find me?'

'Then it's a simple *no comment* from you.'

Celia finished the call and sat frozen, her eyes glazed over. It wouldn't be hard to manufacture the sudden illness Bob suggested. She felt sick, as if she was about to throw up.

'Are you okay? I couldn't help overhearing. That was your solicitor?'

Celia drew herself together. 'Bob. Yes.' She drew her hand through her hair. 'He's going to talk with Julian – Bill's solicitor – and best mate.' She grimaced. 'He'd know all about Bill's peccadillos. Would have, for years. The pair were inseparable. I wouldn't be surprised if... No, I shouldn't malign the man, but I never liked him. Nor he me.

He and Bill go way back. Sorry, Heather, I'm ranting on here. Let me make that tea I promised you.'

'Don't worry about that. You have enough on your plate. I'll be off. I just thought I should draw your attention…'

'Thanks, I'm glad you did. It's a surprise. I never thought Bill… Well,' she tried to smile, 'at least it may have got me out of a round of bookshop visits I wasn't looking forward to. You did the right thing, Heather. Thank you.'

'And if there's anything I can do to help. You know you only have to ask.' Heather picked up her bag, and gave Celia a hug.

'Thanks,' Celia said again and, as the office door closed behind Heather, she poured the now boiling water over the teabag in one of the mugs. Wrapping both hands around it, she took small sips of the warm, soothing liquid as she tried to pull her thoughts together, to reconcile the allegation in the paper with the man she knew.

'I thought we'd lost you,' Val said when Celia finally emerged, her face pale, but sporting a fresh application of her signature red lipstick, the one she'd worn for years and which usually lifted her spirits. Not this time. 'What did Heather want?'

'She had something to show me. I'll tell you later,' she added, as the door opened, and a couple of middle-aged women breezed in, followed by an older trio chattering ten to the dozen.

'Lunch?' Val asked with a sigh, when the shop was finally empty again. 'Want me to dash out for sandwiches? There's a break in the rain.'

'Would you? I don't think I have the energy.'

While Val was gone, Celia couldn't get the newspaper headline out of her head. The photos of Bill and the model were spinning around behind her eyes, threatening to make her dizzy. But alongside all the angst there was a certain degree of curiosity. Keeping one eye on the door to check for the arrival of any customers, she went back to retrieve the paper and started to read the article more carefully than before.

When finished, she tossed the paper back into the bin. Despite the offending headline and the almost life-sized photos, there was little substance. All that appeared to be alleged was that at some unstipulated time, Bill had made some unspecified unwelcome advances to the model in question. Celia sighed with something she recognised as relief. Not outright sexual assault, not rape. Advances, she could believe. She had this morning's example to prove it. But did that count as an assault?

She shook her head in disbelief.

At that point, Val returned. 'Ham and pickle on rye or tandoori chicken wrap? I got a couple of bottles of apple and mango juice too.' She held up a carrier bag.

'Ham and pickle sounds good. Thanks, Val. What would I do without you?'

'And what would I do without Isabella? I'd be mouldering away in that big house on the water wondering if I should top myself now or later.' She laughed. 'No, but really. You saved my life. When David was killed, I felt my life had come to an end. This place has given me a reason to get up in the morning.'

Celia felt a warm glow at her words. It almost took away the distress the article had engendered, almost, but not quite.

'Now, can you tell me what's wrong?' Val asked.

The women had finished their lunch and were enjoying a respite from customers to drink a cup of herbal tea together.

'Heather...' Celia began.

'What did she have to say? You looked like death warmed up when she left. You still don't look great.'

'Thanks!' Celia had tried to get back to normal but knew the stress she was feeling must show on her face. 'Heather brought in a copy of today's paper.' She picked the crumpled paper out of the bin and handed it to Val. 'See for yourself.'

Celia sipped her green tea with peppermint – guaranteed to sooth anxiety – while Val read the article.

Finally, her eyes rose to meet Celia's. 'Hell's bells. What does this mean for you? You're still in the midst of all the book publicity, aren't you?'

'I've spoken to Bob – my solicitor. He seems to think I may be able to get out of the book signings. That would be a relief. Bill's been... a bit too friendly, you might say. He wanted us to have breakfast together this morning. That's why I may have seemed a bit strung-out when I got in. He was acting as if this image of the perfect marriage we're conveying to the media is real, that I am the model wife I'm pretending to be. It was scary.'

Celia shivered at the memory of Bill's arm around her shoulders, his hand on her knee during the television programme, and thought she had some idea to what the model had been referring.

'Wow! You poor dear. No wonder you couldn't speak. Then to see this right after.' She folded the paper then dropped it back in the bin. 'What you need is a drink – something stronger than this tea.'

'Not at this time of day.' Celia managed a grin. 'But I'll have one tonight when I get home. Damn! I promised to see the girls again tonight; to let them know how it went this morning. They may have seen the paper too. Hopefully, they won't get involved in all this.'

*

It was still raining when Celia locked Isabella up for the night. The sky was dark, and a strong southerly wind had blown up, sending sheets of water against her legs as she made her way to the car. Once inside, she took a deep breath. Much as she loved her girls, tonight, all she wanted to do was go home, soak in a hot bath with a glass of wine, then go to bed and sleep for a week.

By the time she pulled up outside her daughters' home, however, Celia was feeling more sociable.

A pale-faced Hannah greeted her at the door and drew her into a warm hug. 'Oh, Mum! How do you feel? Have you seen it?'

So Hannah knew.

'Bob's here,' Hannah said by way of explanation. 'He was passing on his way to dinner with Chris at the Yacht Club and dropped in to see Mia. He told us.'

Bob. Of course! Since he'd fathered Hannah and Ingrid's daughter, he and his partner, Chris, had been frequent visitors at the Cremorne home. But, till now, his visits hadn't coincided with Celia's.

'How are you, Celia?' Bob rose as Celia entered the kitchen. He shook her hand and put his other hand on her shoulder. 'It must be tough for you.'

Tough didn't begin to describe it.

'I haven't heard back yet,' he said quietly so only she could hear. 'Should know something tomorrow.'

'Thanks.'

'Wine, Mum?'

'Thanks, and how's my favourite grandson?' Celia said to Simon who came running to clasp her around the knees. *They mustn't become embroiled in this.* She picked him up, giving him a hug and a kiss, before he slid down again.

Hannah handed her a glass of red wine. 'Bet you need this.'

'I certainly do.' Celia took a gulp. 'Bob told you everything?'

'And Ingrid brought home a copy of the paper. Don't know where they dug out that photo. He looks almost presentable,' she said, referring to the photo the paper had chosen to grace their front page.

'Your dad was a good-looking man, charming too. That pic was taken years ago, when he was playing for New South Wales. He was a fine figure of a man in those days.'

'Hmm.' Hannah didn't appear to be so sure.

'You don't remember what he was like then, before…'

'*I* remember when we all went to Noosa on holiday,' Chloe broke in. 'He was a lot of fun.'

'You were only about six,' Hannah said. 'What could you possibly remember? That was a lifetime ago.'

Celia said nothing. She agreed with Hannah. It had been another lifetime – before she'd realised how much she was under Bill's thumb, how much he bullied her. But they *had* been good years when the children were young, before it had all gone wrong.

'Bedtime,' Chloe announced. 'Let's get this show on the road. Time to say goodnight, Si.' She picked up the little boy and, after a round of hugs and kisses, carried him to the bedroom.

'I should be going, too,' Bob said handing back Mia who had climbed up to sit on his lap. 'Chris has a table booked.'

When he had left, and the children had been put to bed, Hannah filled up their glasses. The table was set for three, the little ones having already eaten, but Celia didn't feel at all hungry.

'You must eat something,' Hannah exhorted. 'You'll really like this new recipe. It's a Jamie Oliver sweet potato and chick pea korma I'm trying out. You can't leave now, Mum,' she said, as Celia picked up her bag.

Celia gave in to her entreaties and discovered she did have an appetite and the curry was delicious, served on a cauliflower base instead of rice.

But, as soon as they finished eating, Hannah wanted to return to discuss her dad and how they could prevent his drama spilling over into their lives.

'We have enough to cope with right now,' Hannah said. 'There was more news today. It looks like the government are going to let everyone vote on the same-sex marriage issue. It seems our future is going to be a matter for public debate.'

She grasped Ingrid's hand tightly, and Celia was aware of a tension in the room which had nothing to do with Bill, the allegation, or his damn book. It was as if the pair had retreated into a private place which neither she nor Chloe could penetrate.

Six

Johnno swung through Wynyard station on his way to the office. His mind was on how to best present his new proposal to the group of potential investors – he'd discovered a perfect location for the new industrial town they had in mind.

He almost missed the headline on the sign outside the newsagency. It caught the corner of his eye as he hurried past, and something made him stop and retrace his steps. There, staring up at him, was a picture of Bill Ramsay and his wife arriving at the book launch he'd attended. Nothing odd about that. He scanned the headline that had caught his eye – Accused Legend and his Model Wife. *Accused? Accused of what?*

The Daily wasn't a paper Johnno normally bought. He read online most days, preferring *The Australian* or *The Guardian*, but curiosity got the better of him and, tossing a few coins on the counter, he picked up a copy.

There was no time to read it now, so he folded the paper, thrust it into his briefcase and continued on his way, his mind once more settling on the task ahead.

The meeting went well, and Johnno was ebullient as the senior member of the group shook his hand enthusiastically.

'Great work, Henderson,' he said. 'I'll have our guys contact you to work out the details, but I can safely say you can go ahead with the acquisition. We're on a winner with this one.'

Johnno smiled. He always loved it when he managed to meet his client's expectations, even exceed them. He retreated to his office with its views over the city and Circular Quay, and stood for a moment appreciating this view of the harbour – a different aspect from the one he enjoyed at home. The sight of the green and yellow ferries docked at their wharves never failed to remind him of Sydney's history, of how the city had grown from its original few streets to the metropolis it was today.

He turned at the sound of a discrete cough.

'Your coffee Mr Henderson.' Tania, the office junior stood at the door tentatively holding out a cup of his favourite blend.

'Thanks, Tania.' He thought of reminding her of his preference to be called Johnno, but her nervous expression stopped him. Why bother? He'd told her so many times to no avail. She wasn't much younger than some of the models he'd dated not too long ago, he thought, watching her leave.

Johnno took a sip of the welcome liquid and realised he must seem old to her – too old to be called by his first name. Hell, how old was she? Eighteen? Nineteen? He was probably as old as her father, maybe older.

Putting such gloomy thoughts out of his mind, Johnno settled at his desk and was about to log onto his computer to set the ball rolling on the new contract and search for a developer, when he remembered the newspaper.

Unfolding the paper, he laid it flat on the desk and, still sipping his coffee, began to read the article. Besides the almost full-page photo, there was scant detail, only a reference to page six. Flipping over the pages, Johnno found a double-page spread itemising the life and times of *Sydney's Golden Couple* including photos of them in their heyday and an excerpt from Bill's memoir.

But, Johnno noticed, there were no recent photos and little mention of Bill's life in the last few years. There was a reference to *two beautiful daughters*, but no photos of them and no quotes from either them or his wife. Naturally, Bill himself was cited as denying any wrongdoing.

Johnno leant back in his chair and propped his feet on his desk – his favourite thinking position. Sexual assault was a serious claim. If this model could get it to stick… But it seemed Bill's publishers were using the accusation to garner all the publicity they could.

Johnno's thoughts strayed to the elegant woman he'd seen at the

Convention Centre. Even then, he'd sensed her vulnerability. *How did she feel about all this?* If what Anna said was true, and Celia was no longer *with* Bill, how humiliating for her. She must be furious.

'Got a moment?'

Johnno's legs dropped down. He folded the paper and put it aside. For the next hour he and his colleague, Allan, worked out the project plan for the new clients and made a list of possible developers. When Allan finally left, the newspaper article was furthest from Johnno's thoughts. He dashed out to pick up a sandwich for lunch, then was back at his desk, fingers busy on the keyboard as he caught up with the day's responsibilities.

It wasn't till well after six that Johnno stifled a yawn, logged out and rose, stretching his arms above his head. His eyes fell on the paper, lying where he'd dropped it that morning. He picked it up and the picture of Celia Ramsay as he'd last seen her came to mind. What was it about the woman? She was beautiful, elegant. But so were many other women. She wasn't the most beautiful, or the most elegant. But there had been something about her – an indefinable quality – that set her aside from all the others, that made her special.

He pushed back the lock of hair that always fell over his forehead – the one women seemed to love, stuck his briefcase under one arm, and closed the door behind him. To Johnno's surprise, the main office and reception area were both empty. He checked his watch again. At this time there were usually a few others still around, finishing off work or chatting about the latest vagaries of the stock or property market.

His phone buzzed.

Where are you, J? We're on the second round. A

Shit! He'd completely forgotten. Friday night. Guy's farewell. His long-time colleague, friend and mentor was retiring, and the office was sending him off royally with drinks at The Sheraton followed by dinner either there or at some other joint – Johnno couldn't remember what had been decided. *How could it have slipped his mind?* He'd been so engrossed in the job on hand, then distracted by the Ramsay stuff.

Fortunately, the elevator was waiting. Johnno pressed the ground floor button. He leapt out as soon as the door opened and hurried along the street, weaving his way among the crowds of young people intent on making the most of the Friday night that heralded the start of their weekend.

He made a conscious effort to slow his pace as he reached the hotel, heading up in the lift and entering the rooftop bar to the raucous jeers of the others.

'Sorry, sorry. How are you, mate?' He clapped Guy on the shoulder and accepted the ice-cold beer one of the others thrust into his hand.

'Bet you need this,' Allan said. 'You work too hard, Johnno.'

'Not like you slackers.' But Johnno knew that was a lie. They were all high-achievers, each trying to outdo the other in the cut-throat industry of investment finance. 'Thanks.' He used his glass to gesture toward the man who'd provided the beer.

'Heard you're all set to make a killing. A new town out west? Well done!' Guy shook Johnno's hand.

'Couldn't have got there without your advice.'

The two men stood a little apart from the others and admired the view – not unlike that from Johnno's own unit.

'Think you'll miss it? All this?'

'Not likely. We're planning the overseas trip. You know, the one you're supposed to do when you retire? The wife's been looking forward to it for years. Then…' Guy paused. 'Who knows? Maybe a place in the country or by the beach. Always had a hankering for Queensland. Spent a lot of time in Noosa when we were younger.'

'Queensland?'

'You're from there, I seem to remember.'

'That's right.'

Just then, there was a yell from one of the others.

'Dinner! We're heading off now. Ross has talked us into Mr Wong. Hope you like Chinese tucker.'

Guy grinned at Johnno who knew it was the other's favourite, and that Ross had no doubt booked a table on the restaurant's lower level – a popular venue for Sydney diners on a busy Friday evening.

Johnno sighed. It was going to be a long night, one which would no doubt leave him with yet another hangover and a gut full of highly salted food. But it was a small sacrifice to make for this group of men whose company and skills he valued above all others.

As the evening drew to a close, he made his farewells and headed home, glad it was within walking distance. He hoped the fresh evening air would go some way to removing the worst of the evening's indulgence.

As he walked down Sussex Street, his thoughts flashed back to the newspaper article and that woman – Celia Ramsay. There was something about her. Something that pulled at him. He shook his head. Maybe he'd had too much to drink.

Marcus and Anna. He'd see them on Sunday. They knew her. He'd talk with them. Find out – what, he wasn't sure. But he knew he needed to know more about Celia Ramsay, maybe even meet her again. Although, he reminded himself, their last meeting hadn't gone too well.

Seven

'Mrs Ramsay – Celia.'

The young woman wearing a smart red pant suit, a large bag slung over one shoulder and a notebook at the ready, accosted Celia as she was fitting the key into the door at Isabella.

They'd caught up with her.

Fixing her most polite smile – the one her daughters called *that look* – she gave the journalist a frosty glare. 'Not here. Not now. I have nothing to say to you.'

'But the public want to hear *your* side. What are your thoughts about the allegation? Do you intend to stand by your husband? How was he this morning? We didn't see you drive off. Have you moved out?'

Damn and double damn. It didn't take them long. How did Bill and that creep Julian intend to play this?

'Sorry. I can't speak now.' Celia finally managed to get the key in the door, open it and close it again, locking it from the inside. Once there, she took a deep breath and headed to the office to brew a cup of calming camomile tea. She was taking her first sip when she heard a persistent knocking. *Surely the woman wasn't expecting her to let her in?*

Looking through the glass, she saw Val's worried face peering in from the other side and hurried to open the door, glancing warily up and down the street. Thankfully there was no sign of the woman in the red pant suit, only a few early-morning joggers, a couple who looked as if they were on their way home from a hectic Friday night, and an elderly woman pushing a canvas shopping trolley.

'What's up?' Val was already in the back shop by the time Celia returned, having left the door unlocked and the shop open for business.

'A journalist. Caught me as I was opening up. I locked her out.'

'Oh no! They know you're here.'

'It wasn't too difficult, I guess. But she wanted to know why I hadn't driven out of our old house.' She bit her lip. 'Bill will have to come clean about the separation regardless of what it might do to his publicity – and his reputation.'

'Will they think you moved out because of all this?'

'I don't care what they think. We do have an agreement of secrecy. But we never thought of being pursued by the press. All of the book publicity was designed to be kept well away from our personal lives. I need to speak to Bob. He promised to call when he had news.'

'You haven't heard?'

'No. It's Saturday, but I need to call him.'

'You do it now, and I'll get set up for the day.'

'Thanks.'

Celia went through to the back, took a seat, and pressed Bob Frazer's number on her speed dial. It rang for a few moments before a sleepy voice answered, 'Bob Frazer here.'

'It's Celia Ramsay. Sorry to ring so early on a Saturday morning, but...'

'No worries.' His voice became stronger. 'You've probably seen yesterday's paper. I have it in my diary to call you today to set up a conference with Bill and Julian Clarke – and maybe the publicity woman.'

'Paper? What paper?' Celia felt the breath rush out of her. 'What did it say?'

'You haven't? *The Daily* had a front-page photo of the two of you at the launch and a double-page spread inside – seems the publicity team is milking this for all it's worth. I thought you must have seen it.'

Celia gasped, a hand going to clutch her chest. *How could they?* Then she realised what Bob had said about a meeting. 'A meeting today?'

'If I can arrange it. If you didn't see it, why are you ringing?'

'A journalist was waiting for me outside Isabella this morning. She wanted to know my reaction and why I wasn't at the house this morning.'

'Shit! That was fast. I presume you didn't say anything.'

'No, but what if she comes back – she or someone else?'

'Not a lot we can do at this stage. Let me see if I can get this set up and get a press statement out.'

'Where does this leave the deal we made?'

'Leave it with me.'

Val looked up expectantly when Celia returned, but any discussion was stymied by a rush of customers which lasted unabated till lunchtime.'

'Whew!' Celia said, when the last one had left carrying two bags of garments. 'Where did they all come from?'

'You don't think?' Val asked tentatively.

'What? The publicity around Bill? The newspaper article yesterday?'

'Yesterday?'

'Bob said there was another in yesterday's paper – more extensive and mentioning me and our marriage. He's trying to set up what he calls a conference.' Her phone buzzed. 'That may be him now.'

But it was Chloe's face Celia saw when she took out her phone. Her heart dropped. It was unlike Chloe to call her in the middle of a working day. Surely the media vultures hadn't got to the girls too?

'Hi honey, What's up?'

'Mum. Did you mean it when you said to bring Owen to Sunday lunch?'

Celia sagged against the counter with relief. 'I certainly did. Have you spoken to him about it?'

'Can we do it tomorrow? Owen says I should have told you before. He accused me of being ashamed of him. We had a bit of an argument. He wants to meet you, to show you he's serious.' Chloe sounded remorseful, and Celia had to smile at this turn of events.

Tomorrow? She tried to think what she had in the fridge and pantry, failing to come up with anything suitable for Chloe and her friend. Maybe she could run out to do a quick shop later today. But there was this proposed conference.

'Mum – are you still there?'

'Sorry, honey. Tomorrow will be good. Around twelve? I'm looking forward to meeting Owen.' She heard Chloe chuckle.

'I think you'll like him. He says his mum remembers you when you were a model.'

Celia's heart sank. No doubt his mum had also seen the papers, knew of the allegation and, like everyone else, was wondering where Celia fitted into all this.

'Not Bob?' Val asked when Celia closed her phone only to have it buzz again. This time it was Bob's name that appeared. She mouthed *Bob* to Val and pressed *accept*.

Five minutes later she hung up, a glazed look in her eyes.

'What did he say?' Val asked.

'It's set for this afternoon at four. In Bob's office. He's drawing up an agenda and an amendment to the original arrangement for us to sign – if all parties agree. I hope we're not too busy here. I feel bad leaving you on your own. If it's anything like this morning…'

'Don't worry. I can cope. You need to get this fixed as soon as possible.'

'Yes.' Celia sighed and pushed her hair behind her ears.

*

The tension in the room was palpable. Celia tapped her foot and gazed at the surface of the table. They were all there. Bob, Bill, Julian and Ria, the publicity bird – a woman in her late-twenties with red-streaked hair who seemed to be captivated by Bill.

'Thanks everyone for agreeing to meet at such short notice,' Bob began. He tapped his pen on the table and shuffled a bundle of papers. 'I think we all know why we're here.'

Celia nodded and heard a few murmurs of assent from the others.

'My client,' began Julian, and Celia saw Bill smile.

They were up to something.

'My client,' Julian repeated, 'Mr Ramsay…'

'You can call me Bill, Julian. We're among friends here.'

Friends?

'If everyone agrees?' Julian's gaze moved around the table. No one spoke. 'Okay. As you know Bill here has had an accusation levelled at him. Untrue of course.'

Bill smirked.

'But the timing is such that it could do untold harm to his reputation and…'

The red-haired woman interrupted. 'In his memoir, Bill appears as everyman's hero, a footy legend, a happy family man, a wonderful husband and father.'

Celia cringed as the woman gave her a glare.

'So,' she continued, 'we need to do what we can to maintain that image to our public.' She smiled across the table at Bill who winked back.

'What we're saying is,' Julian's smooth voice took over, 'we think it would be best if Celia and Bill could be seen together more – a gesture of solidarity, if you like.'

Celia's gut clenched. The colour drained from her face. This wasn't what she'd expected. This wasn't why they were here. She gave Bob a pleading look.

'I don't think so,' Bob said, his voice echoing in the tiny room. 'My client has already been subjected to media interest, been hounded by reporters for something that is none of her doing. As your client knows full well, much of his so-called memoir is a tissue of lies. There has been no happy marriage, wonderful husband and father for some time. If you don't want that truth told, then we need to re-negotiate our agreement. I have an amendment which I've drawn up here.' Bob proceeded to hand around the papers from the bundle he'd been shuffling.

Celia saw Bill's face redden and his mouth open as if to speak, but Julian laid a hand on his arm. 'I speak for my client when I say we're not interested in any amendment. The agreement stands. The book signings in the next two weeks are important engagements, and it's imperative Celia shows her support by attending as his wife, regardless of what the true nature of their relationship might be. As I said already, we – Bill and I, and Ria,' he smiled at the publicity woman, 'would like the couple to be seen – and photographed – together outside of his regular speaking engagements and promotional events. Perhaps having coffee or dinner together, with his grandchildren? Seen as the perfect family man.'

'No!' Celia yelled and stood up. She couldn't help herself. Bob signalled her to sit again and, somewhat abashed, she did so, but she felt a rush of heat through her body. *How could they? How could they contemplate using innocent children, the ones Bill had called bastards so many times and refused to even acknowledge?*

Julian smiled slyly, as if he knew he'd hit a hot button with his mention of her grandchildren. 'Well, maybe not the children,' he acknowledged. 'But Celia?' His eyes met hers with such a gleeful expression she had to look away.

'It looks like we can't come to an agreement today,' Bob said. 'I suggest you look over my amendment, and we all take the weekend to consider how to proceed. We can convene here again on Monday. I believe the first signing is scheduled for Wednesday?' He picked up his papers and rose.

'I don't...' Bill began, but was silenced by a look from Julian, and the two men rose and left, Ria following close behind.

Celia remained seated, stunned by the demands. She covered her face with her hands.

'Don't worry,' Bob said.

'How can you say, "Don't worry"? You heard what they want? I'm not going to be able to get out of the book signings, and Bill won't be content with my attending them. I can't do it!' Her eyes filled with tears.

'Here.' Bob handed her a tissue. 'It's not as bad as it sounds. They made an ambit claim, that's all. And I made a counter proposal.'

'But if you...'

'It won't come to that. They have the weekend to think about it, and I'm willing to bet they'll come to the party when they realise the implications. It's not a case of any publicity is good publicity. They won't want the truth about Bill and your marriage to come out any more than you do.' Bob smiled. 'Now dry those tears and let me take you for a drink and a bite to eat.'

'Thanks.' Celia wiped her eyes. 'But I need to do some shopping. I have Chloe and her new boyfriend coming to lunch tomorrow, and the cupboard is bare.' She managed a weak smile.

Bob checked his watch. 'It's only six. The supermarkets are open till midnight. You need to eat, and Chris is out of town, so I'm at a loose end. How does Italian sound? Baia at Darling Harbour is a favourite of ours, and they can always find me a table.'

'Italian?' Despite her protestations, Celia's mouth watered at the sound of an Italian meal, and Bob was right. She *did* have to eat, and the supermarkets *were* open late. She planned a very simple lunch so there'd be nothing to prepare till tomorrow. 'Okay, you're on.'

It was a lovely evening as Celia and Bob took the leisurely stroll down to the harbour and along Cockle Bay Wharf to the restaurant. This was a part of Sydney Celia loved and didn't visit nearly often enough.

*

Johnno was whistling as he waited for the elevator. Life was good. He might not have a lady on his arm this Saturday night, but the prospect of his latest deal promised him a healthy profit. Maybe enough to take some time off and enjoy a well-deserved holiday. He could take time to search out that holiday shack in Noosa he'd been promising himself. Guy's mention of the seaside town the night before had reminded him of lazy summer days growing up in Queensland, of surfing during school holidays, paddle boarding on the Noosa River, kayaking in the Everglades.

Yes, that's what he'd do. Though maybe *shack* was the wrong word. He had no intention of landing himself with an old place. He'd heard there were some luxury units going up near the river. That was more his scene.

The elevator arrived, and he travelled down to ground level. He jangled his car keys and considered the basement car park, before deciding it was too nice a night to be cooped up in the car and setting off to walk to one of the local restaurants.

A beer in one hand and the menu in another, Johnno glanced down the offerings, knowing in advance what he'd choose. He was a creature of habit, and a plate of oysters to go with the beer followed by a bottle of red and the Angus rump would go down a treat.

He'd finished the oysters and was enjoying his first sip of the *Castello di Querceto Chianti Classico* – a Tuscan wine that was a favourite tipple of his, when he noticed a blonde head at the far end of the room. The woman had her back to him, but there was something vaguely familiar about her and the way she leant towards her companion.

Johnno racked his brains, but there was no resounding flash of recognition. Deciding to ignore her, he checked out his phone, replied to a couple of text messages, deleted a few more without responding, chuckled at some Facebook posts, then closed it up as his steak arrived.

Almost simultaneously, the blonde woman and her companion rose. She turned slightly on her way to the door and Johnno recognised Celia Ramsay, looking as elegant as before. But, even at this distance, he detected a shadow on her face. Johnno quickly glanced at the man who was shepherding her out. It wasn't her husband.

*

Sunday morning saw Johnno making his weekly pilgrimage across Spit Bridge, the rising mist giving an ethereal appearance to the smooth stretch of water.

There was little time for chat as his young namesake, Jonathon, tumbled out of the other car along with Marcus and Anna. The four settled themselves into their sculls before heading out onto the water. So, it wasn't till they were seated around the breakfast table and Jonathon was digging into the big breakfast, that Johnno had a chance to ask about Celia.

But, now that the opportunity had arisen, he had trouble finding the words. He didn't want his friends to think he was interested in the woman. *He wasn't, was he? Not that way. What way was that*, he wondered?

'You're very quiet this morning, Johnno,' Anna said, between bites. 'Everything all right?'

'Great!' Johnno tried to inject a note of enthusiasm into his voice but knew he'd failed.

'Burning the candle at both ends isn't doing you any good, mate. You should listen to one who knows.' Marcus pointed his fork at Johnno.

'And that would be you?'

'Marcus is right about one thing,' Anna said. 'It's time you found yourself a nice lady. I wonder…'

'No setting me up with *a good friend*,' Johnno said, holding his hands up defensively. 'I prefer to make my own choice where women are concerned, even if I may not always choose wisely.' He pushed back a lock of hair as he spoke, hoping his thoughts didn't show on his face. *Maybe if he agreed to meet one of Anna's friends, that friend would turn out to be Celia Ramsay?*

As if reading his mind, Anna spoke again. 'Did you see that awful article about Bill Ramsay – the guy whose book launch you went to? I can't say I'm surprised, but his poor family...'

'Something about an assault wasn't it? I think I saw a headline,' Johnno lied.

'An unwanted sexual advance the paper called it. We all know what that means. He's been playing around for years, and now this. Poor Celia. I can imagine how she's feeling. Just as she was forced into pretending to be the happy couple for the media. Still, Bob will see her right.'

'Bob – your brother?'

'Yes. He won't stand for any nonsense from that ratbag. But it's her daughters I really feel for. He disowned them and now seems to want to claim them as part of his happy family.' She frowned.

Daughters? Johnno remembered some mention of them in the paper. Why should he be surprised? Most people of his age had children, had decided to put down roots, start a family. He was the odd one out, the one who'd refused to conform, continued to play the field long after...

'You said you met her, didn't you?' Anna's voice broke into his thoughts.

'Yes. Briefly. She seemed... cool.'

'No bloody wonder if it was at the book launch. She'd been forced into that mockery – a charade of happy families. Anyone would be annoyed. Cool is probably putting it mildly.'

Johnno felt more confident. Maybe it hadn't been him, but the situation. But last night and the man she was with?

'So she's left him, moved on?' he asked, trying to sound disinterested. 'I think I saw her last night. She was with someone – not Bill Ramsay.'

'She wouldn't be with him! It might have been Bob. I think they were meeting yesterday, and it would be like him to take her to dinner afterwards – his partner's out of town.'

They continued eating silently, Jonathon sneaking surreptitious glances at his mobile under the cover of the table. Johnno knew Anna was turning over something in her mind, so it was no surprise to him when she said, 'Celia Ramsay might be just right for you, Johnno. Right age. Former model. Still an elegant lady despite being a grandmother twice over.'

Grandmother? What the...?

'Grandmother? Isn't she a bit young?'

'She was pretty young when she married Bill. Her grandchildren are still little. Hannah is in her early-twenties, but Chloe was only eighteen when...'

'Too much information.'

Anna smiled delightedly, seeming to sense his interest and disquiet. 'Do you want an introduction? It can be arranged. Jan knows her pretty well. They share a grandson, after all. Though,' she added with a frown, 'I'm not sure she's ready to move on just yet. Not with all the publicity and stuff.'

Jan! Anna's sister – the woman who soundly rejected him and returned to her husband. The only other woman he could have taken seriously.

'No!' The word came out more forcefully than he'd intended. 'No,' he said more mildly. 'I can find my own women, thank you. But it's kind of you to offer, Anna.'

Eight

Celia examined the table setting and gave herself a shake. It was Owen who was on show here today, not her. So why did she feel as if she was going to be judged?

She checked that Bindi had enough food and water, took one more glance in the mirror, and was just deciding if the blue and white outfit she'd chosen to wear was appropriate, when the buzzer sounded to indicate they'd arrived.

'Hello, Mrs Ramsay. Pleased to meet you at last.'

'Please, call me Celia.'

Celia wanted to discard the name Ramsay. It was still her daughters' surname, but now her marriage was all but over, she cringed each time she heard it. She made a sudden decision. She'd revert to her maiden name – become Celia Lang again. That name sat more easily with her. It was the name she'd grown up with – even though she'd been quick to shrug it off when she married Bill.

'Thanks.' The boy – for that was what he seemed to Celia – looked embarrassed.

'Wine?' she offered, bending down to pick up Simon who had, as usual, rushed to greet her and was now clinging to her knees.

'We brought some, Mum. And beer,' Chloe said, taking a bag from Owen and putting it on the kitchen bench. 'I hope you haven't gone to too much trouble.'

'Fine, Mrs... Celia.' Owen smiled, and Celia could see his attraction for Chloe. It was a smile that lit up an otherwise unremarkable bespectacled face surrounded by a mop of ginger hair.

Si slid down from Celia's arms and took Owen's hand, dragging him to the bookshelf where he knew the supply of Dr Seuss books lived. Owen seemed happy to go with the little boy, and Celia saw Chloe watch them with an understanding grin before turning back to her mother.

'Wine for me thanks, Mum, and I'll pour a beer for Owen. What do you think?' she whispered when they were out of hearing of the other two.

'I've only just met him – but so far so good,' Celia replied, opening the bottle of Sauvignon Blanc Chloe had taken out of her bag. 'Si seems comfortable with him.'

'He is,' Chloe beamed, and, for a few moments, Celia had the feeling that everything was right with her world.

Then the present intervened. She remembered Bill's snide comments, remembered Bob's warnings about the possibility of more media interest.

But not today, she decided. Today was all about Chloe and her friend, and she wasn't going to sully it with what might or might not happen as a result of Bill's bad judgement.

The meal passed pleasantly, Owen proving to be easy to talk to and informative about the IT industry. He even offered to set up a website for Isabella, asking if Celia had considered selling garments online. She hadn't and didn't think she was ready to jump into that market, but it was certainly food for thought, and something to discuss with Bel who was still part-owner.

It was only when they were enjoying coffee on the balcony, Si having fallen asleep on the sofa, that Bill's name came up.

'Owen's mum knows Dad,' Chloe said.

Celia's heart raced. *What next?*

Owen cleared his throat. 'Knew is more accurate Chloe. Mum said she'd met you both at a school thing when my sister was in year ten.'

'Oh.' Celia couldn't think of anything else to say, then added, 'I don't believe I remember her.'

'Anne Cunningham. She said… it was when she saw it in the paper.' He reddened, the blush reaching all the way down his neck. 'I'm sorry. I shouldn't have said anything.'

'No that's all right. I can guess. Bill tried it on with almost every woman he met. That's why I wasn't surprised when...' She threw an apologetic glance at Chloe. 'I'm sorry, pet. I know he's your dad, but...'

Chloe tossed her head. 'I don't care. Nothing about that man can surprise me. I stopped considering him to be my dad long ago.'

Celia saw Owen reach over to cover Chloe's hand with his, and a wave of relief flooded her. Chloe would be all right. She'd found a good man in Owen, even if she'd kept him secret for too long.

'I don't know...' Celia began, but was interrupted by the buzz of the intercom.

'Sorry, Mum.' Chloe said, 'I forgot to tell you. I told Jan we were coming here, and she said she might drop round. She hasn't met Owen yet either.' She gave him an affectionate look. 'I hope that was all right?'

'Sure.' Celia went to press the button to allow Jan to enter the building. 'You should have said earlier.'

'Sorry,' Chloe repeated, while Celia wondered how Jan would react to meeting the man who was poised to take her son's place as Si's father. If Jan's son, Simon, had lived, would the couple be married now? Would their relationship have survived? It had been a simple boy-girl affair that had got out of hand on one occasion, and little Si was the result. His father had died unaware of the consequence of their carefree Year Twelve celebration, and now there was Owen.

'Hi Jan, Welcome,' Celia said, opening the door. 'Glad you could make it. Come in and meet Owen.' She saw Jan's face turn pale. 'He's a nice lad. Not at all like Simon, but I think your boy would have liked him.'

'That's what Chloe said,' Jan replied, looking as if she was steeling herself for the encounter.

'Jan.' Chloe rose and came into the room to give her a hug and, on cue, little Si awakened and held up his arms for a hug, too.

This effectively broke the ice, allowing Owen to join the group and be introduced.

'I've been looking forward to meeting you, Mrs Turnbull,' he said. 'I knew Simon, even though he was a couple of years below me. He was a great sportsman. You must be proud of him.'

'Thanks, Owen. That's kind of you. And call me Jan. Mrs Turnbull sounds so old. I see Si has taken to you,' she added, as the little boy ran towards Owen and grabbed him by the leg.

'He's a great little kid. Simon would have been stoked,' he said awkwardly. 'I mean…'

'It's okay,' Jan said. 'It's okay to talk about Simon. I'd rather we did that than forget all about him. By the way, I brought some cake, so I hope you're not all too full.' She gestured to a cake box she'd placed on the bench when she arrived.

'Cake!' little Si yelled, proving that at least one of the group still had a cake-sized space, and making everyone laugh.

Celia brewed more coffee, and they regrouped around the table with the large strawberry sponge cake Jan had provided. The conversation focussed on the young couple and their plans for the future, surprising Celia and Jan by their thoughtfulness and attention to detail.

'We know we're pretty young and haven't known each other long,' Owen said, throwing an arm around Chloe's shoulders. 'I've heard all that from *my* parents. But there's Si who needs a dad.' He gave Jan an apologetic look, and Celia saw Chloe beam at him, her expression so full of love, she was forced to avert her eyes. 'I know I can't replace his real dad, but I intend to do my best.'

There was nothing the two women could say to that impassioned speech. It was clear how much in love the pair were, and Si obviously loved and looked up to Owen too. Both Jan and Celia gave the young couple their blessing, while admonishing them not to rush into marriage.

When Chloe and Owen finally left, Si riding on Owen's shoulders, Jan and Celia looked at each other.

'It had to happen,' Jan said. 'And Owen seems like a nice lad. I just wish…'

Celia wrapped her arms around her friend in a warm hug. 'I know. If only it didn't have to be like this. If only Simon were here.'

Jan shed a few tears, then wiped her eyes. 'This won't do. We should be happy for them. Chloe has chosen well. How are *you* coping?'

Celia knew she wasn't referring to the young couple.

'Oh, you know. Some days are better than others. But there is a bright side. I may get out of any more media appearances. Your brother's been very good. Though I'm not sure I can trust Bill and *his* solicitor. She grimaced. 'I get the feeling they're up to something.'

Nine

Military Road was the usual snarl of traffic as Johnno's car made its way along towards Mosman. He was trying to believe the excuse he'd given himself about having to catch up with his old mate Rod Miller, the local realtor – someone he'd often had cause to be grateful to in the past. The two went back a long way and had collaborated on more than a few lucrative property deals.

But that wasn't the case today. There had been no call from Rod heralding a not-to-be-missed opportunity, no online notification of a land sale to follow up. No matter how hard Johnno tried to convince himself otherwise, he knew the reason for this trip across the bridge had more to do with Celia Ramsay's presence in the suburb, than in any property deal, projected or otherwise.

Nevertheless, as Johnno drew into a parking spot in a side street and walked along, he avoided glancing across at the sign for Isabella. The memories the shop had for him did not show him in his best light. He recalled dropping in to see Jan Turnbull when he thought he might have a chance there. He'd been visiting Rod on that occasion too and, he seemed to recollect, there had been a young girl who…

Suddenly he stopped in his tracks. The young girl Anna had mentioned – Celia's daughter, the one pregnant at eighteen. She must be the same one who'd been living with Jan back then, the one he'd managed to help find a job with Rod. Hell's bells! Had he actually met her? Met Celia's daughter? He'd been so shocked by the whole episode he'd tried to forget all about it.

'Johnno Henderson! You're a stranger. What are you doing over here?' Rod Miller greeted him at the door and led the way to his office at the back of the agency.

'I was passing through,' Johnno murmured, realising how ridiculous he must sound. One didn't *pass through* Mosman. One had a reason to go there. 'Thought it was time we caught up,' he added.

'I was about to take a break,' Rod said. 'Let me buy you a coffee. I usually drop round to Avenue Road Café at this time. Suit you?'

'Sure.'

Johnno waited, idly reading the For-Sale lists lying on a low table, while Rod gave instructions to his staff regarding who might call when he was gone. Then they were outside again and walking briskly along the street. As they waited for the traffic lights to change, Johnno sensed Rod's gaze on him and felt uneasy – as if Rod could read his mind.

But all the other man said was, 'How's business? Not much going this side of the harbour. I think you and your mates have bought up and developed all the available land.'

'So it seems. But you never know what's in the wind and you've been a good friend to me over the years.'

The traffic stopped, and the pair hurried across the road, found a table on the outside of the café, and ordered – two long blacks and a serving of banana bread for Johnno. It seemed a long time since his breakfast which had been leftovers from last night's Chinese takeaway.

As they enjoyed their coffee, Rod quizzed Johnno on his latest acquisitions, and the pair bemoaned the current state of the property market.

'Had a few good sales last year, though,' Rod said with a grin. 'Remember that women's dress shop? I think you were interested in someone there for a bit. The owner, Bel, moved overseas and sold a nice Federation place in Cremorne. Could do with a few more of those. They've become pretty sought after.'

'Sold it? Hmm. Did she sell the shop, too?'

'Did some private deal there with a local woman. Cut us realters out of the mix. Now, that's something interesting. Do you remember Bruiser Ramsay? Played for the state back when... Bit of scandal there. We've had a few reporters sniffing around. He and his wife have a place on the bay, water frontage, boat ramp. What I'd give to have that house on my books.'

Johnno silently cursed. He'd forgotten Rod's tendency to move from one topic to another seemingly unrelated one.

'What's the connection?'

'Didn't I say? The woman who bought the shop – she's Ramsay's wife. Though there are some who say she moved out.' Rod tapped his nose with his forefinger. 'Not what the papers are saying, but the neighbours haven't seen her for months.'

'Wasn't she a model?' Johnno hoped he didn't sound too interested, but Rod didn't appear to notice.

'That's right. Celia Lang, she was known as. Every young man's dream back then. And she's still got it.' He rubbed his chin. 'Not for the likes of me, though I can't speak for a babe-magnet like yourself.' He chortled.

Johnno changed the subject. This was too close to the truth, though he doubted his infamy as a babe-magnet would ever attract Celia Ramsay. It would no doubt have quite the opposite effect.

Coffee over, the pair parted amicably, Rod promising to contact Johnno if anything came up to suit his interests.

Johnno hesitated before strolling down the road towards the shop, Isabella.

*

'It looks lovely,' Celia said to the middle-aged woman who was trying on a calf-length lilac dress. 'I'm sure it'll look wonderful in the wedding party and…' She broke off as the shop door flew open, and her husband strode in, his masculine bulk incongruous in this feminine setting.

Bill's eyes flitted around the shop before settling on Celia whose stomach began to roil. Her eyes blurred. She felt dizzy.

'We need to talk,' he said in the bullying tone Celia remembered – the one she'd thought never to be forced to hear again.

'I'll take over,' Val whispered in her ear, just as she thought she was going to faint. 'Why don't you both go through to the back?'

Celia found her way into the office where she dropped into a chair. Bill followed, taking the only other seat.

'We need to find a way out of this pickle,' he began.

'Pickle? Is that what you call it?' Celia remembered how Bill always managed to make light of any disaster. Some would call it seeing a silver lining. She saw it differently.

'There's no need for our lawyers to get het up about it,' he said in a wheedling voice. 'I'm sure we can come to some arrangement between ourselves. No need for Julian and that man of yours to get involved, is there?'

A strange feeling began to creep over Celia. *What was he about to propose?*

'We're all grown-ups here. And the simplest thing is to give the publishers what they want.'

Celia's eyes widened.

He couldn't be suggesting? But he was.

'All you need to do is move back to the Mosman house. It's still your home. Nothing has changed. Then they can have their photos, right there on the deck, in the kitchen, in your sunroom. And we can be seen out together, just like Ria advised. That'll put paid to all the rumours. You can see that, can't you?' Bill's voice took on a hard tone that seemed to indicate he wouldn't take no for an answer.

Celia felt herself wilt. Then she remembered she wasn't alone any longer. She had friends. She had the support of her solicitor. Her back straightened, her head went up. 'No, Bill. I don't see it that way. I have no intention of moving back into your house or of having any photos taken with you. You lost that right long ago.'

Bill began to pout – not a good look in a man of his age and size. 'Come on, Celia. Don't be like this. We can make it difficult for you – and for those bitches you're trying to protect. You wouldn't want anything to happen to them, would you? To see their faces spread across the newspapers – that lesbian slut, the other tart, and their bastard kids?'

'How can you? They're *your* children and grandchildren too. They…' But Celia couldn't go on. This was worse than she could ever have imagined. A surge of white anger seethed through her. She stood up. 'Get out!' she yelled, oblivious to any customers who might hear her. 'Get out!' she repeated, pointing to the door, where a man was standing.

Celia's breath caught, and a hand went to her throat.

'I think the lady's asking you to leave,' the man said. 'Do you need any help?'

Bill stood up, dwarfed by the newcomer. The comparison was awesome. The two men were around the same age, but whereas Bill appeared as a flabby has-been, the result of too much alcohol and insufficient exercise, the other guy was still in prime condition, his body kept fit by his rowing and frequent trips to the gym, a magnificent specimen of manhood.

Muttering to himself and with one last glare in Celia's direction, Bill left.

Celia gazed at her rescuer in surprise. It was that man again – the one who'd spoken to her after the book launch. *What was he doing here?*

Val rushed in. 'Sorry Celia. I told him you were busy, I couldn't prevent...' She stopped in surprise, seeing the two sizing each other up. 'Do you know each other?'

'Sorry if I interrupted something,' the man said, pushing back an errant lock of hair. 'I heard raised voices. Are you all right?' He moved towards Celia as she slumped against the desk.

'Fine.' She waved him away and sat down again. 'Maybe some water.'

'Here.' Val handed her a bottle of water from the shelf.

'Thanks.' She took a long gulp, then wiped her mouth. 'We'll be right, Val.'

'If you're sure.' Val didn't seem convinced, but went back into the shop.

Celia tried to recall where she'd seen him before. 'We've met, haven't we?'

'Johnno Henderson. We met briefly. At Darling Harbour. After your...' he cleared his throat, '...after the book launch. You gave me short shrift. I'm a friend of Marcus King – and Anna. I was in the area. Hell, I'm not making much sense, am I?' He dragged a hand through his hair. 'I'm just glad I was here when...' He gestured toward the door through which Bill had left.

Johnno, that was it. 'He wouldn't have hurt me. At least I don't think so. It's all words with him. But thanks.'

'Words can hurt too.'

Celia looked at him more closely. 'Last time, at the Convention Centre. Didn't you say you knew me? I don't think...'

'Knew might be too strong. I saw you at a barbecue at Marcus and Anna's.'

'Yes, I remember you saying.' It was coming back to her now. 'I wasn't at my best that day. Not today either. You seem to be making a habit of finding me at a low ebb. What brings you here today? Are you with…?' Celia peered into the shop, expecting to see his lady friend browsing the racks.

'Just me.' He seemed flustered and hesitated before adding, 'I wanted to see you again. Anna said you worked here.' He held up his hands defensively. 'I don't often do this – pursue strangers. In fact, I've never done it before. I'm no stalker. But I'd like to get to know you.' He smiled, and Celia felt a matching smile tug at her lips.

'About…' Johnno gestured to the door Bill had left by.

'Oh, him. I have a solicitor who'll deal with him – and his threats.' Celia felt a surge of energy as she spoke. Regardless of what he might say, what he might threaten, Bill had no real power over her any-more.

'Right.' Johnno shuffled awkwardly. 'I'll be going then. You're busy. Now's clearly not the right time.' He doffed an imaginary hat and walked out. Hearing the outside door close behind him, Celia stifled another smile, drew a hand through her hair, and walked back out into the shop.

'Who was *that*?' Val asked.

'His name's Johnno Henderson. It seems we have mutual friends.' Celia was still bemused by the man's arrival and his awkward explanation of his presence. 'He says he wanted to meet me. His arrival sent Bill packing at any rate.'

'And?'

'There's no *and*. He came and now he's left, and Bob should have called by now.' She checked her watch just as her phone buzzed. 'That'll be him.'

It was, and a few hours later Celia was driving across the Harbour Bridge on her way to yet another meeting in Bob's conference room. This time, she was prepared for Bill and Julian's pre-emptive proposals and knew how she was going to handle them. She'd already told Bob about Bill's visit to Isabella. His response was to recommend she take out an AVO to prevent his approaching her, her children or grandchildren. While Celia was reluctant to do this, she'd agreed it was a possibility if the afternoon's meeting didn't result in a positive outcome.

Unable to eat any lunch, Celia overdosed on black coffee before she left. Her mouth was dry, and she took several deep breaths in an attempt to calm herself before climbing the stairs to Bob's office. Once there, she gratefully accepted a glass of water and tried to appear confident and in control as Bill entered the room with Julian at his side. There was no sign of Ria today.

'Have you considered the amendments I provided?' Bob asked without preamble. 'That my client be excused from any further commitment to the promotion of *your* client's memoir?'

Julian looked at Bill before replying.

'My client has another suggestion. He...'

Bob didn't allow him to finish. 'If it's the suggestion he made to my client when he visited her at her place of work today, he can forget it.'

Julian glanced at Bill in astonishment. Clearly, he didn't know of Bill's visit to Isabella and his attempt to get Celia to return home.

Bill had the grace to look remorseful.

'So, I can assume you're happy to agree?' Bob placed a pen on the paper in front of Bill.

'Steady on,' Bill blustered. 'You can't just...'

'And I'd like an agreement you won't attempt to see my client – or your daughters,' Bob continued.

'*Her* daughters,' Bill said, almost snorting and crossing his arms. 'Why would I waste my time with *them*?'

Celia remembered his threats, but remained silent, her leg jiggling nervously.

'I understand some threats were made,' Bob said without any change of expression.

Julian picked up the pen and handed it to Bill. 'You'd better sign, mate.' He shook his head. 'Sorry,' he said to Bob. 'I knew nothing about this, If I'd had any inkling...'

'Thanks,' Bob said, passing the paper to Celia for her signature, then back to Julian for his as a witness. 'I'm assuming your client understands his position, and we won't have to take out an AVO?'

'What?' Bill half-rose, glowering, but Julian pressed him back into his seat.

'No. That won't be necessary. That's the last thing you need, Bill,' he hissed, as Bill subsided into the chair again, his face reddening.

'Then we're done here.' Bob collected the signed document and rose. Celia remained seated and began to tremble. *Was it all over? Had they won this round?* Knowing Bill, she was sure it wouldn't stop here – *he* wouldn't stop here. But maybe this would give her some respite.

Ten

'They've done it, Mum!'

Celia stopped stirring the pasta sauce to concentrate on her daughter's call, her mobile held firmly to her ear. 'Done what Han?' she asked, her mind immediately going to the journalist who'd approached her at Isabella. *Had they discovered where Hannah and Chloe lived? Had there been another article?* She'd refused to look at any papers or news reports in the hope the whole thing would go away.

'Don't you watch the news? They've got the go-ahead for a plebiscite – or a postal vote is what they're calling it. I'm not sure of the difference.'

'And you're pleased?'

'Pleased they're doing something – yes. I'm not sure what's going to happen between now and November when everyone votes, but Ingrid's already planning for a 2018 wedding.'

Celia let the spoon fall into the mixture. It wasn't Bill's debacle. It was her daughter's future – to be decided by popular vote.

When she didn't respond, Hannah continued, 'It's to be a postal vote managed by the census lot who stuffed up last time – and it won't be compulsory. But it's action at last. We have to be grateful for that.'

There was a loud popping noise.

'That's Ingrid opening the champagne. She's excited.'

More so than Hannah, Celia deduced from her daughter's tone. 'I'm glad for you both, honey,' she said after a pause. 'I'll turn on the news later tonight and catch up. I've been avoiding it this week,' her voice trailed off.

'Oh, Mum. I'm sorry, I forgot. But there's been no more about you and Dad, has there?'

'Not that I'm aware of. Now, you go off and enjoy your champagne and we'll maybe catch up on the weekend.'

But Hannah wasn't ready to hang up just yet.

'You met Chloe's Owen on Sunday? What did you think?'

Celia paused again. Sunday seemed such a long time ago. *Had she really not spoken to the girls since then? Had she been so wrapped up in her own problems, she'd forgotten they'd be keen to hear from her?*

'He seems very nice. Jan thought so too.'

'Yes. Chloe said she'd dropped in. She was hoping it would be easier for her with the two of you there.'

'Jan's okay with it. She knows Chloe would move on and, as Chloe said, Simon would have liked Owen. Little Si seems to like him too.'

'Right. My bubbles await. See you soon. Love you.'

Celia hung up. Now she had more to think about. She checked the messages on her phone she'd ignored earlier, surprised to see one from Jan suggesting they meet for a drink after work next evening.

It had been a long time since Celia had enjoyed Friday night drinks with a friend. Since Bill's book launch and the subsequent media furore she'd scuttled home each night, glad to close the door behind her. And for months before, she felt she'd been living under a shadow waiting for her chance of freedom. But, suddenly, she felt her spirits lift. A night out was just what she needed. She texted back her agreement, only to receive the reply that Jan's sister, Anna, would be coming along too. *It'll be a girls' night out,* Jan texted. *The Oaks at seven. J.*

Celia was surprised yet pleased. She'd only met Jan's sister a couple of times, both times at barbecues when they'd had little chance to talk. She knew their brother, Bob, better and it would be good to get to know the third member of the family.

*

Friday was always busy at the shop, many women choosing to buy something new to wear on the weekend. By five-thirty, both Celia and Val were exhausted.

'I intend to go home, have a hot shower, and spend the evening with a glass of wine and a good movie,' Val said, as they locked the door and began to check the day's takings.

'You go on, then,' Celia said. 'I'm meeting a couple of friends later so no lazy evening at home for me.'

'Good,' Val said, much to Celia's surprise. 'It's about time you did something for yourself. Your life seems to have been in limbo ever since we met again – since we've been working together. You need to get a life, Cee – meet some people.'

Celia grinned at the old pet name Val had coined for her when they'd both been in the modelling game. She hadn't heard it for years, her friend choosing to always be circumspect and calling her Celia at work.

'What about you?'

'I get out.' Val started to enumerate her activities with her fingers. 'Choir, yoga, pilates, tennis, book club…'

'Okay, okay. I get your point. But I have my girls.'

Val grimaced. 'Don't you ever think you use them as an excuse?' She put up her hands as Celia started to object.

'Like you, you mean?' Celia was perfectly aware that, like her, Val had no intention of replacing her husband in her life. It was something they'd discussed. But while Val thought she'd never find a man who could live up to her husband, Celia knew she'd have trouble ever trusting one again. 'It's a girls' night out.'

'That's a start. I've been worried about you.'

Celia's eyes widened. Val, worried about her?

*

It was ten past seven by the time Celia found a parking spot and hurried into the courtyard behind The Oaks. The place was filled with noise, Friday night being the beginning of the weekend for many of the young local professionals. Her eyes searched the tables until they finally settled on Jan and Anna sitting in a corner almost hidden behind a large table of young people who appeared to be celebrating something besides the end of the working week.

Glad she'd taken time to slip home for a quick shower and to change into a more casual outfit – tailored black pants with a blue and white striped blazer over a white shirt – Celia weaved her way through the crowd.

'Sorry I'm late.' She slid into the empty seat and dropped her bag at her feet. 'Have you been here long?' she asked, seeing both already had glasses of wine which were almost half-empty.

'You mean these?' Jan held hers up. 'Anna and I had some family stuff to discuss so we arranged to meet a bit earlier.' She emptied her glass in one gulp. 'Now we can start the evening properly.' She passed Celia a menu. 'Choose what you want. We've already decided.' She stood up. 'I'll get more drinks in. 'White or red?'

'White. Chardonnay please.'

'Why don't I get a bottle?' She looked at Anna.

'Fine by me. But remember, we're all driving.'

Jan disappeared in the direction of the bar.

'I'm glad you could come,' Anna said, when the two were alone. 'I've been wanting to get to know you better. And I'm so sorry for what you're going through.'

'Thanks,' Celia muttered. Was it always going to be like this, now – people feeling sorry for her? Maybe she shouldn't have come. She hated being seen as a victim.

'It must be hard,' Anna continued. 'Jan told me you'd agreed to be part of your ex-husband's book publicity – and now all this media coverage. It can't be pleasant.'

'No.' Celia was grateful Anna seemed to understand. 'But he's not my ex – not yet. Your brother…'

'Oh, good. You're using Bob. He helped me when I…' Anna seemed to think better of what she was about to say, falling silent just as Jan returned flourishing a bottle in one hand and three glasses in the other.'

'Wow, it's a crush in there. We should order soon, or we'll be waiting all night. Have you looked at the menu?'

'Not yet.' Celia hid her confusion by burying her face in the large menu and making a careful study of its contents.

Finally, she raised her head. 'The grilled salmon with cauliflower sounds good. What are you two having? Thanks,' she added as Jan pushed a glass of wine towards her.

'The chicken for me, and Anna's chosen the baked eggplant parmigiana. Shall we order?'

Once the orders were placed, Celia took a gulp of her wine hoping Anna had forgotten their earlier conversation or, at least, wouldn't return to it. She wanted a relaxed evening out, not one where she was forced to rehash the chaos that was her life these days.

To Celia's relief, the conversation turned to a discussion of grandchildren, each of the women resorting to their mobile phones to share recent photos which were duly admired. Celia marvelled that she'd reached an age where grandchildren could help provide a bond. She and Jan had a special one, sharing Si.

'You're both so lucky,' Anna said with a sigh. 'My little Susie is in the States, so we mostly only get to visit via Skype or Facetime.'

This led to Anna talking about her daughter, then her and Jan's parents, who Celia had met a couple of times. It wasn't till they'd finished eating and were on their last glass of wine that Anna returned to Celia's predicament.

'What you need,' she said, waving her glass in the air, 'is a new man in your life. Take it from someone who's been there. I was pretty down when I met Marcus and … Well, suffice to say, we're gloriously happy. I can honestly say he changed my life.'

Celia gave her what she hoped was a polite smile. 'I don't think…'

'Anna's right,' Jan said. 'Is there anyone on your horizon?'

Celia shook her head and took a sip of wine, but she couldn't help but picture the blond heartthrob called Johnno Henderson.

Anna seemed to consider for a moment. 'I know the perfect man for you,' she said after a long pause. 'Right age. Intelligent. Funny. Charming…What?' she asked as both Jan and Celia burst out laughing.

'You sound like a used-car salesman,' Jan said between breaths. 'Who *is* this paragon?'

'Marcus has a mate. We go rowing together, and I think he's perfect. If I hadn't met Marcus first…' But her eyes softened at the mention of her husband's name, and Celia felt a flash of envy. 'Johnno…'

Celia flushed, embarrassed Anna seemed to have read her innermost thoughts. She was too flustered to hear Jan's gasp of astonishment.

'We've met,' Celia heard herself saying in a small voice.

'Yes,' Anna said. 'He told us he'd met you at your… at the book launch.'

A blush suffused Celia's neck and face. She wanted to hide but there was nowhere to go.

'You're blushing,' Anna said, 'Have you...?'

'He came into Isabella to see me.' She looked down at her hands which were trembling.

The eyes of the other two women widened.

Anna was first to recover. 'He did? Well, he's even more of a dark horse than I thought. The cunning devil.'

Celia turned even redder. 'You've been talking about me to him!'

'I may have mentioned you. But he said...'

'What?'

'He could find his own women. Looks like maybe he did.'

There was a moment's silence.

'Jan knows him, too,' Anna said with a sideways glance at her sister. It was Jan's turn to blush.

'It was when I'd left Graham. There was nothing to it. He's way too young for me. But he made a good companion.' She smiled as if in reminiscence.

'Oh, I think there was a bit more to it than that,' Anna said.

'Not really.' Jan paused, as if wondering how much to divulge. 'I may have led him to believe...' Jan's face turned even redder, the blush spreading down to her collar. She fidgeted. 'But when it came to it, I couldn't. I love my husband and I think it took that experience to make me realise how much.'

'What's he like?' Celia couldn't hide her curiosity.

'Just as Anna said. He's intelligent, funny, very charming. He has a veritable bachelor pad with fantastic views over Darling Harbour, black leather sofa, super sound system, corner bar, the lot. And the bedroom...'

Celia put her hands over her ears. 'Sounds like a player.'

'He was, but that was more than three years ago,' Anna interrupted. 'He's changed. I should know. As I said, Marcus and I see him every Sunday. He's not getting any younger and...'

'None of us are,' Jan said.

They laughed, all conscious of their attempts to hide the grey beginning to show between hair appointments.

'No, really. He's ready to settle down with the right woman.'

Both looked pointedly at Celia.

'You don't think... No.' She shook her head, but it was a tiny shake as she remembered how he'd come to her rescue, how he'd seemed understanding, how....

'He *is* rather dishy,' she said.

'And charming. *And* he knows how to treat a woman.'

'But he's always gone for young models you say. I'll never see forty again, and I'm no model.'

'Have you looked at yourself in the mirror lately? You could give any young model a run for her money. You've barely changed since you left modelling. Besides, he's tired of that scene. He even dined out on his own last Saturday and...' Anna buttoned her lip.

Jan and Celia looked at her in surprise.

'Oh, well, you'll probably find out anyway. He saw you, Celia. You were with someone. I expect it was our brother.'

'I did have dinner with Bob last Saturday, but I didn't see Johnno. We went to Baia at Darling Harbour. Oh!' Celia put a hand up to her mouth. 'That's where he lives, you said.'

'He's stalking you,' Jan joked, only to retract it when Celia turned pale. 'No, I didn't mean that. He wouldn't. He's not like that. I found him to be pretty genuine. He was totally accepting when I rejected him. Don't think it had ever happened to him before,' she finished with a grin.

'So?' Anna asked. 'Can we set up something? Get you two together?'

'I don't think so. I'm not ready to meet anyone just yet. I may never be. After Bill,' she sighed, 'I don't know if I can ever trust a man again, not even one that comes as well-recommended as this one.' Celia tipped up her wine glass and drank the last few drops. 'I should be going now. Thanks for this evening. It was good to get to know you better, Anna, and to catch up with you, Jan. I'd love to do it again, but no matchmaking. Okay?'

Jan and Anna smiled in what Celia took to be agreement. But as she drove home, she wondered if Johnno Henderson would try to contact her again.

She shivered, not sure whether it was with anticipation or apprehension.

Eleven

It was Sunday and the day was too glorious to be inside. It would be a beautiful day to visit the zoo, and Si loved seeing the animals. A call to Chloe was all it took, and Celia was on her way to pick up the little boy.

Si was jumping up and down with excitement as they walked through the zoo shop on their way in. He wanted to loiter beside a display of toy monkeys, but Celia managed to move him on with a promise to spend more time there on the way out. She hoped he'd forget, but was sure he wouldn't, and they'd end up adding to his collection of soft toy animals.

'But I don't have one like that,' he complained as she juggled her bag and the map she'd picked up, trying to work out how many of the shows they could fit in while still going around most of the exhibits.

Once in the zoo proper, however, Si was easily distracted, and they were soon part of the crowds of parents, children and tourists wandering around.

'This is where Grandma Jan works,' Celia said as they passed the Education Centre.

'Now?'

'No, not today. Today she'll be home with Grandpa Gray and Uncle Andy. She'll be here tomorrow. What would you like to see, today?' Celia asked, knowing that already at almost four, Si was a regular visitor.

The little boy looked up at her, his small face so like his mother's at the same age, that her heart jumped. He was so trusting. Chloe had been the same. And now she was a mother herself. Celia swallowed.

'The monkeys, please, and the birds and the giraffes and the seals and...' Si was pulling on her hand as he tried to lead her to all the animals he wanted to see.

'Okay!' Celia laughed at the eagerness in the little boy's voice and the confident way he reeled off his list of preferences. 'We'll see what we can fit in.'

They wandered slowly around, Si clearly enjoying showing off to his grandmother, while she marvelled at how well-informed he was. She knew Chloe brought him here a lot, but it appeared her daughter had also been at pains to educate him. She supposed he'd also been here with Jan. The family pass which Chloe had insisted Celia use today meant there was no charge for the little boy. And having the zoo right on their doorstep was a big plus.

'Here, Grandma!' Si pulled Celia towards what she could now see was the Squirrel Monkey walk. She remembered reading about its opening in December. 'It's my favourite!'

Since he'd said that about every exhibit so far, Celia smiled but, as they made their way along the boardwalk which stretched through the exhibit, she was as enthralled as the little boy. The small animals had such cheeky faces as they leapt and swung along the ropes and through the branches, stopping momentarily on the top of a pillar to nibble a piece of fruit before resuming their seemingly endless chase.

The little boy was mesmerised by the monkey troupe and would most likely have been happy to spend the rest of the day laughing at their antics. Celia checked her watch and the map. 'If we want to see the bird show, Si, we need to leave the monkeys.'

Reluctantly, he agreed to move on, with one last lingering look at the little creatures.

'Have you seen the birds, Grandma?' he asked, swinging on her hand. 'They fly right over...' He held his free hand over his head, eyes wide with delight.

'Not for a long time,' Celia replied. 'I came here a lot with your mum and Aunt Han when they were little – just like you.'

'Like me?' Si's look of astonishment that his mother and aunt had ever been like him made Celia laugh aloud. She should have done something like this long ago. Young children were so innocent, so untouched by the vicissitudes of life. It was impossible to feel sad or angry in this company.

They reached the location for the bird show with time to spare. Celia had forgotten what a wonderful setting this was with the backdrop of Sydney Harbour. What other city had a zoo right on the harbour like Sydney? If there was one, she wasn't aware of it. It was perfect. They managed to find seats close to the front of the amphitheatre and settled down to wait.

'I'm hungry.' Si slipped his hand into Celia's. She was glad she'd come prepared and reached into her bag to pull out a pack of raisins.

'Something to drink?' she asked, holding out a bottle of water, but Si shook his head, intent on opening the small cardboard box without spilling the contents.

The show began, and the constant arrival of birds kept Si's attention, while Celia's began to wander. She wished she could remain here in the cocoon of happiness forever, or at least for a few days. A few days with no worries, no Bill, no media, no...

A tug on her arm dragged her back to the present.

'This is the best bit.'

Celia remembered this trick, watching as a galah landed on the keeper's wrist.

'I need someone's help,' the keeper said. 'I need someone with a gold coin.' There was some laughing behind them and someone obviously stood up, because she then asked the volunteer to stand out in the passage-way and hold a gold coin in an outstretched hand.

Si wriggled beside Celia obviously eager for this particular part of the show.

Their eyes followed the bird, turning as it soared over their heads to grasp a coin from the hand of a teenager standing beside... Celia's breath caught in her throat. Surely that was Johnno Henderson sitting beside another long-haired youth. Their eyes met, and he gave her a rueful smile. She quickly turned away. Could this be a coincidence? It had to be. There was no way he could have known she'd be here. She'd only decided this morning.

Celia let her breath out slowly. She was becoming paranoid. The zoo was filled with people. Sydney was a big city. It was the weekend. There was no reason why he shouldn't be here too.

She bit her lip, completely missing the rest of the act where the coin was returned, and sitting through the remainder of the show in a daze. The commentary flowed over her unheard, until the words, 'Remember to always look up,' brought her back, and the sky was filled with the sight and sound of a flock of white, then black cockatoos.

'All done,' Si said in a sad voice, standing up.

By the time Celia joined him and they made their way up the steps to the path, most of the audience had disappeared. Celia was busy watching her and Si's feet, so was surprised to hear her name.

'Hello, Celia.'

Her head jerked up. Her stomach churned. It was him!

'Johnno.'

'And this is?' He gestured to the small boy who looked down at the ground.

'Simon. My grandson. And...?' Celia raised an eyebrow in the direction of the two teenagers who were loitering nearby, one of whom being the boy who'd taken part in the bird show.

'My nephews. The taller one is Dylan and the one hiding behind him is Nathan. My brother's boys.'

'Hello, boys. Enjoy the show?'

The pair muttered and wandered off, evidently unwilling to participate in what promised to be an adult conversation.

'Sorry.' Johnno pushed back an errant lock of hair and grimaced. 'Teenagers! But they've been pretty good so far. It was their idea to visit the zoo and Dylan was stoked to get chosen for the galah deal. Put Nate's nose out of joint I think. Are you having fun with Grandma or is it Nana?' he asked, turning to Celia with a smile.

'Grandma,' she said. 'Why don't you answer Mr Henderson, Si?'

'Oh, Johnno, please!'

'Yes. I like watching the birds,' Simon said with a burst of confidence. 'But the monkeys are my favourites.'

'I think they're everyone's favourites,' Johnno replied easily. 'We're about to find a bite of lunch then take in the seal show. Why don't you both join us?'

Celia was about to politely refuse when Si piped up again. 'I'm hungry, Grandma, and you said we'd see the seals after lunch, too.'

Celia realised she was beaten. Cursing inwardly, she smiled. 'Okay. I think...'

'Food market's just up there,' the boy named Dylan said, suddenly becoming animated at the mention of food. 'Nate and I'll head on and grab a table.'

The pair were off before Johnno could reply. He held up his hands in a gesture of resignation and they followed more slowly, Si pulling at Celia's hand in an effort to catch up with the older boys.

'You have no children of your own?' Celia asked as if she had never discussed him.

'God, no! Sorry, that sounded... I...' Johnno rubbed the back of his neck. 'I've never married. Brother Dan is the one to keep the family name from disappearing. But you have...?'

'Two girls.' Celia realised he probably knew that, knew all about her. If he hadn't read it in the paper, then she was sure Anna had filled him in, just as she'd filled Celia in about Johnno. 'You've probably read all about us.'

Johnno nodded, and Celia saw a look of sympathy in his eyes, before it disappeared, to be replaced with one of annoyance as they arrived at the food market to find Dylan and Nathan engaged in a wrestling match.

'Steady guys. Remember our deal?'

The boys broke apart. 'Sorry, Johnno,' Nathan said, 'it wasn't my fault, Dylan...'

'Not another word or I take you both home. No lunch, No seal show. No ice creams. No movie.'

The pair looked abashed and hoisted their backpacks as if ready to leave.

'Grandma, I'm hungry!' Si's voice broke into the silence, causing the older boys to suddenly notice him.

'Hey matey,' Dylan said, bending down to Si's level. 'How about we find a table where we can watch the elephants?' He reached out to the little boy who, to Celia's surprise, let go of her hand to grasp Dylan's.

Johnno scratched his head. 'I'll never get used to them. They can drive me mad, then turn around and do something like that. He'll be fine with them,' he added, as if anticipating Celia's uneasiness.

'Sure.' But she watched carefully as Si strolled off, one hand in each of the boy's for all the world as if he'd known them forever.

'Well,' she said, 'he hasn't... Until recently there haven't been many men in his life. His dad died, and he and his mother live with my other daughter and her partner. His uncle – his dad's brother – isn't much older than these two. But now Chloe, his mum, has found a...' Celia hesitated. What was Owen? More than a boyfriend, not yet a partner, or was he? 'A significant other is what they call it, I guess,' she said with an embarrassed laugh.

Johnno and Celia joined the three boys at a table. The older two had shed their backpacks and were keeping Si amused pointing to the exploits of the elephants in the nearby enclosure.

'Are you ready for lunch?' Johnno asked, producing cheers from the older boys and a hesitant glance towards Celia from Simon.

'I'll...' Celia began.

'Let me. I got you into this,' Johnno said. 'What's it to be, guys?'

While Dylan and Nathan opted for burgers and Coke, Si whispered in Celia's ear.

'Just sandwiches for us, and juice for Si. I'd love a coffee.'

'Coming up. Help me carry it all back, Dylan?' Without waiting for a reply, Johnno strode off, followed by a reluctant Dylan.

Left alone with Nathan and Si, Celia asked the older boy, 'Do you and your brother often go out with your uncle?'

Nathan kicked the table leg for a moment before replying, 'Depends. Sometimes, if he's busy we don't see him for ages, then he appears, and we have a day like this. He usually goes rowing on Sundays, but he was free today. Johnno's different from Dad. He doesn't treat us like kids. It's as if he's one of us – like a big kid – except when...' He dropped his eyes. 'He won't stand for us mucking up like we were. But he's okay, is Johnno. Are you his girlfriend?'

'No!' Celia was aware the word came out too harshly. 'No,' she said in a gentler voice. 'What makes you think that?'

'Well,' Nathan seemed to be considering the question, 'you're pretty and wear nice clothes. You look like a model. But,' he frowned, 'you seem a bit older than Johnno's usual girlfriends and there's...' He gestured towards Simon with his head.

Celia smiled inwardly but was saved from replying by the return of Johnno and Dylan bearing trays of burgers, chips, sandwiches, Cokes, juice and, much to Celia's relief, two cups of coffee.

The boys quickly demolished their share of lunch and asked

permission to take Simon closer to the elephants. After a questioning look at Johnno, and receiving a nod, Celia agreed, and the boys set off with the parting reminder from Johnno: 'Don't go too far. Remember the seal show starts at two.'

Left alone with Johnno, Celia didn't know what to say. Here she was, sitting beside the man who'd approached her twice, who she'd denied being interested in – even to herself – and whose presence, she now admitted, made her pulse race.

She sighed.

'He's a nice little boy. You must be proud of him.'

'Yes.' *How inane*, she thought. *We have nothing in common. How could Anna possibly have thought we'd be a good match?*

'You must have wondered why I came to your shop and left so suddenly.' He cleared his throat and took a deep breath. 'I came because I couldn't stop thinking about you, because I wanted to see you again, because I read that stuff about your... about Bill, and it infuriated me. I knew you must be hurting and I wanted to do something to help. Then, there he was, and you were so angry. You looked magnificent and I...' He pushed his hair out of his eyes. 'I'm sorry. I know I'm not making much sense.' He fell silent.

Celia stared at him in astonishment. *What was he trying to say?*

She took a sip of her coffee to discover it had gone cold.

'What I'm trying to say is that I think I came there that day to invite you to dinner, then...'

'You weren't sure, or you changed your mind?' Celia asked, a smile tugging at the corner of her mouth.

'A bit of both.' Johnno smiled ruefully. 'The situation wasn't right. I got cold feet. But now we've had lunch together, albeit well chaperoned, maybe you'd consider a repeat performance – without the kids?'

'Another lunch at the zoo?' Celia felt a wild laugh bubble up.

'I think I can do better that that. Do you like seafood?'

Bemused, Celia nodded.

'How about Doyles at Watson's Bay?'

Doyles, the renowned seafood restaurant on the beach at one of Sydney Harbour's most famous bays, and one which Celia loved, though she hadn't eaten there for years, not since... She dismissed the memory of her last visit there as a family when the girls were in their teens. On that occasion, Bill had taken exception to something, whether with the food or Celia she couldn't recall, didn't want to. But it hadn't spoiled the restaurant for her, or her memory of the delicious seafood menu.

'I'd love to.'

'Great. I'll be in touch about that. Meantime…' he checked his watch, 'we'd better make tracks if we want to see the seals do their thing.'

They collected the boys, made their way up the path – Simon choosing to walk between his two new friends – and soon found places in the tiered seating facing the seal pool. The show progressed with the commentary and so much yelling and applause, it would have been difficult to carry on a conversation, even if Celia hadn't been filled with apprehension at what she'd just agreed to.

The seals slid, swam, leapt and performed for their audience who relished every minute of their antics. They laughed at the shark impersonation, and thrilled at the many tricks, before the creatures finally disappeared, and the show was over.

'Home, now, I think,' Celia said, grasping Simon's hand as they stood up to join the rest of the audience in leaving the area. 'Thanks for lunch – and the company,' she said to Johnno. 'Nice to meet you, boys,' to Dylan and Nathan, but they were already moving off, heading for whatever they planned next.

'I should go.' Johnno pointed to the boys. 'Dinner. I'll be in touch.'

Celia watched his back as he ran to catch up with his nephews. Meeting him had been so unexpected, as had lunch and the invitation to dinner.

'Can I have a monkey now Grandma? I've been good.'

Celia had been so caught up in her thoughts, she hadn't noticed they'd already reached the main entrance and shop. Si was holding up one of the toy Spider Monkeys, a hopeful look in his eye – one she found it difficult to deny. She took out her purse to make the purchase, and they returned to the car, the tired but happy little boy clasping his new toy tightly.

On the drive back, Celia's thoughts were in a whirl. *What had she just done? Had she really agreed to dinner at Doyles with Johnno Henderson?*

Twelve

'I took your advice, Anna,' Johnno said, as he tucked into a large piece of steak.

'What advice would that be?' His friend's wife seemed to be racking her brains as to which of the many pieces of advice she'd offered – and he routinely ignored – he was referring.

'Boy this is good stuff, Marcus. Great marinade. You must tell me your secret.'

'Don't change the subject, Johnno.' Anna raised her fork threateningly. 'Advice?'

'Well, I was at the zoo with the terrible two – the bro's boys. You should take Jon there, you two. We spent the whole day and there was still lots we didn't get to see.'

'You're doing it again!'

'Okay.' Johnno forked up a piece of steak before continuing. He enjoyed teasing Anna like this. She was so quick to rise to the bait. 'It was while we were at the bird show. You know…' He held up his hands in surrender as he saw Anna about to interrupt again. 'Celia Ramsay was there with her grandson.' He cut another piece of steak and pierced a cherry tomato with his fork, enjoying the expression of frustration on Anna's face.

'And?' Anna asked.

'Why should there be an "and"?'

'You said you'd taken my advice, you annoying man. Does that mean…?' Johnno saw her expression change and a knowing look appear in her eyes. 'You did, didn't you? You invited her out.'

'Steady on, Anna. The guy only said he'd seen her,' Marcus interrupted. 'Even Johnno doesn't work that quickly.' He gave a sideways glance at his friend, something dawning on him. 'Did you?'

'Ha! You fail to recognise my undoubted charm with the ladies,' Johnno said. 'Well, it wasn't that simple. We had lunch together – all five of us. We got on well. The little guy took an instant liking to my two so we all went to the seal show together, and, yes, I invited her to dinner – to Doyles, Watson's Bay.'

'Doyles? I'm impressed.' Anna said, then turning to Marcus asked, 'Why don't we go there sometime? I love eating by the water.'

'Soon,' Marcus replied, 'but I want to hear the rest of this story.'

'That's it. No more to tell. She agreed. We went our separate ways. End of story. I thought you guys would be pleased I was planning to date someone you've been trying to set me up with.'

'Ye…es,' Anna said slowly.

'What's up, hon?' Marcus asked. 'You were all for doing a bit of matchmaking. Why the gloomy face now that Johnno has met the woman?'

'She's still very vulnerable, Johnno. I wouldn't like to think… I mean… You won't…'

'You're thinking of your sister,' Johnno said frowning. 'I liked Jan a lot. I wasn't playing around. That incident really shook me. Sent me running back to younger women.'

'That's exactly what I mean,' Anna said. 'I don't want to see Celia hurt again. She's been through enough with that bully of a husband. Anyway, when we last spoke, she said she wasn't ready for another relationship.'

The two men gazed at Anna in surprise. Marcus was first to regain the power of speech. 'You mean you've already spoken to Celia about this – about Johnno? Women! I suppose it was that night you met with Jan and her?'

'Steady on.' Johnno dropped his knife and fork with a clatter. 'You've discussed *me* with *her*? Already? And with Jan Turnbull? Hell!'

'We didn't say anything detrimental. Quite the opposite. If I remember correctly, you were described as intelligent, funny and charming.' Anna grinned. 'You can't take exception to that.'

'She's got you there, mate. More wine?' Marcus picked up the wine bottle and refilled Johnno's glass. 'Anna?'

Anna held out her glass.

There was a silence, interrupted by the slamming of a door inside the house.

'That'll be Jon,' Anna said, rising. 'I'll let him know we're out here.' She disappeared.

While she was gone, Marcus took a sip of wine before saying, 'You really shouldn't tease Anna, you know.'

'Yeah, yeah.' Johnno grinned, and lifted his glass.

'And this thing with Celia. Are you serious?'

'Come on, mate. It's a date – dinner. I'm not about to take her to bed, though…' His eyes gleamed, then he caught sight of his friend's expression. 'No, nothing like that. She's a nice lady, good company. She's had a rough time, and I've no intention of adding to her grief. But I did say I was tired of the round of young know-nothings, and you two tried to foist this woman onto me. What's the harm in a dinner date? And it isn't a lot of fun eating at Doyles on your own.'

'There is that,' Marcus conceded with a smile. 'But, given your history…'

'I'm a changed man,' Johnno said matching his smile, as he polished off his wine.

'Hi, Uncle J. Leave any steak for me?' Marcus and Anna's son appeared and took an empty chair.

'How was the game?' Marcus asked. 'And don't make yourself too comfortable. There's a steak and some sausages for you in the kitchen, plus a potato and salad.'

'No need.' Anna appeared carrying a laden plate and a can of Coke and set them down in front of Jon.

'Gee, thanks,' the boy said, opening the can with a loud hiss and taking a long draught.

'You spoil that boy,' Marcus said to Anna, shaking his head. Then he turned back to his son. 'The rugby?'

'Okay. Smithy played a blinder. We won.' He began to eat the steak as if he hadn't seen food for a week.

'See what you have to put up with when you have a teenager in the house,' Marcus said to Johnno, his indulgent smile belying his words.

'Ignore your dad,' Anna advised. 'Glad you won, Jon. Does that mean you go into the semi-finals?'

'Yeah, yeah,' Jon muttered, as he continued to eat, wolfing down the meal in record time, before mumbling something about homework and disappearing inside the house.

'So much for that,' Marcus said, gazing after his son seemingly perplexed. 'What happened to my enthusiastic communicative little boy?'

'He grew up,' Anna said. 'It happens. Wait till he discovers girls.'

'He hasn't?' Johnno asked.

'Don't!' Marcus drained his glass. 'I don't think I'm ready for that yet.'

'You said you were tied up this morning when you both had to give the rowing a miss – something about your folks?' Johnno asked Anna.

'They're beginning to find it more difficult to do things around the place. Even though they're living in a villa in a retirement village, there's still a bit of maintenance. Dad had a fall when he was trying to clean the gutters yesterday, so we went over there this morning. I provided some TLC while Marcus finished the job for him. Neither he nor Mum like being beholden to us for anything, but sometimes they're forced to give in.' She sighed. 'It's not pleasant – this getting older.'

'You're right. I should make the effort to go up and visit *my* olds.'

'They're in Brisbane, like Marcus' folks?'

'Sunshine Coast. They moved into a resort-styled place in Caloundra. Nice part of the world.' That made Johnno remember his notion of finding a place up there himself. He was about to speak again, to share his thoughts, when Marcus broke in.

'How's business? Going well?'

Johnno never knew if Marcus and Anna really understood what he did. As academics, in his view, they lived in an ivory tower with no awareness of how the real world operated. But they always expressed an interest, and he always tried to give them an answer in terms they'd understand. This latest one wasn't too difficult.

'Really well. I'm just about to pull off something that could make a huge difference, not just to me, but to…' He hesitated. He liked to keep his deals under wraps till they were all signed and sealed. But these guys weren't in a position to blow the deal. Hell, they'd barely understand it.

'Imagine an entire new town, out in the west of the city – homes, shops, schools, hospital, factories, maybe even a university. What would that do for the community? Affordable living, everything nearby, no need to travel to work.'

'Wow!' Anna said. 'And you can do that? Build it?'

'Not exactly.'

'What Johnno means is that he can help to set it in motion, arrange the finance, gather the right people together. Is that right, mate?'

'That's about it.' It wasn't exactly, but it was enough for them. 'Still a way to go, but if it all comes together…'

'Hey, we should drink to that.'

'A bit previous. Nothing's signed yet.' As he spoke, Johnno made a mental note to get onto it first thing Monday. It was over a week since he'd had a meeting with the developer. They'd got the proposal off a few days later and should have heard back from him by now. Hopefully everything would move smoothly. The last thing he needed right now was any delay. In addition to his plans for his cut of the deal, the company needed an injection of funds. This one was going to be to everyone's benefit.

They chatted on about this and that, till the sun began to set, a cool breeze started to rustle the leaves and a few drops of rain spattered on the table.

'Time to move,' Anna said, gathering the dirty dishes and making for the house.

'I should be going, too.' Johnno rose and, picking up his empty glass followed her into the kitchen, Marcus in his wake.

'No need to rush off. One for the road?' Marcus asked, once inside with the door firmly closed against the weather.

But Johnno's mind was already elsewhere. He was thinking of the next day, of the calls he needed to make, the meetings he needed to prepare for, the emails he expected to receive and the replies he'd formulate. 'Thanks, but no. I have a few things to do tonight to prepare for the week ahead. It's been good, guys. Thanks.' He hugged Anna, gave her a peck on the cheek, slapped Marcus on the shoulder and called a goodbye – which didn't elicit a reply – upstairs to Jonathon. Then he was in his car and driving home. All thoughts of the day and Celia were pushed to the back of his mind as he began planning what his strategy would be to move the proposed development to the next stage.

Thirteen

'Morning Val.' Celia looked up from the computer as her assistant walked into the office. 'Good weekend?'

'Yes, thanks. You?'

'Good.' Celia leaned back, thinking how much seemed to have happened since she'd seen Val at close of business on Saturday. It was only one day, but the zoo trip and the subsequent dinner invitation from Johnno Henderson seemed to have swelled out to fill her whole weekend. 'I took Si to the zoo.'

'The zoo? Well, that's not exactly what I meant when I urged you to get out more, but I suppose it's a start. I don't expect you'll meet anyone there.'

'As a matter of fact, I did.' Celia fingered the card she'd found in her bag when she got home. A white card with John Henderson, a mobile number and an email address – all in black embossed lettering. There was no more information. He must have slipped it in when she wasn't looking. It had been burning a hole in her pocket ever since and now it lay on her desk as if accusing her. Would he call, or wouldn't he? He could easily find the shop number – and email address. She knew that. Or was slipping his card into her bag a way of asking her to call him? She covered it with her hand, sliding it under a sheaf of papers.

Celia immediately regretted her words. She could see Val was eager for more information. But, before she could ask, or Celia could volunteer more, there was the sound of the door opening.

'Would you...?' she asked gesturing to the shop.

Val went through, and Celia could hear her friendly, 'How can I help you? Are you looking for something in particular, or are you happy to browse?'

Always the professional, Celia thought, blessing the day she'd caught up with her old friend again. She turned back to the invoices she'd been checking, but found it difficult to concentrate. Sliding the paperwork off the desk and into a folder, she closed the computer and joined Val in the shop just as the door opened again and Hannah walked through with Mia in a stroller.

'Han! What are you doing here?' Celia said, bending down to tickle her granddaughter under the chin. 'Where's my beautiful girl then?' The little girl chuckled, and Celia straightened up to gaze at Hannah.

'Hi, Mum. Sorry to put this on you without warning. Can you look after Mia for a bit? Just a couple of hours. I need to meet Ingrid in town and…'

'Meet Ingrid?' Celia asked, completely ignoring the request to mind her granddaughter in her place of business. 'But you live together. What couldn't you…?'

'She wants me to meet a marriage celebrant,' she whispered. 'The woman is only available today, and Ingrid's keen to get into her schedule.'

'Marriage celebrant?' Celia's voice rose even as Hannah put a finger to her lips, and both Val and the customer looked round to see what the disturbance was. In a quieter voice, Celia added, 'It's not even legal yet. Don't you think it's a bit soon to be booking a celebrant?'

'I do, but Ingrid's keen to get the show on the road. She reckons once it is legal, there'll be a rush and she wants our next child to be…'

'She's pregnant?'

'Possibly. Mia?' Hannah asked again, checking her watch.

'Surely. But Isabella isn't a creche.'

'Thanks a million, Mum.' Hannah leaned forward to give Celia a hug, just as the door opened again.

'Well, isn't this a sight for sore eyes,' Bill's voice boomed.

There was a stunned silence, broken only by Val farewelling the customer, and the door closing behind her.

'Dad!'

'Bill!'

Hannah and Celia spoke together.

'Isn't this a nice family get-together. I suppose this is your bastard,' he sneered.

'Your granddaughter,' Celia said. 'And you're not supposed to be here. You agreed.'

'Julian agreed. I did no such thing. You're still my wife and…'

'I think you should leave.' Val's calm voice took them all by surprise.

Bill swung around to face her. 'And you are?'

'Val Russell. I work for Celia and I understand you have no business here, so you should go.'

Celia stared at her, surprised at her temerity in facing up to the bully, while Hannah carefully manoeuvred the stroller through to the office.

'Too ashamed to face me?' Bill yelled after Hannah.

'You haven't spoken to her in years. Why should she have anything to say to you now?' Celia asked. 'And I believe you've been asked to leave.'

'I only wanted to…'

But Celia had no interest in discovering what he wanted or didn't want. 'I'm calling my lawyer,' she said, making a move toward the office. 'He did mention an AVO if you came here again.'

'No need for that. Can't we…?'

But Celia heard no more. She was already in the office with Hannah and Mia. Hannah closed the door.

'Sit down, Mum. You're trembling. He can't be allowed to get away with this. Call Bob.' She handed Celia the phone. Celia took it, then laid it down.

'Not now.' Her legs felt like jelly. She wasn't able to talk to anyone. How dare he come here like this – just walk in as if… She put her head down on her arms on the desk. 'I'll be right in a minute.'

'You need to take out that order. Make it legal, Mum.'

'No, Han. He *is* your dad. I can't.'

'But he can't just walk in here like that. There has to be some way of preventing it.'

'I'll handle it.' Celia raised her head, feeling her strength returning, a white anger beginning to fuel her. 'You go along and meet Ingrid and your celebrant. Plan for happier times. Mia will be fine here. And, yes, I'll call Bob,' she said, seeing the concern on Hannah's face.

There was a loud bang from the shop, startling the two women.

'The door,' Celia said. 'I bet Val's managed to get rid of him.'

'This time,' Hannah said. 'But what if he comes back?'

'I said I'd take care of it and I will. Now go!' She opened the door and ushered Hannah out, leaving it open so she could keep an eye on the little girl.

'Thanks, Val,' she said, when Hannah had gone. 'How did you do it?'

Val held up her mobile. 'I threatened to call the police.' She chuckled. 'That saw him off in no time flat. You *are* going to call your solicitor?'

'Not you too!' But Celia returned to the office and picked up the phone.

After speaking with Bob, who promised to have a strong word with both Bill and Julian and threaten further legal action, Celia was reassured. She didn't want to go down the AVO route if it could be avoided.

When the phone rang again she thought it was Bob ringing back, so was surprised when it was Johnno wanting to make arrangements for the promised dinner at Doyles.

Despite Celia's earlier uncertainty about seeing Johnno again, she still retained the remnants of her anger at Bill's arrival. That fuelled her sufficiently to agree to meet Johnno on Wednesday. She did draw the line at having him pick her up, preferring to arrange to meet him at the restaurant. She told herself this was so she could leave when she wished, and to avoid any awkwardness at the end of the evening.

She hung up with a sense of relief and a quiver of anticipation. She hoped Bill would hear about her date. That would show him she was no easy target, that she no longer considered herself to be his wife, or to be bound by that ridiculous agreement. She was a free agent and could dine with whoever she wanted.

And there was a small part of her that buzzed with excitement at the notion of seeing Johnno again.

Fourteen

Johnno checked his emails again. Still nothing. He drew out his copy of the documents he'd sent over to the developer to determine he'd got everything right. He scanned the front page – yes, there it was – Vernon Wright and Company. He matched it with the card in the file. Then he flipped through the other pages, all exactly as they'd discussed. He was about to pick up the phone when Allan popped his head into the office.

'Heard back from Wright yet?'

'No. Just about to call him.' Seeing a worried look on his colleague's face, his scalp prickled. *Did Allan know something he didn't?* 'Why? What have you heard?'

'Nothing specific. But there's some talk about another developer being caught out with dirty dealings. No name at this stage, but… I wondered.'

'Can't be Wright. We'd have heard.' But would they? If the guy was in trouble, wouldn't his first thought be to save his skin? Johnno's project would be way down the list. 'What exactly is being said?'

'A para in the *Fin Review*. It just states that the Corruption Watchdog is investigating yet another NSW developer for fraud – no names.'

'Haven't got to the papers yet, today.' Johnno frowned. He'd been so buoyed up about his meeting with Celia Ramsay yesterday, he'd forsaken his usual habit of checking the papers first thing, in favour of calling her and booking a table for dinner. He scratched his head.

Damn! He'd been delighted at her quick acceptance of the date. But that's what women did to you – interrupted your routine and made you miss crucial information. 'I'll call them now. Put my mind at rest.'

'Let me know how it goes. I need to get things finalised.'

'Will do.' He picked up the phone as Allan left.

After a few moments, Johnno's call was answered by a harried-sounding Vernon Wright. At the sound of Johnno's voice, Vernon seemed to calm down, and became apologetic.

'Had a few dramas this end,' he said. 'Nothing major. We're still on track. Can you give us a few more days?'

Johnno agreed, but pressed his lips together in a grimace. Dramas? Didn't sound good. He opened his computer to check the item Allan had referred to. There it was and, as Allan had said, there was no indication of the company in question. He leaned back in his chair. He'd been down this road before and, as a result, examined each company carefully before making any approach. Wright had checked out.

This one had to work. He had a lot staked on it. It was the one that would see him make a name for himself. He just had to wait. But patience wasn't his strong suit.

He wandered out into the office, taking a few moments to chat to his fellow consultants before deciding he needed some fresh air.

'Back in ten,' he said to Tania as he strode out and pressed the button on the elevator, heading down into George Street and towards his favourite coffee shop.

A long black in his hand, he opened his mobile and checked the article in the *Fin Review* again. It still said the same as before. No company was named. Johnno sighed and closed his eyes.

Until Allan poked his head into the office he'd been feeling on top of the world. He had a good feeling about this Celia woman. She came highly recommended by Marcus and Anna, though why that should bother him, he wasn't sure. And he resented Marcus' implication he'd hurt her, his admonition to treat her carefully, that she was vulnerable. He'd been around the block a few times. He knew how to treat a woman.

He opened his eyes suddenly, understanding this wasn't the sort of woman he normally dated. He dragged a hand through his hair. That's what his friend had been getting at. Celia was no young model out for a good time. There were no killer heels, no carefully manicured nails, no human Barbie doll. She was a real person and one who'd suffered, who was still suffering.

She was a mother, a grandmother, even. God, that made him feel old! And she'd been badly burned already by the bastard she'd been married to – was still married to. He knew he needed to tread carefully here. He'd screwed it up with Anna's sister, and had no intention of making the same mistake again. Still… He rubbed his chin.

They were a lot alike – Celia and Jan. Both mature, independent women in a vulnerable situation. Was he taking advantage of the that? He didn't think so. In fact, he intended to make sure that wasn't the case. He planned to move cautiously with Celia, be a friend, maybe even get to know her daughters – he'd already met the younger one. He thought back. It must have been around four years ago, when he'd visited Jan in the shop, in Isabella, and Chloe – that was her name – had been looking for a job and he'd recommended Rod Miller Realty. The girl had worked there for a bit when she was pregnant. From memory she'd been a pretty little thing, not unlike her mother.

Johnno wondered if the girl remembered him, and his frequent visits to see Rod. Back then, they'd had quite a few deals going together and he strongly suspected at least one of the young girls on the staff had a crush on him – one which he'd no doubt encouraged at the time.

How he'd changed. He now recognised the futility of the relationships he'd pursued, the girls he'd flirted with, the… Johnno shook his head. *He* knew he was a changed man, but how did he convey that to Celia Ramsay, a woman who'd no doubt heard all about his earlier exploits and been warned about him.

He drained his coffee and checked his watch. The ten minutes he'd intended had stretched to thirty. He needed to get back to work.

As he strolled back, dodging the tourists and weekday shoppers, he reminded himself that Celia was acting cautiously too. Her refusal to be picked up, her determination to meet him at Doyles – all spoke of self-preservation. She wasn't going to be an easy person to get to know.

Fifteen

What was she doing?

Celia argued with herself as she drove across the city to the Eastern Suburbs and weaved her way through the streets to Watson's Bay.

Okay, it was only dinner, but it was a date. On the spur of the moment and, she acknowledged, fuelled by anger at Bill, she'd agreed to a date with a man she barely knew – a man she wasn't even sure she wanted to know. And a date! When had she last been on a date? Did she even know how to behave?

Celia thought back to the conversation with Anna King. Anna had rung her around lunchtime that day – a surprise call. Anna had never called her before. Her words had been a shock.

'You're a sly one.'

'I beg your pardon?'

'You and Johnno Henderson. You pretended you didn't know him. Now you're dating.'

'I didn't. We're not.'

Then a conversation had ensued, during which Anna revealed Johnno had told her and Marcus about meeting Celia at the zoo and that they'd warned him to take care.

'He says he's changed and he may be right. I know I suggested you meet him, but now... I don't know... I wouldn't like you to think we encouraged him. He could charm the birds off the trees. Maybe he pulled the wool over our eyes too. Although...'

While Celia was grateful for her friends' concern, she was mildly annoyed they felt free to discuss her like that. Did it mean Johnno was really interested in her, or that he was playing with her affections? *What was she thinking? What affections?* She had no feelings for him, fond or otherwise. She considered him a pleasant companion, a... Okay, he was a handsome devil – charming, too. She'd give him that. And he'd caught her in a weak moment.

She was so busy over-thinking the evening ahead that she arrived at her destination without noticing. Well, it was only one dinner, and it was in a lovely restaurant. She stepped out of the car, pressed the key to lock it and walked towards the entrance.

'Here you are.' Johnno was waiting to greet her. He was wearing a black leather jacket, the collar of a pale blue shirt showing at the neck, his mouth curved up in a lazy, lopsided smile, his hazel eyes twinkling.

She'd forgotten just how handsome he was. No man should be that good-looking at his age. Celia made a snap decision to put all her misgivings aside and enjoy the evening. It would be something to look back on during the lonely nights ahead, during what promised to be a difficult divorce settlement and further battles with Bill.

*

Wow, wow, and wow!

The exclamation echoed in Johnno's head. If he hadn't known Celia was close to his own age, he'd have taken her for mid-thirties at worst, late-twenties at best. Dressed in a smart red pantsuit, a black frilly something edging the jacket, and wearing heels that almost took her to his height, she was hot.

'Hello.' Her voice was tentative, as if she wasn't sure she was in the right place – or didn't want to be here.

'Shall we go in?' He reached out a hand, but she evaded it, merely walking beside him, so close he could smell her perfume. It was one he recognised – a spicy blend he was familiar with, though he couldn't recall just which of his former women friends had favoured it. It spoke of a different side to the elegant woman beside him – one which intrigued him even more.

'Sorry I couldn't arrange a full moon for you,' Johnno said once they were seated, and immediately berated himself silently. That was something he'd say to his usual date – a way of trying to set the romantic scene for later in the evening.

'Sorry,' he repeated, 'I didn't…' He floundered. Damn it! He was nervous. He – Johnno Henderson – was acting like a teenager on his first date. *What was the matter with him? What was the effect this woman had?*

But it didn't appear to have fazed Celia. She looked up into the almost black sky and smiled.

'A new moon, or almost. My mother used to say I should turn the coins in my pocket and make a wish on the new moon.'

'And what would you wish for?'

Celia sighed, closed her eyes briefly, just long enough for Johnno to note her clear skin and long eyelashes, then opened them again, a wistful expression in their grey softness. She linked her fingers together on the table. 'I'd wish…' She paused. 'I'd wish it was a year from now, and I had my life sorted.'

The waiter's appearance bearing two large menus saved Johnno from replying.

After studying them carefully, both decided to order oysters and to share the seafood paella for two, and, after some consideration, Johnno ordered a bottle of *Pierre Brevin Sancerre* to accompany their meal.

'I don't drink much,' Celia demurred.

'That's okay. We don't have to drink the entire bottle.' Johnno settled back in his chair, feeling more comfortable, but noting Celia's hands fiddling with the cutlery. He knew he had to put her at ease, or the evening was going to be a disaster.

'Would it help to talk about it? I know I'm almost a stranger but sometimes it's easier to talk to someone who's completely uninvolved.'

Celia didn't respond immediately, looking out onto the darkened water instead, and making Johnno wonder if he'd made a dreadful blunder.

The waiter arrived with the wine. Johnno inspected the label, tasted it and nodded to him to fill Celia's glass.

When the man had gone, Celia picked up her wine, took a sip and held the glass, tracing the moisture on the outside with one finger. After a few moments she met Johnno's eyes.

'You may be right. As you no doubt have heard, I left Bill a couple of years ago and was in the process of arranging a divorce when...' She took a gulp of wine, almost choking. 'Sorry. When my solicitor – do you know Anna's brother, Bob?'

Johnno nodded. He'd never met the bloke, but knew of him.

'He's very thorough and has been a great support. Anyway, he discovered from Bill's solicitor – a weasel called Julian Clarke.'

Johnno nodded. He knew Clarke.

Celia continued. 'Bill had signed a contract to write this memoir – the one that's just been published. Well,' Celia cleared her throat, 'I was a bit short of cash at the time and Bob managed to arrange... Heck this sounds so mercenary.'

Fascinated, Johnno shook his head and sipped his wine.

'We signed an agreement that I'd get some of the divorce settlement up front in exchange for my agreeing to be part of the media stuff around the book launch.' She shook her head. 'I had no idea it would take so long, that my life would be on hold until...' She took another gulp of wine.

At this rate, he'd have to order another bottle.

'Anyway, that's all gone out the window with this allegation, and it looks like I might finally be able to set the divorce proceedings in motion.'

'And the other day – in the shop – Bill?'

'He's a bully who can't take no for an answer,' Celia said bitterly. 'He has the crazy notion I'm still his wife – well, I suppose, legally, I am. But not in any other sense. Haven't been for ages. Bill doesn't seem to accept that. My solicitor thinks I may have to take an AVO out against him, but I don't want to.' She placed her glass back on the table. 'I probably shouldn't drink any more.'

The restaurant was beginning to fill up, and Johnno was glad he'd made a booking. He knew there could often be a long wait for those who'd failed to plan ahead. By the time their oysters arrived, the room was humming with chatter and peals of laughter.

The pair were silent as they swallowed down the salty delicacy.

'I'm glad you're a fan of oysters, too,' Johnno said.

'Love them,' Celia said, 'though it took me a while to get used to the slippery sensation.' She laughed.

Good, Johnno thought, *she's beginning to relax*. Celia had seemed on edge ever since she first arrived, and the way she'd taken her first gulps of wine had confirmed that. But now she'd shared a bit about her ex – all of which he'd already heard – it was as if she'd shed a burden.

'Tell me a bit about what you do,' she said, surprising him. 'I've been boring you with *my* tale of woe. You work in the city, don't you? Your business card didn't give much away. That was a bit sneaky, you know, slipping it into my bag.'

'Sorry!' Johnno felt himself redden. The business card thing was something he'd started doing more years ago than he cared to remember. He'd found it piqued curiosity in the young women he went around with. But Celia wasn't one of those – and he'd made his first mistake. 'Not sure why I did that,' he lied, seeing her give him an apprehensive glance.

Then, he remembered her question. 'It's a bit complicated.'

'Try me.' Celia set down her cutlery, leant her elbows on the table, chin in her hands and met his eyes with an unflinching gaze.

'I'm a bit of a management consultant. I work in the finance business – usually with investors and developers. It's difficult to explain exactly what we do.'

'So you work in a company? In the city?'

'That's right. And I liaise with people in real estate and investment. I guess you could say I'm a bit of a middle-man.'

'Hmm.'

Johnno could see Celia was puzzled. He'd never had to describe his business to anyone before. Most of the women he'd dated in the past only cared that he had money and could take them to nice places.

'So give me an example. What are you working on now, for instance?'

'Imagine a new town on the outskirts of the city…' Johnno described the project in much the same way he'd described it to Marcus and Anna. But Celia wasn't so easily satisfied.

'So what can go wrong? I'd hazard a guess a project like that isn't all smooth sailing.'

Johnno swallowed. He still hadn't received the documents back from Wright. Celia had hit the nail on the head.

'Bill had some business deals – real estate and such. A few of those didn't work out exactly as he anticipated. In fact, he nearly lost his shirt on one of them.' She gazed into space, clearly lost for a moment – remembering. 'So, yours are always successful?'

'Not always,' Johnno admitted, 'but mostly. I do a careful risk analysis before I make any moves, and ensure I deal with honest companies and individuals – as far as I can.' The image of Vernon Wright flashed before his eyes. *He'd better not have got it wrong this time.*

Johnno sensed a presence at his side and looked up with a smile of relief at the waitress who'd come to remove their plates. She simpered at him as she picked up his plate more slowly than necessary. Just in time, he stopped himself from winking – his customary response on such occasions, often followed by the slipped business card and a follow-up call.

It was actually a relief to have put all that behind him, and to be spending time with someone who was interested in him for more than what she might get from him. *Was* Celia interested? He hoped so. He certainly wanted to see her again, though he didn't want to do anything to prejudice her divorce proceedings. He had no intention of being cited as "the other man", though the publicity around Bill Ramsay's extramarital peccadillos made that possibility extremely unlikely.

*

Unobserved by Johnno, Celia had watched the interaction with the waitress with amusement. Given the early days of her marriage to Bill, she wasn't entirely immune to the temptation of a good-looking man where young women were concerned. Back then she'd just sighed and ignored it. Then, as the years went on, she'd ceased to worry, sure the coterie of fans that followed the game were thrilled to be the target of their hero's attention. But now, given the recent revelation, she wasn't so sure.

She hadn't expected to experience the same adulation for her current dinner date. She gave Johnno more serious consideration, watching him while he paid the bill and made easy conversation with the cashier.

She'd thought him a handsome devil earlier, but now she took time to examine him more carefully. She could see how some would consider him to be a hunk. Standing there, the black leather jacket hanging open, a curl of blond hair peeping out of the open-necked shirt, he could be mistaken for a blond Greek god.

As she watched, an idea took root in Celia's mind. She'd already toyed with the hope Bill might hear about this date, but it was only one dinner. What if they became what was commonly known as *an item*? What if she was seen about town on Johnno's arm? That really would put Bill's nose out of joint and would scupper all his happy family talk.

She smiled inwardly, a smile that appeared on her lips as Johnno turned towards her and took her elbow.

'Ready to go? I'll walk you to your car. Where are you parked?'

Celia allowed him to keep his hand on her arm, intent on her plan and stifling the quiver of excitement his touch triggered. At the car, she pressed the control to unlock it and turned to face Johnno.

'I enjoyed tonight. Can we do it again?'

'I'd love to,' Celia replied, slipping into the car before he could attempt to kiss her, either on the cheek or the lips. That wasn't part of her plan.

Sixteen

'For you, I think. Hand-delivered just now.'

The thick envelope plopped down on Johnno's desk. He looked up at Tania's smiling face, then focussed on the package. He turned it over to see the sender listed as Wright and Company.

'Isn't this the one you've been waiting for?'

'Thanks, Tania. And could you...?'

'Coffee coming up.' She turned and left, her hips swinging in an unspoken invitation.

Johnno pushed back the stray lock of hair – the one that seemed to get him into trouble with young women like Tania. But no more. He picked up a letter opener and slit the envelope before flipping through the pages. Yes, it was all there, signed and initialled as required.

He leant back with a sigh of relief, just as a large mug of black coffee was placed on his desk.

'Thanks.'

He took a gulp of the hot liquid, almost burning his throat as he swallowed and, still holding the mug, called Allan into his office.

'Here it is. All signed and sealed. Must have been some other developer who went bust.'

'This time,' Allan said, his words seeming to be a prediction of more to come.

Johnno shrugged it off. 'Can I leave it to you to get things moving? Keep me informed of the progress and...'

'I know – send you the project plan and a weekly report – or would you like it daily?'

'Weekly's fine.' Johnno had worked with Allan for a number of years and knew he was an efficient project manager. He'd see the project milestones were met and would manage to keep all parties informed and happy. It would be a lengthy development, one of the biggest he'd undertaken so far, but he had no doubt it would be a success.

Buoyed up by the fruitful conclusion to what had been a stressful week business-wise, Johnno could at last look forward to the weekend. 'Is there anything else?' he asked, as his colleague hovered in the doorway.

'Have you seen *The Daily* this morning? No,' Allan said answering his own question, 'I don't suppose you read it.'

Johnno was puzzled. *What had* The Daily *to do with them – or him?*

'It's just that...' Allan shifted awkwardly, still clutching the Wright document. 'Didn't you say you'd been to Bill Ramsay's book launch – the footy star who's been up for sexual assault?'

'Alleged,' Johnno corrected him.

'Whatever. Well, there's another article today. Seems his daughter's been photographed in one of those marches for same-sex marriage. Her and her partner. There's a child, too. Bet he didn't have *that* in his memoir.' Allan disappeared, leaving Johnno gazing after him. All he could think of was what this would do to Celia and her daughter. Damn Bill Ramsay! He could take care of himself. But Johnno knew Celia had been worried about the media discovering her daughter and grandchildren. It seemed they didn't have to look very far.

He picked up the phone to call Celia.

*

The shop had been surprisingly busy for a Friday morning. 'Whew,' Celia exclaimed when a noisy group of elderly women finally left with only one purchase – and that a silk scarf. 'Where did they all come from?'

'I think this may be what brought them, though they were too polite to say. Some people like to enjoy others' discomfort.' Val held out a copy of a newspaper which one of their customers had dropped. It was folded open at the gossip column.

Celia threw a curious glance at Val as she picked up the offending item and read the headline: *Whose daughter is marching for her lesbian rights?* Below the headline was a photo of Hannah and Ingrid waving a placard on which were the words *Marriage Equality Now.* There followed a paragraph identifying Hannah as the older daughter of Bill Ramsay, former football player and author of a recently released memoir, and Celia Lang, former model, now owner of the fashion boutique, Isabella, in Mosman. It went on to wonder why Hannah's sexual preferences hadn't been mentioned in her father's book and to speculate about his other daughter.

Celia threw the paper down in disgust. 'How could they? They should have known.' But it wasn't clear – even to her – whether she was talking about the reporters or her daughter. Bill would have a field day with this – or would he? Celia could imagine his anger and disgust. And, no doubt he'd be asked for comment.

'Do you think that's why we've had so many women here this morning? They've come to see how I react to having my daughter's private life spread across that rag?'

'Could be. That march was last week, wasn't it? It took them a long time to latch on. Someone must have alerted them, and they checked through all the shots taken on the day.'

'I should ring Han. Hell, this is just what I was afraid of. They've been leaving Bill alone since that last outburst, and I thought the girls had escape the media scrutiny.'

She went into the office, took a deep breath and picked up the phone to call Hannah, but the call went to voicemail. 'Have you seen today's paper, Han? Call me!'

No sooner had she finished the call, than her mobile rang. Without looking to see the caller ID, Celia said, 'Han?'

But it wasn't her daughter's voice.

'I'm sorry, Celia. I just saw the paper.'

Celia felt herself go limp. Johnno had seen it too. By now all of Sydney would have seen it. She wasn't angry with Hannah and Ingrid for protesting for something they believed in, something that would change their lives. She'd done a bit of protesting herself in her younger days – against uranium mining – but she'd managed to avoid getting her name and photo in the papers. Bill would go spare.

'I did, too,' she managed to say.

'Have they contacted you?'

'Han and Ingrid?' Celia was puzzled.

'The reporters.'

'Oh!' Celia's hand went to her chest. Of course. It was to be expected that she'd be their next target. With a bit of luck, they still wouldn't know where the girls lived, but it would only be a matter of time. She'd need to contact them, warn them. 'No, not yet. But they mentioned Isabella, so it's no secret where I am. It may have bought me a bit of free publicity.' She grimaced.

'There's that.' Johnno was silent for a moment. 'I wanted to invite you to dinner again, but the timing may not be...'

'No.' Celia remembered the plan which she'd hatched in the restaurant. 'The timing's perfect. I don't intend to let a bit of publicity intimidate me, prevent me from going out, being seen in public. I'm not going to be a victim.'

There was silence at the other end of the phone, and Celia wondered if she'd sounded too forceful. 'What I mean is that I won't change my life because it may cause a bit of bad publicity for Bill. Unless you feel you'd rather stay away,' she added, suddenly realising that, as her companion, Johnno might also become a focus for the gossip columns. Though wasn't that exactly what she wanted?

Celia heard an intake of breath.

'How about tomorrow night? I have an invitation to an opening at a friend's gallery in Paddington. Or is art not your thing? Fabian dabbles in what I guess is called Pop Art. It's not everyone's cup of tea, but he's an old friend and I promised I'd look in. We could have dinner afterwards.'

Celia pictured Johnno. No doubt he was sitting at a desk in some high-up glass-fronted office, his blond hair falling over his face, his eyes full of doubt waiting for her response.

'That sounds interesting, though I'm no art critic. I'm one of those plebeian people who knows what they like, but can't explain why.'

'It starts at six. Is that too early for you?'

Celia considered. She usually closed up at five on a Saturday and liked to get everything ready for the following Monday before leaving. Maybe... 'I could come straight from here. I...' She tried to work out the route to Paddington, to judge the traffic at that time on a Saturday evening, to think what the parking might be like.

'Why don't I pick you up? I have to be over that way on Saturday.'

'But…'

'You can always get a taxi back,' Johnno said, seeming to recognise her reluctance.

'Okay. Thanks.'

'I'll be there around five to give us time to navigate Saturday night traffic on the bridge,' he said, echoing her concerns.

*

The crowd was different to what she was used to, and Celia wasn't sure whether to be pleased or disappointed that this wasn't somewhere she'd bump into her soon-to-be-ex-husband.

Bob Frazer had called her yesterday, and they'd set up an appointment for the following week to get her divorce proceedings underway.

Celia was sipping her second glass of champagne, feeling quite mellow and laughing at Johnno's description of the piece of art they were studying, when she had the distinct feeling she was being watched. Turning carefully, she was transfixed by a glare from none other than Julian Clarke. *What was Bill's lawyer doing here?*

There was, of course, no reason why he shouldn't be here. But, as far as Celia knew, Julian had never been a patron of the arts. Like Bill, he was more likely to be at a sporting event.

Oh shit, he was coming towards them. Celia nudged Johnno's arm.

He turned just as Julian reached them.

The glare had become an angry scowl. 'You shouldn't be here,' he hissed. 'Not with him.' His scowl expanded to include Johnno, who merely appeared amused.

'Steady on, Clarke,' he said. 'Mind your manners or I'll get you thrown out.' He looked around as if seeking Fabian or one of the security men employed for the evening.

'Johnno!' The soft voice seemed to float on a waft of an expensive musky fragrance. Its owner was a svelte young woman with jet-black hair and a haughty expression. She slipped her arm into Julian's in a proprietary gesture.

'Siri, honey,' Julian's tone softened as he turned toward the woman, 'this isn't any of your business. Why don't you fetch me another drink?'

But it seemed the woman wasn't about to leave.

'Aren't you going to introduce me, Johnno?' she asked, ignoring Julian's stunned expression.

'You know Henderson?' Julian asked in a tight voice.

'Of course, darling. Doesn't everyone? But I don't think I know his companion. Though you do look a tad familiar.' She favoured Celia with a long stare. 'I know. You're...' She frowned, as if trying to recall where the two women might have met.

'Celia Ramsay – Celia Lang that was.' Johnno resolved her confusion. 'She was a top model before your day.' He threw an apologetic look at Celia.

Siri's face cleared. '*I* know where I've seen you,' she said. 'You're Bill Ramsay's wife.' She turned to Julian who was clearly embarrassed by this conversation and eager to remove both Siri and himself from their company. 'Why didn't you tell me Bill would be here, darling?' She gazed around the room in bewilderment.

'He's not,' Julian said shortly.

'So...'

Celia saw it dawn on Siri that she was here as Johnno's companion, partner, plus one, or whatever it was called.

'You and Johnno? Well!' She smiled slyly.

Just one word, but it spoke a thousand. It told Celia that Siri and Johnno had once been an item. She wondered what he saw in her, Celia, when he'd been used to squiring around beautiful young women like Siri.

For a moment Celia felt old; old and used up. Then Johnno squeezed her arm. 'Celia's with me,' he said, and Celia could hear the pride in his voice. 'And you two?' he raised an eyebrow as if he knew the answer but wanted confirmation.

'I'm Siri Clarke, now, aren't I, darling?' she simpered, holding out a hand to display a wide golden band and a large diamond ring.

Julian ran a finger round the inside of his collar.

'Congratulations,' Celia said, feeling that some sort of comment was called for. Johnno seemed to have been struck dumb. *Hadn't he known about Siri and Julian Clarke? Did he still harbour feelings for her?*

She was exactly the type Jan and Anna had said he went for – or used to, she reminded herself. He was with *her* tonight.

'We need to go.' Julian began to steer his wife away from them, throwing one last, 'You'll be hearing about this,' over his shoulder as he strode off, Siri tottering to keep up with him, hindered by her tight skirt and heels even higher and narrower than Celia's.

'An old flame?' Celia asked a still silent Johnno when they were alone again.

'Ye…es. I didn't…' He seemed to pull himself together. 'I knew she was married, but I didn't know… Julian bloody Clarke, of all people. He must be…' Then he seemed to recollect himself, perhaps realising he was much the same age as Julian. 'Well,' he let out a long breath, 'there's no accounting for taste.'

'Where there's money…' Celia murmured.

'What? Oh, right. That's probably what she saw in me, too. Or thought she did.'

No, Celia thought, maybe Johnno's apparent wealth *had* been part of his attraction, but there was no way anyone could compare Johnno's handsome, devil-may-care outlook and appearance with Julian Clarke's staid conservative exterior and, from what she knew of Bill's old mate, his chauvinistic attitude to women. No, Siri had definitely sold out there.

'Maybe we should go too. Hungry?'

'Mmm.' But the recent confrontation with Julian Clarke with its reminder of Bill and her impending divorce had soured the evening for Celia. She'd dearly like to go home, have a hot bath, pour herself a glass of wine, and not have to think about Bill, the media, the girls, or anything else.

Johnno was looking at her strangely. *She hadn't said that out loud, had she?*

'Dinner?' he asked again. 'I thought maybe we could try Thai – or would you prefer Italian?' he added when Celia didn't respond.

'Sorry. I'm afraid I'm not good company. Seeing Julian – he's Bill's solicitor. It took me by surprise. Then…'

'Siri. Yeah. That was a bit of a shock. Fancy settling for someone like him.'

'You know him too?'

'From a long time ago.' Johnno's lips formed a grim line. 'But don't let's talk about *them*. I'm concerned about you. Look, you're shivering.'

Celia realised she was indeed shivering. It wasn't anything to do with the temperature in the room which, if anything, was on the warm side. She drew her grey cashmere wrap more closely around her. 'Sorry, I don't know...'

'What you need is a drink, not the namby-pamby champagne they're serving here. And my guess is you've had enough of crowds of people for one night. What if we go back to my place?' He held up his hands defensively. 'No ulterior motive, I promise. I can offer you a glass of some good Scotch, and we can order in a takeaway. How about it?'

Weakly Celia agreed and allowed herself to be led from the gallery, poured into Johnno's yellow convertible, and driven off into the night.

Seventeen

Celia stretched her arms above her head, remembering the previous evening. Jan had been right about Johnno's apartment. It was definitely a bachelor pad, designed to his taste. But, despite the expensive fittings and appliances, there had been something sad about the place. It felt as if it belonged to someone who rarely spent time there, who was really a lonely person.

Travelling up in the lift, Celia had wondered if she was making a huge mistake, Johnno's comforting arm around her shoulders doing nothing to dispel her concern. But, once they arrived there, he was the consummate host – pouring drinks while she stood on the balcony admiring the view and joining her only to hand her a glass of Scotch before leaning on the railing to point out the sights on the other side of the harbour.

She propped herself up against the pillows, leaning her head on upraised knees and linking her arms around them. Celia examined her feelings, surprised to find she'd enjoyed Johnno's company. After a couple of whiskies, he'd brewed coffee and they'd sat together on the black leather sofa – the babe-magnet – while Johnno explained his earlier relationship with the new Mrs Clarke.

If he was to be believed, it had never been serious on his part, with Siri making most of the running, but he had admitted how, until now – and he'd given Celia a strange look – he'd chosen to spend time with women who were flattered to be seen with him and asked nothing other than to be fêted and mentioned in the gossip columns.

She shivered. It sounded exactly what Anna and Jan had said about him. He'd been apologetic, assured her that wasn't who he was now. *But could she be sure? And hadn't she formulated a plan to use him too?* She winced, remembering how cold-hearted she'd been after their dinner at Doyles. He didn't deserve to be used that way. Maybe she needed to come clean with him. Do a bit of confessing herself. She wondered what his reaction would be.

Well, it wouldn't be today. Today was Sunday – Celia's one free day in the week – and she intended to spend it with her daughters. Hannah had rung on Friday to invite her to lunch, indicating they had news. She suspected Ingrid was pregnant. Another grandchild – a brother or sister for Mia. Celia stretched her legs out again in delight at the prospect.

Her phone buzzed.

She checked the text.

Enjoyed last night. How are you this morning? Can we do it again? Are you free next Sat? J

Notwithstanding her earlier thoughts, a jolt of anticipation flooded Celia. He wanted to see her again! Well, of course he did – how else could her plan work? But she knew that the emotions swamping her had nothing to do with any plan of hers, and everything to do with Johnno Henderson himself.

She remembered his genuine concern, his carefully worded questions, his openness in revealing his past and how his nearness had made her uncomfortable – in a good way. Celia could picture his blond hair, his hazel eyes, his… As she felt an unfamiliar tingle and her mouth became dry, she took a deep breath and headed for the shower.

*

'Hi, Mum,' Hannah greeted Celia at the door with a warm hug and led her inside, right through to the family area which seemed full of people. There were not only Ingrid and Chloe – both busy placing platters of cold meats and bowls of salad on the large table – but also Bob and his partner, Chris. Mia was happily ensconced on Bob's knee, and Si was running around, pretending to be a train and getting in everyone's way.

'Mrs... Celia.' Celia looked around to see Owen holding out a glass of champagne.

'Thanks, Owen.' She hadn't seen him when she walked in. Now he and Chloe joined the two men, Chloe picking up Si and hugging him tightly to prevent him sliding down again.

Hannah and Ingrid stood together in the doorway, with beaming smiles on their faces.

'Now we're all here,' Hannah said, 'Ingrid and I have some news. We – thanks to Bob and Chris,' she nodded in their direction, 'want to announce that Mia will have a little brother or sister in March.' She pointed to her partner. 'Ingrid's pregnant.'

'Yay!' Chloe said, and, although clearly not understanding what was happening, Si cheered too.

At that, Bob handed Mia to Chris and stood up, raising his glass. 'I think we need to raise our glasses to the new member of this family,' he said.

'Congratulations to you both.' Celia joined in the toast, then moved to enfold Hannah and Ingrid in a joint hug.

'Now we can eat,' Ingrid said, ushering everyone to places around the now laden table.

'So, March?' Celia said to Hannah when they were all seated, and Ingrid was busy handing around the large well-filled platters.

'Yes. Brilliant timing, Mum. Ingrid's planning our wedding for Valentine's Day. It's a bit tight. She'll be pretty big by then, but...'

'As long as the legislation is passed.'

'It will be.' But Hannah didn't sound totally convinced. 'There's another rally next Sunday and we're all going – Ingrid, Bob and Chris, that is. Chloe and Owen will babysit.'

'Is that a good idea? Last time...'

'It's a great idea.' Hannah's voice rose belligerently. 'After the ads last week, we need to do everything we can to counteract the naysayers. You did see them?'

'Yes.' Celia thought it would have been difficult to have avoided seeing the television ads in which mothers, or actors – it wasn't clear which – warned viewers of the dangers of legalising same-sex marriage. 'But the publicity... Your dad...'

'Damn Dad. He's nothing to do with me, with any of this. If

anything, the media focussing on our relationship to him will help our campaign. Though I don't expect him to like it.'

'No.' Celia was about to say more, but the arrival of a platter of seafood and the necessity of selecting several pieces prevented her. By the time she'd added several prawns and a piece of salmon to her plate, Hannah was already chatting to Owen on her other side.

The conversation flowed as the group demolished the food and consumed more wine, till both Mia and Simon began to wilt.

'I'll put them down for their nap,' Chloe said, rising and disappearing with the two young ones.

Bob slipped into her vacant spot at Celia's side. 'Still okay for this week?' he asked. 'There could be good news.'

Celia's eyes widened but, realising this wasn't an appropriate time for questions, just nodded.

'No more sign of Bill?'

Celia shook her head. 'But Hannah…'

Bob put a finger to his lips. 'She and Ingrid will do their thing. Chris and I'll be right with them at the rally. We won't let anything happen to them. We'll make sure they're not harassed by the media,' he added, clearly seeing her shocked look.

'Right.'

'Mum, can we have a word?' Celia turned. While she'd been talking with Bob, Chloe had returned, and Hannah and Ingrid had started to clear the table. Chloe was standing behind Owen, her hand on his shoulder.

'Excuse me,' Celia said to Bob.

'Not here. Can we go outside?'

Puzzled, Celia rose and followed the two out into the courtyard where Bindi was lying in a sunny spot. Chloe and Owen settled themselves in two of the cane chairs set around a glass table, and Celia joined them. She noted Owen gripping Chloe's hand tightly. *Something was afoot.*

'Owen and I… we've decided…' Chloe threw a glance at Owen so full of love that Celia almost had to look away. Her heart thudded. It reminded her of how she'd felt about Bill in those early days – before everything went to hell. Chloe was speaking again. 'We don't want to wait any longer. We're sure we love each other and,' she took a deep breath, 'I'm moving into Owen's flat next weekend. But there's a small problem.'

'Oh?'

'It's Bindi.'

As if hearing her name, the cat rose, arched her back and padded over to rub herself against Celia's ankles. Her hand automatically went down to scratch the little creature's ears, resulting in a loud purring sound.

'What about Bindi?'

'Where Owen lives... it's not very big. He's renting and...'

'Animals aren't permitted in the complex,' Owen finished.

'So?' Celia still didn't understand where she came in. 'Bindi's quite happy here, isn't she? You can see her when you visit.'

'That's just it.' Chloe pouted. 'Ingrid's being quite stubborn about it. She says it's not suitable to have an old cat like Bindi where there are two young children – one a baby. She's gone on and on about it, and...' Chloe's voice broke. 'We thought maybe you could take her.'

'Oh!' Celia was stunned. *Did she want a cat? What were the regulations in her own apartment complex? But Bindi was a delightful cat and she would be company.* For the first time since moving into her beautiful unit, Celia admitted to herself that she did get lonely at times.

'Can you at least think about it? Bindi can be a bit grouchy now she's getting older. Si's careful with her, but Mia's too little to understand and when she treats her roughly, or pulls her tail, Bindi can turn on her. Han hasn't said anything, but I've noticed she picks up Mia when Bindi's around. Ingrid's worried for the new baby. I want to move in with Owen, but I can't...' Her eyes filled with tears.

Celia began to understand. Bindi had been a gift for Chloe's seventh birthday. That meant she must now be around fourteen – a good age for the cat who'd been Chloe's constant companion till now. When Bill had thrown Chloe out of their home, Celia had found out where she'd gone and taken the cat to her – left her on the doorstep. She'd risked her husband's wrath to reunite the pair, and they hadn't been apart since. This was something else she could do for her daughter. And the very fact Chloe was putting her love for Owen before her beloved pet was a testament to their devotion.

'I'd love to have Bindi,' she said, adding, just as Chloe was about to throw her arms around her, 'I just have to check the body corporate rules, but I don't think there'll be a problem.' Celia seemed to recall seeing a neighbour entering the lift with a small dog.

'Oh, Mum!' This time, Chloe gave her a tight hug, then turned to Owen with a beaming smile. 'I told you Mum would agree. She loves Bindi almost as much as I do.'

'And you're right. She will be good company.'

Bindi leapt up into Celia's lap and turned around several times before settling down, head on her paws which were kneading Celia's lap.

'See! It's as if she knows,' Chloe crowed.

'You've settled it, then?' Hannah said, joining them with a tray of mugs. Ingrid followed with a plate of chocolate biscuits.

'You all knew.' Celia accepted one of the coffees and, picking up a biscuit, took a bite.

'It seemed the obvious solution,' said Ingrid. 'Bindi's an old cat. She's not good around littlies. They tend to annoy her and when she gets annoyed the claws come out and... Anyway, you're all alone in that big unit. She'll be good company.'

She sat down and was soon joined by Hannah. 'The boys have gone,' she said. 'So, Mum, it's going to be you and Bindi?'

'I'm not quite over the hill yet.' Celia didn't know whether to be amused or annoyed at her daughters' concern for her welfare. She wondered what they'd think if they knew how she'd spent the previous evening, if they'd seen her with Johnno Henderson. They might not be so ready to write her off, then.

Johnno had called her the promised taxi, but this time she hadn't evaded his goodnight kiss. It had only been a peck on the cheek, the sort of farewell graze any friend might give to another at the end of an evening together, but it had left her wondering if she was playing with fire.

Eighteen

Celia's heart was thumping as she stepped onto the bus which would take her into town for her meeting with Bob. She'd decided not to drive, as parking in the city at this time of day would be too difficult and, besides, the bus trip would help calm her nerves.

She so hoped this would be the beginning of a short but successful process and she'd have her divorce from Bill in no time – in less time than she'd already been waiting. It seemed to have been going on forever – this feeling of being in limbo. She wanted to be free, though what she would do with that freedom, she had no idea.

The bus drew into Wynyard before she fully appreciated it, the trip across the bridge passing in a blur as she contemplated a future without Bill breathing down her neck. What would it be like to be a free agent? Free to…? Do what? The image of Johnno Henderson came unbidden into her mind. She felt a small quiver in the base of her stomach at the thought of him and the way she'd felt at the touch of his lips on her cheek. Without thinking, her hand rose to touch the spot, then she cursed herself as a fool and let it drop, just as the bus came to a halt.

She rose, patted her hair and pulled down her skirt. Today Celia had chosen to wear a smart navy suit with a white blouse and, before she left home, felt she could handle anything. Now she wasn't so sure.

She took a deep breath as she climbed the stairs to Bob's office, and another as she pushed open the heavy glass door.

Once she'd been ushered into his office, Bob greeted her with a smile and, removing his glasses, held out his hand. 'Morning, Celia. It was good to see you on Sunday. Nice to think our family is growing.'

Celia just wished he'd get on with it. She hadn't come here for small talk, though she appreciated Bob's attempt to put her at ease.

'You said you had good news?'

'Yes. Take a seat.' Bob sat down himself and replaced his glasses. 'Tea? Coffee? Water?'

'Water would be good.' Celia's mouth was dry, and she could feel the fluttering in her stomach starting again. *Would what she was about to hear change her life or be more of the same – another delay?*

Bob went over to a water cooler Celia hadn't noticed and filled a paper cup, handing it to her before resuming his seat.

'Well,' he said, with a wide smile. 'I do have better news for you. In terms of the divorce proceedings, we can make a start. Last time, if you recall, we needed Bill to agree to the divorce. That's no longer the case.'

'No?'

'Now you've been separated for more than the requisite one-year period, we can institute divorce proceedings on the basis of the fact you've been living separately for that time. I have the documents here. With your agreement, I'll send copies to Julian Clarke to have Bill's signature, then it's only a matter of time.'

Celia swallowed. It couldn't be this easy, could it? Her thoughts were going round in circles. She pictured Bill's face when he saw the documents, when he realised she meant it – she really was going to divorce him. And Julian knew about Johnno – or might think he did after seeing them together. Hell, this could well end up in a worse mess than before.

'What if he doesn't sign?' she asked, trembling.

'Let's face that if it happens, but I expect Clarke will advise him to agree. He really doesn't have any option. If he refuses, we can take him to court – family court. But I can't imagine he'd want to go through that with all the publicity it would entail.'

'No.' Celia imagined a long, drawn-out court case, the attendant media interest when he was still marketing the book which depicted them as a family unit with Bill as the happy family man and doting father. She thought of Hannah and Ingrid and the rally they planned to attend with Bob and Chris on the following Sunday.

Then she remembered Julian Clarke again and his not-so-subtle warning. 'One thing.' She leant forward. 'Julian Clarke...' Celia cleared her throat. 'Last weekend, I was at an art gallery opening and met him and his new wife.'

She saw Bob's eyebrows go up. He hadn't known about Siri. 'He was most unpleasant. He practically threatened me.' Celia could still feel the chill of Julian's glare.

Bob seemed about to speak, but Celia held up her hand to stop him. 'I was with someone,' she said quietly. 'A man.'

Then she lifted her head and straightened her back, gaining confidence despite feeling unsure of the outcome. She had nothing to be ashamed of. 'His name's Johnno Henderson and...'

'I know the name. He's a mate of Marcus, my sister's husband, isn't he? We've never met, but I've heard them mention him.'

'Could that make a difference?' Celia asked urgently. 'I mean, could Bill use that against me in some way?' She wasn't quite sure what she was asking. Was she asking if Bill could involve Johnno in the divorce proceedings, or if it could stop everything?

'Not if we state the years of separation. There would be no need for any co-respondent. I would imagine any reference to your own,' he coughed, 'infidelities wouldn't stand up to scrutiny given the allegation against your husband. But, if you're worried about it...'

'Oh, there hasn't... We haven't...' Celia blushed. 'Johnno's just a friend. We've only just met. There's been no...' Her voice died away, embarrassment making her wish the floor would open up and swallow her. Bob didn't want to hear about her non-existent sex life. He was her solicitor, for God's sake. He dealt with documents, divorces, property settlement, wills and the like. He wasn't a counsellor.

'Hmmm.' Bob coughed, and removed his glasses, while Celia took a gulp from the cup of water she'd been holding tightly with both hands. She placed the empty container on the desk and folded her hands together.

'So, what's the next step?'

'Right.' Bob replaced his glasses and, picking up a pencil, tapped on his teeth. Celia wondered if he knew he was doing it. Seeing her looking at him, he quickly put down the pencil and fingered the document on the desk, turning it around to face Celia.

'You should read this. You may want to take it away and consider its contents.'

'No, I'll read it now, if that's okay with you.' Celia wanted this over and done with. And if Bob thought the divorce could go ahead based on their separation, well and good. It had been going on long enough.

Celia picked up the document, feeling Bob watching her as she perused it, trying to make sense of the legal language. It all seemed okay till she came to the division of property. She read the section again and again, then raised her eyes to meet Bob's. He was tapping his teeth again. She wondered idly if anyone had ever told him about it. It seemed to be a nervous habit, though what had he to be nervous about?

'This division of property bit.'

'You're not happy with it? I assure you it's standard practice in a divorce such as yours, An equal share of the property and all assets. I've ascertained from Clarke – not without a degree of difficulty,' he grinned, 'that this is a complete list of Bill's assets, and you'll see I've included any future profits from his memoir.'

Celia's eyes scanned the list again. 'But…' She bit her tongue and swallowed hard. She'd had no idea of many of these so-called assets. The house in Mosman – yes, the boat, the book, Bill's super – though how she could be entitled to a share in that she wasn't quite sure. But the investment property in Bateman's Bay, the shares in what appeared to be companies mining gold and – she peered again – diamonds in West Australia. It was all news to her.

Bill had kept information about his financial dealings very close to his chest in the later years of their marriage. She'd had no idea of his worth. Unlike their early years together, when they'd discussed and argued over the expenditure of every dollar. As Bill's fame had grown – along with his income from playing in a top team – he'd told her it was all taken care of by his financial advisor, and not to worry her pretty little head about it.

He took me for a fool, she thought, not for the first time. But Celia was nobody's fool and now, according to Bob, she was entitled to half of the farm.

'You're surprised?'

'Surprised is putting it mildly. I had no idea there was so much. And I get half?'

'That's what the law says.'

'Where do I sign?' Celia grinned inwardly, imagining Bill's face yet again when he and Julian saw the document. No more hiding now. And when the proceeds of the book were added, she'd be a rich woman. With all the attendant publicity it seemed to be flying off the shelves, top of the Amazon charts, and book of the month with several booksellers.

By the time Celia walked out of Bob's office she felt she was walking on air and was dying to share her news. Reaching the pavement, she stopped and took out her mobile to call someone, anyone. But to her dismay, there was no reply from Hannah and Chloe, and Jan's phone went to voicemail too.

Who else could she call? Celia immediately thought of Johnno. But she couldn't, could she? She fossicked in her bag to where she'd slipped his card, took it out and gazed at it, her thumb rubbing the embossed name before, taking her courage in both hands, she tapped the number into her phone.

It rang and rang, and she had almost given up, when the voice she remembered so well answered. 'John Henderson.'

She thrilled at the professional tone, one she wasn't familiar with. So, at work he was John, not Johnno. It didn't suit him.

'Hello?'

Realising she hadn't replied, Celia spoke quickly, 'It's Celia, Celia Ramsay.' That was one of the first things she'd change. She no longer wanted to use that bastard's name. 'I'm in town and I wondered... no, it's probably a bad idea.' She heard a chuckle on the other end.

'What did you wonder?'

'I'm about to have coffee.' She glanced around to see she wasn't far from her favourite bookshop. It had a lovely café area upstairs, and a bookshop was anonymous, wasn't it? 'In Dymocks,' she said. 'If you're not too busy.'

'I'd love to join you.'

Celia could hear the amusement in Johnno's voice and wondered if she'd made a huge mistake in calling him. But he'd agreed, hadn't he?

'I can be there in ten minutes.' He hung up, and she was left staring at the phone with the realisation she had no idea where in the city his office was. Ten minutes. It couldn't be too far away.

Looking carefully in both directions, Celia hurried across the road and headed towards the bookshop, only to be faced with a huge display of Bill's memoir at the entrance, including a larger-than-life photograph of him. She should have been prepared for this, but she wasn't, and it shocked her to see his face staring out at her.

Skirting the display with her head down, she made her way upstairs, choosing a seat at a corner table. The place was busy, and no one was looking her way. They wouldn't recognise her anyway, she hoped. It was Bill's face on the cover, not hers. But Celia was in many of the photos inside, she remembered, seeing a woman at a neighbouring table open a copy and begin to flick through the pages.

'Hello.'

Celia looked up with relief to see Johnno's tall figure filling the space between her and the woman.

'Have you ordered?'

'Not yet. I only just got here.'

'What would you like?'

'Skinny cap, please.'

He was off again, soon returning to join her. This morning he looked very much the professional in a striped grey suit, white shirt and a red tie. Celia had read somewhere that red ties were power ties, but Johnno didn't need a tie to set him off. He exuded confidence and looked as attractive as usual as he smiled across the table.

'Saw the display downstairs,' he said with a grin. 'Seems to be doing well. I guess any publicity is good publicity.'

'Yes.' Celia fiddled with a napkin, folding it this way and that, eyes lowered.

'So,' Johnno said when their coffees had been served, 'I'm delighted to hear from you, but what prompted this invitation? You said you were in town. Not at Isabella, today?'

'No.' Celia scooped up the chocolate from the top of her coffee and sucked it off the spoon, trying to work out what to say. Now they were here, she wasn't sure if she wanted to confide in Johnno. It was *her* divorce, after all. It concerned her and Bill. No one else. But...

She took a drink and met his eyes across the top of her cup. 'I've been to see my solicitor.'

'Bob Frazer – right? The plot thickens. And?'

His eyes were filled with something that was more concern than amusement, she thought, so she ploughed on. 'About my divorce. I told you...'

'It's been hanging fire for the past two years – yes. Can it all be resolved now?'

'So it seems. Bob was very helpful. He always is. Evidently, the past two years apart have been the good thing. It means we can now be divorced due to that – without Bill's agreement – though he still has to sign the documents.' She grimaced, then hesitated.

'Well that's good, isn't it?'

'I guess so.' Celia used her spoon to stir the brown liquid, before picking up her cup and cradling it in both hands. 'It all seems very straightforward including my half of everything. That's what worries me.'

'You expected more?'

'No! Of course not. I didn't expect half, and certainly not half of what Bill seems to have amassed over the years. I never imagined there was so much.'

'From what I hear, that's what a divorce is all about – splitting the assets. Each getting a fair share. In fact,' Johnno rubbed his chin, 'I've even heard of the wife receiving more than half – some sort of reckoning on the work she's done keeping the home and raising the children. You do have two children.'

'But what if... what if Bill doesn't think it's fair?'

There, she'd said it. The doubt that had been niggling at her ever since she read the document, the document she'd signed.

'Can he object?'

'Bob says his solicitor – Julian Clarke who you know – will advise him not to contest it. But I'm not too sure about Julian, and I know Bill. He'd never agree to my getting half of everything he owns, especially since...'

'Does he know about me – about us?'

Celia started to say there was no *us*, then remembered Julian Clarke's angry face. 'I expect he does by now. After last Saturday. I doubt Julian was at pains to keep it to himself. He was no doubt on the phone to Bill as soon as we left. And Bill...'

'He'd not be best pleased?'

'That's putting it mildly.' Suddenly the elation she'd felt when she left Bob's office began to dissipate, and a feeling of misery began to take its place.

'Well, I hope it doesn't mean you're going to stop seeing me. I had hopes that on Saturday…'

'I can't do Saturday,' Celia said, ignoring the question. 'I have Bindi.'

'Bindi? Do I know her?' Johnno appeared puzzled – a frown appearing between his eyes and making Celia long to smooth it away.

'Bindi's a cat.'

'I'm being stood up for a cat? Well, that's a first.' Johnno gave her a cheeky grin.

'Not… We didn't have an arrangement, I didn't think you… Oh!' she finally said as her companion began to laugh at her confusion. Celia drained her cup before continuing. 'Bindi is Chloe's cat. She's getting old and a bit bad-tempered, I'm afraid.

'Chloe's moving in with Owen, her new partner, next Saturday, to a unit which doesn't allow pets. Bindi can't stay where she is as Ingrid and Hannah – more Ingrid I suspect – feel she's becoming too aggressive to be around small children. Mia is only eighteen months and there's another on the way.'

Celia noted Johnno's surprised expression. 'You don't know the half of it,' she said, 'but that'll keep for another day. Anyway, my darling daughters decided I must be lonely in my big new apartment and that giving Bindi to me is the perfect solution – killing two birds with one stone as it were.'

'And Saturday?'

'That's the handover day and cats take a couple of days – at least – to adjust to new surroundings. So, I need to stay home with her to acclimatise her.'

Celia saw another frown appear on Johnno's face, then it cleared.

'I know,' he said. 'If I'm not being too presumptuous, why don't I join you – and Bindi – on Saturday. I can bring along a DVD and we can order takeaway, and I promise I'll still be on my best behaviour – no…'

'Ulterior motive,' they said in unison and both laughed.

Celia hadn't considered Johnno might invite himself to Cremorne for the evening. How did she feel about it? She considered, surprised to sense a frisson of excitement. But would a man-about-town like Johnno be satisfied with a boring evening in at her place?

'Maybe,' she said after a long pause. 'How are you around cats?'

'They love me. You should have seen me with the big cats at the zoo. Why…'

Celia laughed. 'Okay, but forget the takeaway, I can cook something. It won't be *cordon bleu*, but better than a takeaway. I'll guarantee you that.'

'Seven o'clock? I'll bring wine.'

Johnno checked his watch and began to rise. 'Sorry. I need to get back. It's a working day for me. You too, I would imagine.'

Celia checked her watch too, surprised to realise how much time had passed.

They stopped outside the bookshop, standing awkwardly together. Celia looked down at her feet, hoping he wouldn't kiss her in this public spot, yet yearning for some form of contact.

'Well, I'll see you on Saturday.' Johnno smiled his disarming smile and put a hand on Celia's shoulder, giving it a warm squeeze, then he was off, striding down the street – a man on a mission.

Celia gazed after him, unable to still the fluttering in her stomach.

Nineteen

Celia put the final touches to the chicken casserole, adding a few extra mushrooms and sloshing in a good dollop of white wine, before pouring herself a glass, checking on Bindi and heading off to the bedroom. She just had time for a quick shower before getting dressed and setting out the tray of nibbles she'd planned to serve before dinner.

Chloe and Owen, along with Simon, had arrived early afternoon carrying the cat in her large cat basket, with Simon bringing along a box of cat toys. 'For Bindi to play with, Grandma,' he said, 'So she feels at home and won't be bored.'

Boring? Is that how they thought of her home? Probably not. She was becoming paranoid if she was going to start comparing herself to a cat!

They'd only stayed long enough for the handover and a brief coffee, saying how much they had to do to get Chloe and Simon settled in before bedtime. It seemed that Owen's unit was in North Sydney and overlooked the expressway – noisy, but both Owen and Chloe insisted that they got used to the traffic noise – and there was a large pool which more than made up for any inconvenience.

'You must come and see it. Mum. What about tomorrow?' Chloe had asked, eagerly supported by Simon.

But Celia reminded them of her need to stay home till Bindi was settled in, so they'd made an arrangement for the following week.

Tomorrow – that was the day of the rally. Celia quivered, her chest tightening as she contemplated what Hannah and Ingrid had in mind. They'd shared their placards with her the previous evening when she'd dropped in after work. It seemed they had no intention of taking a back seat – they were going to be right at the leading edge of the protest.

Celia comforted herself with the knowledge of Bob's promise to 'look after them' but wondered what he and Chris could do in the face of any media barrage.

Calmed by the shower, Celia sipped her glass of wine as she dressed for dinner in a softly flowing turquoise dress with white trim and slipped on her favourite pair of heels – ones which would take her up to Johnno's chin. Thinking of her dinner guest brought a flush to Celia's cheeks. She had to keep reminding herself he was only a friend, and that she was using him in a plan to annoy Bill. But she couldn't entirely convince herself. The way she felt when he was near, the thrill of his touch, all spoke of an attraction she was trying hard to ignore.

She wasn't ready for this. Would she ever be? She needed to get the stuff with Bill sorted first, before she could think of forming any sort of relationship. Friendship was fine, but anything else was off limits.

Returning to the kitchen, Celia broke open a bag of corn chips and unscrewed a jar of salsa, placing them on a tray. She sliced a couple of carrots and zucchini and added them to the mix along with an avocado dip she'd made earlier. There, that should do it.

She turned on the oven. It would be ready for the casserole by the time Johnno arrived, and the chicken dish would go well with the baby potatoes and green beans she'd prepared. She let out a long breath. Everything was ready.

Celia went over to her sound system – unfortunately not as state-of-the-art as Johnno's – and searched through her music collection for something appropriate – not too raucous, not too romantic. She finally settled on a nostalgic collection of classical music, hoping Johnno wasn't a purist where classical music was concerned.

The music had only just started, the initial chords echoing through the house, when the buzz of the intercom signalled Johnno's arrival. Celia checked her watch – he was dead on time.

'Come right up. It's number thirty-two, third floor,' she said into the speaker, before berating herself for telling him what he already knew. She took a deep breath. She wasn't nervous, she wasn't. She – hell, she was as jumpy as a cat on hot bricks.

Celia took a quick glance around the kitchen and dining table. Everything looked fine, except... She moved to quickly put her empty wine glass in the dishwasher. No need for Johnno to know she'd needed Dutch courage to prepare for the evening.

She opened the door with a welcoming smile.

'Hello. You found it all right?' What a dumb thing to say. Of course he found it, he wouldn't be here otherwise. Johnno didn't appear to notice her gaffe, instead giving her a peck on the cheek and holding out a bunch of flowers and a bottle of wine.

Celia gestured to him to take the wine into the kitchen, following with the flowers which she put into a vase and set on the kitchen bench to be properly located later.

'Nice,' Johnno said, looking around, and going immediately to the glass door opening out on to the balcony. 'Middle Harbour isn't it? What a spectacular view.'

'Not quite as busy as Darling Harbour. I like the tranquillity.'

'You can almost see the rowing club from here,' Johnno said, his gaze never leaving the wide stretch of water in the distance. He turned, almost bumping into Celia who was standing close behind him. They laughed awkwardly.

'A drink?' she asked to smooth over the difficult moment, 'and something to nibble while dinner cooks?'

'Thanks. Let me get the wine.'

They moved in unison to the kitchen. Celia passed two glasses to Johnno who poured the wine and took the glasses to a coffee table facing the view, Celia joining him with the tray of nibbles.

'I...'

'Do...'

Both spoke at once, then laughed again. Bindi chose that moment to appear and, to Celia's surprise, after sniffing around his ankles, leapt onto Johnno's lap.

'Who have we here?' he asked, fondling the cat's head to the accompaniment of a loud purring from the little animal. 'Are you Bindi? Are you the cat who's going to be company for this lovely lady?'

Celia relaxed into her seat, glass in hand, and enjoyed the picture they made. Johnno seemed at home here. As if he belonged. Stop that, she told herself. This is his first visit – perhaps his only one. No need to get any ideas, ideas which, if she were honest with herself, she'd already entertained in the small hours of darkness when she found it difficult to sleep.

'Don't let her bother you,' she said, picking up a carrot stick and dipping it into the avocado mixture. 'She knows she's not allowed to...'

'She's fine.' Johnno managed to pick up his wine with his free hand, continuing to stroke the cat with the other. 'She's a lovely creature. Manx?'

'Yes.' Celia relaxed her vigilance. 'As I told you, she was Chloe's pet.'

'And now she's yours?'

'Seems to be.'

Having had enough petting, Bindi let out a loud miaow and jumped down, slipping away to find her favourite spot. As soon as she'd arrived, the cat had checked out the entire apartment before settling in a corner by the window – the corner which caught the first sun each morning. How had she known? But cats were like that – fey creatures who were a law unto themselves. Bindi had quickly made herself at home here, and Celia knew that, by the time she left for work on Monday, it would be as if Bindi had always lived here.

'Good music,' Johnno said. Now that the cat had left his lap, he too leant back and helped himself to some corn chips. 'A fan of this stuff?'

'Not really,' Celia said apologetically. 'I thought... I didn't know your taste in music, so...'

'You chose something neutral. Good choice. I enjoy jazz too, and a bit of folk.'

Celia felt a warm glow – her taste too. 'I have...' She began to rise, but Johnno gently pushed her back down. 'This is fine. Plenty of time for others later.'

They chatted amicably till dinner was ready.

*

Johnno set down his cutlery with a heartfelt sigh. 'That was delicious. You're a good cook, Celia.' He wasn't accustomed to being cooked for by his women. Mostly they would have fled at the thought of entering a kitchen. That may be why he often ate out. He'd become accustomed to entertaining in restaurants and was now well-known across many of Sydney's night-spots. A home-cooked meal was a treat.

'That was a treat,' he said, his words echoing his thoughts. 'I only get a meal like this at my brother's, or when Anna and Marcus invite me to dinner.' He emptied his glass.

'Your parents?' Celia asked.

'They're back in Queensland. On the Sunshine Coast to be exact. They moved into a retirement village there a few years ago. Seem to enjoy it. I don't get up as often as I'd like.' He rubbed his chin reflectively, remembering how he intended that to change. 'In fact,' he said, surprising himself with the urge to confide in her. 'If all goes well with this project, I intend to buy myself a place up there – a weekender. Somewhere to go to get away from the hustle and bustle of the big city. Where's your favourite getaway spot?'

'Well, this is pretty good,' Celia said, pointing to the darkening vista outside her windows. 'But I know what you mean. I love the Sunshine Coast too. I remember spending holidays up there when the girls were little. We would take a house in Noosa for the entire school holidays, Bill would join us when he could, and...' Her eyes glazed over as if remembering happier times. 'But I haven't been there for ages. Makes me think I should do something about that now. There's nothing to stop me. It would be lovely for little Si, too.'

'Except you have a business to run.'

'True. But I have a good assistant and we have a list of casuals.' She seemed to be reflecting on how it could all be managed.

For a moment Johnno was tempted to suggest they go there together. Spend a weekend in the resort town. He could imagine lazy days on the beach, long lunches, sunset drinks... No. This wasn't one of his good-time girls who would be thrilled to spend a dirty weekend with him with no expense spared. This was a mature woman. One he planned to treat with respect, get to know better before making any move that might frighten her off. He was well aware of the danger of being censured by his friends – and by the lady herself.

Trying to change the subject, Johnno pointed to the window. 'I mentioned the rowing club earlier. Marcus and I, plus Anna and their son – he's called Jon, too – we meet there every Sunday early. It's wonderful out there on the water in the rising dawn. You should join us.' Johnno hesitated, wondering if he'd overstepped the mark. A few dates in public places was one thing. Tonight had been different, but it was all due to the cat. To introduce her to his friends, to invite her to be part of that private side of his life – that was something else altogether.

'Yes, I think Anna might have mentioned it,' Celia said with a smile.

Shit, he'd forgotten she knew them – Anna at least, and Jan. The rowing club was where he and Jan met, that first time. And he'd screwed that up right royally. She'd never been back to the rowing – not when he'd been around anyway. Had he frightened her so much she never went back? She'd seemed to enjoy that morning.

He could still picture her in the scull with Anna, he and Marcus in the other, breakfast afterwards, then… Then he'd messed up, or maybe it was doomed from the start. Jan had still been married, albeit living apart from her husband. But he'd never got the impression with Jan that divorce was on the cards, and she'd still been dealing with the death of her son. That same son who'd fathered Celia's grandson, he remembered.

Hell, what a mess! Why couldn't he have found someone with no ties to anyone he knew, with no baggage, no hang-ups? But then she wouldn't have been half as interesting. After the episode with Jan, he'd vowed to keep away from married women. Yet, here he was, with another friend of the King's, another married woman.

Johnno suddenly realised Celia hadn't answered him about the rowing. He'd become engrossed in his own thoughts, and she'd begun to clear away the dishes. He heard the bubble and hiss of the coffee machine through the hatch in the kitchen.

Had his question even registered? Had she chosen to ignore it, or had she already been thinking of the next part of the evening. He'd promised a DVD and had one in his jacket pocket.

Johnno decided not to follow up on the rowing. It had been a mad idea anyway. Why would she want to rise at the crack of dawn to meet him and his friends on the harbour on what promised to be a chilly Sunday morning?

'That DVD I mentioned. I brought along an old copy of *Cabaret*. Hope it's to your taste. Shall we watch it with our coffee?'

Celia appeared with a platter of cheese and biscuits which she took over to the coffee table and switched on the television. 'Sounds good. I've always loved that movie. Can you set it up while I fetch the coffee?'

Johnno took the DVD from his pocket and set it up ready to play. By the time it was starting, Celia had joined him with coffee – long black for him he noted. So, she'd taken notice of his taste. That was a good sign.

They were sitting together on the sofa – a respectable distance apart. As the film progressed, Johnno automatically stretched his arm along the back of the sofa, but took care not to let it drop around Celia's shoulders. Although not touching, he could detect her fragrance – the spicy one he'd recognised on a previous occasion. It spoke to him of the woman she was, could be, given the right timing.

He had trouble concentrating on the movie, thinking instead of the woman beside him, wondering how he could make an impression on her, how he could make himself part of her life.

At the end of the film, he stretched. 'Well, guess it's time to go. Thanks for the lovely meal. I enjoyed the evening.'

'Me, too.' Celia rose to join him and accompany him to the door. Johnno took her by the elbows and pressed his lips to her soft cheek, inhaling her fragrance.

'Thanks again. I'll be in touch.' As he turned to go, Celia spoke.

'About the rowing. I'd love to come along.'

Twenty

Celia woke with a start as the alarm on her mobile buzzed. Sunday – her one free day in the week, the day she generally slept late, pottered around the flat, then caught up with her girls. What had possessed her to agree to go rowing? And Bindi? She'd promised herself she'd stay home all weekend to see the cat settled in her new home.

As if reading her mind, a ball of grey fur leapt onto her bed and small paws began kneading her arm. 'Oh Bindi, you dear thing! You've made yourself at home here so quickly It's almost as if you've always wanted to be here. Are you glad to be away from those pesky littlies who liked to annoy you, pull on your tail and ears?'

Bindi responded with a loud purring reminiscent of the sound of a lawn mower starting up. 'Okay, so you don't need me to stay home. Is that what you're telling me?'

Talking to a cat! She really was getting past it Celia reckoned as she carefully slid out of bed, leaving the pet to curl up in a ball in the warm space she'd left.

Once in the shower, an air of excitement took hold. It was still dark, but she could imagine the dawn breaking over the water, the cool breeze in her hair and... Johnno.

As he'd instructed, Celia dressed casually. After she'd agreed to go along, Johnno had taken time to suggest she dress warmly.

'It can be cool on the water in the early hours, but you'll quickly warm up with the exercise,' he'd said. 'And we usually have breakfast afterwards. Maybe a layered outfit?'

Celia had been amused at his awkwardness as he attempted to recommend what she should wear, but it had been too late to call Anna for advice.

She pulled on a pair of grey track suit pants and a white tee-shirt, throwing the track suit jacket across her shoulders. There wasn't time to brew the coffee she'd have liked, so, filling Bindi's water and food dishes, and leaving the balcony door open to allow the cat to go in and out, she gulped down a glass of orange juice and went out to the street. Johnno had insisted on picking her up as it was on his way, and Celia felt it would have been churlish to refuse.

She'd been right. Waiting outside the block of units for Johnno to arrive, the sky was beginning to lighten, though the stiff breeze made her don the jacket she'd carelessly thrown over her shoulders. Before long, Johnno's yellow Saab came into sight and drew up beside her. Throwing open the door, his familiar voice told her to 'Hop in,' and they were off.

They didn't speak much on the way, Johnno merely asking if she'd slept well and before long, they were driving across Spit Bridge, the sky turning rosy pink, then golden. It was certainly worth the early start, but would she enjoy the actual rowing? Celia hadn't taken part in any real exercise since... she couldn't remember when. When the girls started school, she'd joined a tennis club and, for a time, had enjoyed the weekly get-togethers which were more a way of catching up on gossip than actually playing tennis. Of recent years that had gone by the board and her exercise had been restricted to walking at lunchtime or climbing the stairs at home and instead of taking the lift in shopping centres.

She braced herself. Rowing would be a real test of her fitness. She might look slender and fit, but Celia knew appearances could be deceptive and hoped she didn't embarrass herself.

'We're here.' Johnno's voice broke into her thoughts as the car came to a stop beside another, larger vehicle out of which Anna and Marcus were climbing.

'Where's my godson today?' Johnno asked.

'He had a couple of friends for sleepover last night,' Anna explained, 'and the three of them were still out for the count when we left. We may need to go back there for breakfast to make sure they haven't wrecked the place and don't sleep the day away. He has rugby this afternoon.'

'Help me with the sculls, mate?' Marcus asked Johnno.

The two men disappeared in the direction of the club house while Anna joined Celia by the car. 'Lovely to see you here,' she said. 'So, you and Johnno?'

'No. Not really. I just...' Celia wasn't sure how to explain her presence. To the outsider, it must look as if she and Johnno were an item – was that the term these days? 'We had dinner together last night and he invited me along,' she said weakly.

Anna grinned. 'That's usually how it starts,' she said. 'But I'm pleased to see you two together. He's a good man and deserves to be happy – as do you.'

'We're not...we didn't...' Celia felt herself redden as Anna's implication hit home. 'I mean, I barely know him. We had dinner; he went home. And he picked me up this morning. He has to pass my block to get here.' Celia could hear herself babbling. She didn't want Anna to think... But, hadn't she considered it? Her blush grew even stronger, remembering her torrid dreams.

'It's okay,' Anna assured her. 'Whatever you and Johnno do or don't do is your business, nothing to do with us or anyone else. I just hope neither of you gets hurt in the process. You've been hurt enough already, and Johnno...' She glanced over to where the two men were now carrying the rowing sculls out and placing them on the water. 'Johnno's a very special person. We want him to be happy, to find the right woman. I think my sister hurt him more than he let on at the time. They weren't right for each other – the timing was wrong for Jan, and she was too old for him. But the experience damaged him and sent him rushing back to the dolly birds he's been seeing for years.'

Celia laughed at the expression 'dolly birds'. It was one she hadn't heard for a long time. But it told her something about Johnno, something she'd already figured out. She remembered Siri.

'I won't hurt him,' she said, wondering if she was the one who'd end up being hurt yet again. How could anyone tell?

'We should join them,' Anna said, and Celia saw that the sculls were now on the water and Marcus was waving to them. 'You and I can go in one and let the men go together.'

Celia was relieved. For her first experience to be with Anna seemed like a good option. She knew nothing about the sport, had only just learned to call the boats sculls. She looked down at her clothing, realising how inappropriate it was compared to the lycra outfits of the other three. As if sensing her discomfort, Anna said, 'You're okay. If you make this a regular thing, you can get the proper gear, but no one worries about how you're dressed and there's no one else around to see.'

Sure enough, when Celia glanced around, they were the only four on the river this morning. Suddenly she felt energised. 'Okay,' she laughed,' let's go. But you'll have to tell me what to do. I'm a complete novice. I don't know one end of the boat – sorry, scull – from the other.'

'Fine,' Anna said. 'We'll take it slowly to start with, and you'll soon get the hang of it. You appear to be fit. I shouldn't think it'll take you long to work it out. Though you'll probably be a bit sore tonight, using different muscles from what you're used to.'

As they joined the men, Celia tried to hide her surprise. She hadn't noticed Johnno's outfit in the car, but here, standing with the early morning light behind him, it was as if there was a halo encircling him, and he looked indeed like the Greek god she'd compared him to back at the restaurant. The lycra was tight across his chest and thighs forcing her to look away for fear she'd blush again.

'Right ladies?' Marcus said. 'You okay to take Celia, Anna?'

'Sure. We already decided,' Anna replied as the men stepped into their scull and moved off, the craft making scarcely a ripple on the still water. 'Now, you need to get in carefully,' Anna said, 'Don't tip it up, and sit facing the far end.'

Celia stepped in and, as instructed, took hold of the oar. She was learning. Before they set off, Anna explained the terminology and how to manoeuvre the craft, then they were off, skimming the water in a movement so... Celia couldn't think what to compare it to. It was out of this world. The men's scull was far ahead, and Anna made no attempt to catch up, seemingly content to go at Celia's much slower pace.

When they stopped mid-stream for a breather, Celia exhaled loudly.

'What do you think?' Anna asked. 'Enjoying it?'

'It's spectacular,' Celia said, breathlessly. 'The air, the water, the...'

'You're a natural. Jan never did get the hang of it and she only came once. I hope we'll see you here again. We do it every Sunday.'

'Oh, I don't think...' Celia couldn't imagine making this a regular occurrence. What if Johnno didn't want to repeat it with her? Asked someone else, or...

'Well, maybe not every week. But you're most welcome to join us when you can.'

Celia knew she'd love to come again. She felt exhilarated by the whole experience, but would it depend on Johnno? On her being invited again? On whatever happened – or didn't – with their relationship? Did they even have a relationship? It was all too much to think about right now.

Anna seemed to be aware of her concerns. 'It doesn't need to depend on Johnno. You're welcome to come on your own. And...' she bit her lip. 'Johnno...'

But Celia knew from what he'd told her that Johnno came every week, so that meant he'd always be here.

'We're not the only ones who go rowing,' Anna said. 'You can join the club and come at another time.' She met Celia's eyes. 'Though I hope you don't. I hope you and Johnno...'

The men passed them on their return journey, waving as they went by.

'We'd better get back. Why don't you join us for breakfast?'

'But I thought you were going home?'

'At our place. You'll have to put up with three teenagers. But if you don't mind that?'

'Thanks.' But Celia wondered how Johnno would feel about having her around over breakfast. She needn't have worried.

'We're invited for breakfast,' he told her when all four were once again on dry land. 'Okay by you?'

Celia threw Anna a grateful smile. 'That'd be good, though...' she looked down at her casual outfit, now streaked with perspiration.

Anna dismissed her concern. 'I'll probably change into something similar once we get home. And it'll only be us and the boys. They'll be too wrapped up in themselves to even know we exist.'

Driving to Anna's, Celia could see the beads of sweat on Johnno's forehead. 'Had a good workout?' she asked, resisting the temptation to wipe them off.

'Great. How did you like it? You and Anna seemed to be going okay.'

'I loved it.' Celia couldn't hide the enthusiasm in her voice.

'So, you'd like to do it again?'

Was that an invitation?

'Maybe,' she said cautiously. 'If…'

'You're welcome to join us anytime.' She saw him glance at her out of the corner of his eye. 'If you don't mind our company.'

'But what about their son? Doesn't he usually come?' Celia didn't see how it would work with an uneven number.

'Oh, don't worry about Jon. He actually prefers taking out a single scull – says we oldies hold him back. And,' he said reflectively, 'he seems to be finding other activities more attractive these days. I think there might be a girl involved.'

'How old is Jon?'

Johnno thought for a moment. 'He's in Year Ten so I guess that makes him around fifteen or sixteen. I guess I should know exactly. He *is* my godson, but I'm useless on dates and things like that.' His mouth turned up in the lazy grin Celia had noted and which she found especially attractive. 'We can ask him over breakfast if you like.'

'No, it's fine.' Celia had no intention of being so intrusive with a teenager she didn't know. She had a vague recollection of meeting him at the barbecue she'd attended at Anna's home a couple of years ago, and she'd heard Jan mention him a few times.

*

Celia thrust a hand through her hair as the car drew up at the top of the flight of worn stone steps she remembered from her last visit.

'It's a lovely spot,' she said.

'Was Anna's parents' place and Marcus bought it when they decided to downsize.'

'Mmm.' Celia hadn't realised. So, Anna and Jan – and Bob – had grown up here? How nice to have that sort of continuity. 'Marcus…' she began.

'Second marriage. The first went belly up. She's in the US now. They lived there before it all fell apart and Jonathon stayed with her till… It's not my story, but best you know.'

'So Jon's not Anna's son?'

'Stepson. But as near as makes no difference. She loves that lad, and he's devoted to her, too. He pined for his dad, so Marcus and Lauren came to an agreement. Jonathon spends part of his holidays over there – big house in LA, lots of money. But money's not everything.' Johnno frowned.

'No.' Celia thought about this for a few moments. 'I guess we should go in.'

'Right.' Johnno slid out and stepped around to help Celia out of the car. 'Watch yourself on these steps. They can be lethal. I almost lost it myself one night, coming here in the dark. There are lights, but it's still a bit dicey.'

His hand on her elbow, Celia cautiously descended towards the old house set in the midst of a beautiful garden. She tried to remember if she'd noticed it on her last visit. She must have, but it had been a bad time for her. Her one lasting memory was having Jan give her Bob's business card. She'd been loath to call the lawyer, knowing it meant the end of her marriage, but, after lots of friendly advice, she'd taken the plunge.

Now, she knew she'd be forever grateful to Jan for her assistance, and to Bob for his ongoing services. It was almost at a conclusion, after dragging on for two whole years while Bill's book was written, edited and printed. It was a long haul, but almost over.

'Hi. You got here at last!' Anna greeted them at the door, now dressed in white tracksuit pants and a blue skivvy. 'Come along in. Marcus is cooking breakfast, and I've just been rousing the boys. They were still asleep, and Jon's room smells like a track meet.' She laughed, clearly enjoying it all the same. 'Teenage boys – who'd have them? Yours are both girls, aren't they?' she asked Celia.

'Yes. And well past their teens, thank goodness. Girls can be a problem, too.' Celia grimaced, remembering how Chloe had fallen pregnant at seventeen and Hannah had 'come out' at much the same age.

'Sorry.' Anna put a gentle hand on Celia's arm as if suddenly remembering the drama of Simon's birth.

'Glad I don't have either problem,' Johnno said. 'I'll join Marcus and see what I can do to help.' He disappeared in the direction of what Celia assumed to be the kitchen.

'Let's go outside,' Anna said. 'Leave the boys to it. Marcus is pretty good in the kitchen. I'm not so sure about Johnno. But my guy will find him something to do.'

The women had no sooner settled in a couple of sturdy wooden chairs with colourful cushions, than Johnno appeared with two mugs of coffee.

'I've been delegated to bus-boy duties,' he said. 'The master chef is cooking up a storm, while you two ladies take it easy here in the sun.'

'If he doesn't need you for anything else, maybe you'd have another go at the three lads,' Anna said. 'They may listen to you, and I need Jon to be up and ready for rugby in the next couple of hours.'

'Your wish is my command.' With a mock salute, Johnno disappeared into the house.

Celia laughed. 'He's just a little boy at heart.'

'You're right there. How are you two getting on? Really?'

Celia fumbled for words. 'He's a nice man. Good company. But…'

'You don't want to get involved?'

'It's not that exactly.' Celia hesitated. She couldn't reveal her master plan to use Johnno to thwart Bill. Anna was his friend – the wife of his best mate. And Celia wasn't quite sure her plan was a good one. The past few times she'd seen Johnno, she'd enjoyed his company. Maybe…

As if Anna could see her weakening, she asked, 'You do find him attractive, don't you?'

'Who wouldn't? That's probably the problem. He's too attractive. How can I compete?'

'He's never brought a woman to meet us before, never included anyone in the more private part of his life. I think you should at least consider he's serious – as serious as Johnno ever is.'

'Or could be,' Celia countered. 'What if he's just a perennial bachelor, unable to commit. What if I get involved, then he…' She realised she was voicing her worst fear – that her so-called plan had really been a safety mechanism to protect herself. *But had she – protected herself? How did she really feel about this man who'd stormed into her life?*

'You really think he could make a commitment, form a real long-term relationship?' she asked.

Anna hesitated. 'I really don't know. What I do know is that he's behaving differently to how I've seen him behave with any other of his women. Oh,' she said, 'I don't mean to say you're just one of a string of women who…'

'Johnno said there was breakfast.'

Anna's son, hair awry and still wearing what looked like last night's outfit, followed by two other young men similarly attired and in equal disarray, appeared in the doorway and threw themselves down on a bench. 'It's still early.'

'Have a good time last night?' Anna asked. 'And did you think to wash and change before you came down? We have guests. This is Celia.'

'Uh?'

Celia smiled. Girls weren't so different from boys after all. She could easily recall when her girls would arrive at the breakfast table on a Sunday morning in a similar state of untidiness, yawning and complaining that it was the crack of dawn when it was almost lunchtime.

'Morning, boys,' she said, unsurprised to receive only a few grunts in reply.

'Breakfast!' Marcus and Johnno appeared carrying large trays with platters of scrambled eggs, bacon, hash browns and toast. There was also butter, jam, a large jug of orange juice and a bowl of fruit.

'Food!' Jonathon and his friends seemed to come to life and drew their bench closer to the table, while the adults arranged themselves around the other sides.

Johnno handed around the plates and cutlery.

'Let the grown-ups serve themselves first,' Marcus instructed, 'then you boys can demolish what's left.'

Johnno filled large glasses with orange juice. 'Freshly squeezed,' he said proudly.

'Remember you have a game today,' Anna reminded Jonathon. 'What about you boys?'

'Ed's playing, but Nick has a bye,' Jon said, munching on a piece of toast and gulping his juice. 'You coming along, Dad?'

Marcus looked over at Anna and raised an eyebrow. Anna nodded.

'Who are you playing?' Johnno asked, between mouthfuls.

'Fort Street.'

'Oh! Maybe we'll come too. What do you think, Celia? Fancy watching a bunch of schoolboys bash each other in the name of sport this afternoon?'

Celia was about to refuse. Sport wasn't really her thing. She'd had enough of it when Bill was playing, and she'd been expected to attend every game. She hadn't been to a game since. She looked at Johnno, his wistful, lopsided smile, then across to Anna and Marcus, waiting for her response.

'Sure,' she said. 'I'd love to. But I'll need to get changed first.'

'Me too,' Johnno said. 'Let's finish here. I'll drop you off and pick you up again at around...' He glanced at Marcus.

'The game starts at two – at the Knox grounds.'

'...one-fifteen?'

Celia calculated that would give her plenty of time to shower and change. She probably wouldn't need any lunch after this big breakfast, but could fit in a quick herbal tea and maybe biscuits and cheese to sustain her through the afternoon.

On the way home, Johnno was in good form. 'I'm glad you agreed to come this afternoon,' he said. 'I'm not a great sports fan, but I like to support the lad when I can. And you'll be company for Anna. She doesn't get to many of Jon's games. This should be a good one – both teams are vying for the final and they're evenly matched. Jon's a strong player.'

*

The game was more fun than Celia expected. Sitting on the sidelines with Anna, in collapsible green canvas chairs, drinking coffee from the flask Anna and Marcus had thoughtfully brought along, Johnno's occasional hand on her shoulder and the chat with Anna all made the afternoon pass quickly.

When the game finished – with a draw, much to everyone's dismay – Jon ran over to the group.

'Okay if I don't come back with you?' he asked. 'Some of the guys...' He nodded towards a cluster standing nearby clearly awaiting his return.

'On you go,' Marcus said. 'But home for dinner. Okay?'

'Oh, Dad! We planned on getting some pizzas and going back to Ed's place.'

Marcus and Anna exchanged a glance.

'Okay then. But nine o'clock curfew. School tomorrow.'

He ran off.

'Only the guys?' Johnno asked with a grin nodding towards where a group of teenage girls were following the boys' progress with interest. 'Does Jon have a girlfriend?'

'Oh, Lord no! Not yet, I hope,' Anna said in alarm. 'We have enough teenage angst to cope with without... Sorry,' she said realising Celia was listening.

'It's okay,' Celia said. 'It's over. Chloe was seventeen, almost eighteen – as was Simon. And I wouldn't be without little Si. Now there's Owen, and it looks like they're becoming a real family. These things happen, no matter how good a parent you are. We just have to do what we can, hope for the best, and learn to cope with whatever happens.'

'You're a wonder,' Anna replied. 'But I'd rather not have to cope with any boy-girl thing just yet.' She rose and began to fold up her chair. 'What are you two up to now?' She looked questioningly at Johnno who looked at Celia.

'Dinner later?' he asked Celia.

'Oh, I don't think so.' Celia was stunned. They'd already spent almost the whole day together and now Johnno was suggesting dinner? 'I promised to drop in on the girls. Han and Ingrid were at that rally today, and I want to hear how it went.' She bit her lip remembering her earlier concern. 'I just hope...'

'They'll be fine. I'm sure of it. Sounds like they have their heads screwed on.'

Obviously overhearing, Anna butted in. 'That's the one Bob and Chris were going to, isn't it? Were they joining forces? They'll look after the girls. There's too much at stake for them to allow anything to happen to them.'

Johnno appeared puzzled. 'What...?'

'Oh,' Anna said casually. 'Didn't you know? Bob donated his sperm to father two of Celia's grandchildren. We're all one big happy family.'

*

'So, how was the rally?' Celia asked, when Mia was in bed and the adults were all seated with glasses of white wine.

'It was brilliant!' Ingrid's eyes glowed. 'You should have been there, Celia. There must have been around thirty thousand people, all waving placards and wearing tee-shirts like ours.' She pushed out her chest to show the rainbow logo on the one she was wearing.

'There were lots of rainbow flags, flowers and glitter,' Hannah added. 'We went all the way to Town Hall and Bill Shorten and Tanya Plibersek both spoke in favour. It was so exciting.'

'Then,' Ingrid said, 'Alex the Astronaut sang *Not Worth Hiding* and we marched down to Circular Quay.'

'Then when people began to leave, we took the ferry home,' Hannah finished.

'It's going to happen. It's actually going to happen,' Ingrid said. 'Let's drink to that – and to our wedding.' She held up her glass and, somewhat reluctantly, Celia thought, Hannah clinked glasses with her.

'I'm not so sure, Mum,' she said. 'There was certainly a lot of support there today, but there's a lot of opposition too. What if…?'

'What do Bob and Chris think?' Celia asked. She had a lot of respect for Bob's opinion

The girls looked at each other.

'I don't know,' Hannah said. 'I think they're hopeful too. But they're older.'

As if that made any difference where love was concerned. But the young seemed to think life stopped somewhere around thirty-five. What would they think if they knew about her and Johnno? But there was nothing to know, was there?

'Mum?'

'Sorry, Han. I was miles away. What did you say?'

'I was asking how Bindi was settling in.'

'Oh, fine. She's made herself at home already. In fact, I should be getting back to her.'

'So soon?'

But Celia could see the two girls were tired and she suddenly felt the need to be on her own.

She drove home feeling content. The girls were happy. Soon there would be a new baby. And Chloe was settled with Owen. All that remained was for her divorce to go through without any major hassles and life would be good.

When Celia entered her unit, Bindi was there to greet her, rubbing against her legs and purring loudly. While the room was still dark, she could see the lights across the water, the moon shining on its surface. She did love this home she'd made for herself.

Turning on the light, she went into the kitchen intent on making a mug of hot chocolate and taking it to bed with a good book. She was surprised to see the answer machine light blinking and pressed play to listen to her messages while the milk heated.

There were four messages, all from Bill and all were the same curt demand: *Call me!*

Twenty-one

By the time Celia and Val had exchanged news about their weekends and brewed a first cup of tea, it was time to open up and, unusually for Monday, they were immediately inundated by customers. It seemed the warmer weather over the weekend had brought them out looking for spring and summer clothes.

As a result, Celia had no time to brood over Bill's messages. If she'd given them any thought at all, it was to assume he'd spoken to Julian or seen the divorce papers, and was in a rage about what he probably saw as an unfair division of assets. She had no intention of returning his calls.

When the shop phone rang around lunchtime, Celia wasn't unduly surprised to hear Bill's voice.

What did surprise her were his first words.

'Why can't you keep your daughter under control!' he bellowed, so loudly she had to hold the phone away from her ear.

'I beg your pardon?' *What on earth was he talking about? Not the divorce, then.*

'That lesbian bitch of yours got herself on television last night – parading around the city like a depraved...' He paused as if unable to find a word sufficiently disgusting.

'The rally was on television?' Celia asked to gain time. Of course, it would have made the news on all channels with the leader and deputy leader of the opposition both speaking to the crowd.

'As if you didn't know,' he blustered. 'And there she was at the front, holding up a placard that said,' he gulped, 'Love is love, or some such rubbish and wearing one of those rainbow tee-shirts. How am I supposed to respond to the calls I've been getting this morning? My phone's been running hot. It's not...'

'Bill,' Celia tried to remain calm. 'Hannah is *your* daughter too, remember. I guess that's why they're calling you.' She couldn't help a smile escaping. 'And she's a grown woman – a mother – she's perfectly entitled to do as she pleases. And it pleases her and Ingrid to march for what they believe in. We did it in our day.' Though Celia couldn't recall Bill actually joining her on any of the marches, despite his claimed support of the causes.

'That was bloody different,' he roared. 'Back then, we had real causes to march for. Not this... this... tearing down of the tenets of our society.'

'I can't agree with you there. Hannah and Ingrid are a couple in love. A couple who, as the law stands at the moment, aren't permitted to make a public commitment of it. If that's all you have to say...'

'No,' he yelled, 'it's bloody not.'

Celia's heart dropped. She could hear the menace in Bill's vice and held the receiver away from her ear to avoid hearing the string of expletives, she knew from experience would follow

'What the hell do you mean by these papers Julian wants me to sign? Divorce? There'll be no divorce. You'll be sorry you ever met that poncy lawyer. I hear he's one of them, too.'

And the father of your granddaughter, Celia thought, as she gently put down the receiver. She sat motionless for a few moments, lost in her thoughts, before sighing and returning to the shop.

'Bill?' Val asked.

'Yes. He wanted to rant on about the girls going on the rally yesterday. Evidently, they were on telly last night and he's ropable. Also, he's got hold of the divorce papers and he's not a happy bunny'

'You expected that?'

'Yes.' Celia sighed again. Was this going to be the start of a protracted battle with Bill and Julian Clarke over the division of the assets? She didn't want or need that. Despite Bob's urging, she'd be happy with less if it meant it could all be settled more quickly.

Saying as much to Val brought a forceful disagreement.

'Don't sell yourself short,' Val exhorted. 'After all you've told me about your husband, you deserve at least half. If it were me...'

But it's not you, Celia thought. *And no-one else can comprehend what I've been going through, how I just want it to be over.* 'We'll see,' she said. 'Now, we need to get this new delivery sorted and displayed. If I do the window, can you ensure they're all priced correctly?'

Celia collected the few items she'd had in mind and began to put together her new window display. The former owner, Bel, had been right. She did have a flair for it, and the creative work took her mind off everything else. It was soothing and calmed her right down. By the time the window was finished, showing a *Spring Carnival* display for those customers fortunate enough to attend the races, she was in a more positive frame of mind.

As a result, when her next call came in – from Johnno – she was able to respond with a smile in her voice.

'You sound cheerful,' he said.

'You should have caught me an hour ago,' Celia replied. 'But no, best you didn't. How are you this morning?'

'All the better for hearing your voice. I wondered... You know I mentioned that new town project I'm working on?'

Celia nodded, even though she was aware Johnno couldn't see her, and began to clear a space on the counter, only half-listening. What had Johnno's latest project got to do with her?

'Well, I have to go there – do a recce – on Thursday. Are you able to play hooky and join me?'

'Oh, I don't know. I've left Val a few times recently.' She glanced across the shop to see her colleague mouthing, 'Johnno?'

Celia nodded, to which her friend gestured Celia should agree to whatever he was suggesting. 'Let me get back to you,' she said, after a pause.

'We could make a day of it,' he suggested. 'Take a picnic and...'

'I said I'll let you know,' Celia laughed, with the distinct feeling she was being railroaded and not sure if she liked it. Though the thought of a whole day together – just the two of them – did have some appeal.

'What did he want?' Val asked as Celia hung up.

'Only for me to spend the day with him on Thursday.'

'Go for it.'

'I don't know.'

'You like the guy, don't you?'

'Yes. But a whole day. I can't expect you to keep coping when I dash off on personal business.'

'Forget it. You're the boss; you can do whatever you like. You do trust me, don't you?'

'Of course. It's not that. I just don't know if it's wise to spend so much time with him.'

'What are you afraid of? Has he given you any reason to distrust him? To think he's up to something?'

'No,' Celia said hurriedly. 'Quite the opposite. He's always been the perfect gentleman. It's just that…' She put her hands flat on the counter, and her eyes glazed over as she considered what she was afraid of. 'I don't want to get too involved. He has the reputation of being a player, squiring young models, the perennial bachelor. He says he's changed. His friends say he's changed. But can I believe them?'

'You're afraid of getting hurt,' Val summed up for her.

Celia realised that was exactly what she was afraid of. She was afraid of getting too fond of Johnno Henderson, then ending up being hurt yet again.

'At my age…' she began.

'Balderdash. You're no age at all. You're in your prime – and methinks you've found a man who recognises that and who appreciates your more mature charms.'

'Is that what they are?' Celia laughed.

'Well, we oldies have to have something going for us – older and wiser – well, with more life experience at any rate.'

'So you think I should go? He wants us to spend the day together out west of Sydney at the site of some proposed new town development he's involved with.'

'Sounds interesting. And what's in it for you – besides time together?'

'A picnic. The chance to get to know him better. An insight into the man – what makes him tick. His work. I don't know.'

'Sounds like quite a lot to me. It also sounds as if you've already made up your mind to go.'

'Maybe.' Celia let a small smile escape. 'Are you sure you're okay with this? You can take a couple of days next week to make up. We can always get one of the casuals in if there's a rush.'

'That would be good. My youngest is planning her wedding and has been on at me to help her shop for the dress. I've been putting it off, but…'

'A wedding? You didn't say.'

'No. You had enough going on in your life. I didn't want to burden you with my family affairs. The wedding's not till next April, but Bettina wants to have everything in place. She was born organising.'

Celia felt somewhat chastised. Val had been quick to ask her about her life, and provide support, while remaining quiet about her own family. She vowed to be more interested in future.

A wedding! It made her think of Hannah and her and Ingrid's proposed wedding.

'We might be having a wedding in the family too,' she said slowly.

'Chloe?' Val asked.

'Hannah and Ingrid. Though…' Celia remembered how Chloe and Owen had looked at each other. Maybe a second wedding wasn't too far off either. She shook herself from her thoughts. 'Yes, anyway, that would be great. You deserve some time off. Let me know which days and we'll get it sorted.'

'That's brilliant. Thank you.'

'Thank *you*,' Celia touched her friend's arm, 'and now it's lunchtime. Do you want first shift?'

'Okay,' Val said. 'Can I pick you up something?'

'That would be great. Roast beef on rye. And a mango juice would be good too.'

Val collected her bag and, as the door clanged behind her, Celia's mood changed again. *Was Val right? Would Chloe and Owen be thinking of marriage? They were so young. She'd not been much older than them when she and Bill… And look how that turned out. But they weren't like she and Bill had been. And Owen seemed like a nice guy, kind, thoughtful. Bill had been neither of those. Handsome, charming, well-known… all of that. Yes. And then the arrogance, the bullying, the…*

Her thoughts were interrupted by the door opening.

'What can I do for you today?' Celia asked, as Heather walked in, a smile on her face.

'I'm not really in the market for anything to wear today. I just wanted to pop in to see how you were doing. I've been following the news about your husband and saw your daughter on telly last night. I thought you might need some TLC.' Heather's eyes met Celia's in concern.

Celia didn't know Heather well. She'd been Bel's friend, not hers. But Celia knew the former owner had often used Heather as a sounding board and friendly ear. And she *had* been kind enough to share the news about Bill with her.

'You're thinking deep thoughts,' Heather said, leaning heavily on the counter. 'I don't have a lot of energy these days, and the walk up the hill has tired me out, I'm afraid. But you look as if you need someone to talk to and I've always been able to provide a friendly ear. If I can help in any way...'

But I don't know you well enough.

As if reading her mind, Heather continued, 'Sometimes it's easier to talk with someone completely uninvolved. And it can help a person sort out their thoughts to talk about what's bothering them. Stop me if I'm being presumptuous, but maybe we could take a tea or coffee together, and you can share what's worrying you. A problem shared is a problem halved, as they say.' Heather cocked her head to one side.

Celia looked askance at the woman standing there, her grey bob surrounding a round cheerful face, and suddenly she knew this was someone she could trust, someone who wouldn't offer kind words or platitudes. She made up her mind.

'Val's fetching lunch. But I can duck out for a quick one when she gets back. Can you wait till then? There's a chair.' She pointed to the other side of the shop where what they called the 'husband's chair' sat.

'Thanks,' Celia said to Val when she arrived back with her sandwich and juice. 'Do you mind if I pop out for a bit? Heather's invited me to coffee.'

'No.' But Val appeared puzzled as Celia took her lunch through to the back shop and returned carrying her bag.

Heather followed Celia out, and the two women walked slowly along the road to the nearest café. Once there, Heather flopped into a seat gratefully. 'I've been told I really need to get one of those walker contraptions, or a motorised scooter,' she said, taking a deep breath. 'Can you imagine? But I suppose it'll come to that. I'm just grateful to get around at all.'

'Has your emphysema been troubling you again?' Celia asked, frowning.

'It'll catch up with me one of these days – but not today,' the older woman said with a chuckle. 'Now let's order. Tea or coffee for you?'

They ordered two cups of peppermint tea, Heather complimenting Celia on her choice. 'It always has a calming effect,' she said. 'And you looked to me like you needed some of that this morning. Now, what's that husband of yours been doing to upset you so much – besides getting his name in the paper?'

'You don't want to know.' Then, realising that's exactly why they were here, Celia began to recount Bill's recent tirades. 'And now I don't know if it's going to go on for another two years,' she said at last.

'What does your solicitor say?'

'Oh, he's optimistic, though I haven't spoken to him today.' Celia wondered if she should have called Bob immediately she'd hung up on Bill, but didn't see how it would change anything.

'You may think I'm just an old woman,' Heather said, 'and one who's never married. But that doesn't mean I don't know men. I've had a few relationships in my life, and I've stood on the sidelines and watched a few others. Maybe that's why I stayed single. And let me tell you, it's an ill wind…'

Here we go, thought Celia. *More platitudes and recommendations to make the best of things.*

'The best thing you can do for yourself is to find someone else,' Heather said, surprising Celia into almost choking on her tea. 'Is there anyone else on the horizon?'

'Well…'

'I knew it!' Heather exclaimed. 'You can't fool me – or not for long anyway. And I can't see a lovely woman like you being alone for long. Now, this man. Is he someone you're attracted to?'

'Maybe,' Celia said, unwilling to give too much away.

'Well, then.' Heather sighed. 'That makes it easy. Why not just do what your heart tells you?'

'My heart?' Celia pondered. It had been a long time since she'd followed her heart. All of her decisions for the past few years had been made by her head. Consulting her heart had only led to grief.

Heather seemed to be waiting for a response.

'My heart?' Celia repeated, an image of Johnno immediately filling her thoughts. 'I...'

'What do you feel when he's around? Are you caught up in the moment? Considering what to do next? Does he make your heart race?'

Celia's heart was racing at the very thought of Johnno. 'Yes!' The word erupted unbidden.

'Then that's your answer.' Heather sipped her tea and gazed out of the café window allowing Celia to regain her composure.

'And that's it? That's your advice?'

'It's what you knew yourself. I only helped you find what was in your heart.'

'But...'

'I know. You didn't want to admit it. You'd prefer to think he was just a pleasant companion, maybe even a distraction from the muddle your life's in with Bill, the divorce and everything it entails. Maybe you even told yourself seeing him would be an annoyance to your husband?'

Celia cringed at the truth of her words.

Heather continued, 'Admitting you felt some... affection for this man might mean you put yourself in a vulnerable position. But, my dear, what is life if we always avoid being hurt? What is life without the risk? Without life's highs and lows, it's a very boring place. At least, that's been my experience. I've been hurt more times than I care to remember. But I regret none of it. It's all what they call life's rich pattern, and the memories keep my old body warm at night. You'll see. If it's to be, it'll turn out all right. If not, you can chalk it up to experience and start again.'

Celia looked at her companion with fresh eyes. Who'd have thought it? Heather looked and seemed as if she'd been on her own all her life – a veritable spinster schoolmistress, devoting her life to her career and good works. Her words painted a picture of a different person entirely – one who had loved and lost and loved again – and didn't regret a single moment. Could Celia be like her? Could she throw caution to the wind and allow her emotions to take over? Could she allow herself to fall for Johnno regardless of the possible cost?

Twenty-two

'I'm glad you could make it,' Johnno said, as the car left the centre of the city and sped through the suburbs. 'I want to show you a bit of my life – a part I don't often share.'

Celia felt the wind in her hair, and an emotion she couldn't identify swept through her. It was akin to relief. Relief to be out of the city; relief to be with Johnno; relief to have decided to – as Heather had advised – follow her heart.

'Tell me about where we're going and what we're about to see.'

'I want it to be a surprise. But, I will say this. I plan to be on the forefront of development with this project. It's going to be unlike anything Sydney has seen before, unlike anything Australia has seen. It's to be modelled on a development in the Netherlands – one which is self-sufficient in terms of power, industry, schools, universities, aged care – a total community on the outskirts of the city. Everything within reach. No need for lengthy daily commutes.'

Celia could see it was something Johnno fervently believed in. He was full of enthusiasm.

'But you don't do it all yourself?'

'Hell no! I'm working with a developer – Wright Constructions. They have the experience and know-how. And a group of investors provide the money. I'm just the middle man – the one who had the vision, got them all together. And the one who carries the can if it all fails,' he added ruefully. 'But it won't, not this one.'

'You sound very sure.'

'I am. I know there have been a few disastrous attempts in development in the past little while, but Wrights are a sound firm. It should take around ten years for the project to come to fruition, but I wanted to show you the greenfield site, so you can imagine how it will look.'

Without Celia noticing, they'd left the built-up area behind and were now driving through market gardens and acreage.

'Here we are,' Johnno said, turning up what appeared to be a country lane and coming to a halt at the edge of an empty field.

He helped her out of the car and they stood gazing at... nothing. There were only a few trees and a large empty paddock.

'Just imagine,' Johnno said. 'In ten years this will have disappeared. Instead there will be streets and well-designed homes and offices, schools and a university, sports fields, an entire community. It's planned to be an IT hub – light industry only – no pollution. Here, let me show you.' He drew a folder out of the car and, leaning against the bonnet, opened it to reveal pages of drawings depicting the town of the future.

Celia examined the pages, the sun beating down on her, while Johnno enthusiastically described what it would eventually look like. Although impressed by his vision, she couldn't help but think of the open spaces that would be violated by the uprooting of trees and bushes. Surely there was wildlife living there. What would happen to that when the bulldozers moved in? But she said nothing of this, unwilling to spoil the moment. She was flattered he'd chosen to share it with her.

Eventually, Johnno seemed to realise her interest was waning. 'Let's find a sheltered spot for lunch,' he said. 'I know just the place.' Taking a basket from the boot, he grasped Celia's hand and led the way across the field.

Glad she'd worn jeans and flat shoes, Celia accompanied him to a cosy spot under a large pepper tree.

'See,' Johnno pointed out, 'there was a house here once. And this was part of the garden.' Sure enough, Celia could see the remnants of a stone cottage, the walls almost totally gone, with only a few overgrown bricks remaining to tell the story of its past.

'There were soldier settlements here after the first World War,' he said. 'Not that the occupants could make a living from the size of the acreage they were allotted. Some were turned into the market gardens we passed along the way, but this stretch has been abandoned for years. We'll be bringing life back to the place, not despoiling it.'

Had he read her mind?

Johnno spread a tartan rug on the ground and opened the well-provisioned picnic basket, obviously provided by some expensive delicatessen. There were two miniature chicken pies, a loaf of sour dough bread along with packages of various cheeses, a couple of apples, a small container of grapes, two slices of pecan pie and two mini bottles of white wine. There were also plastic plates and glasses, and even a square of paper tablecloth.

'A veritable feast,' Celia said, as she tucked her legs under her and accepted a glass of wine.

It was a perfect day for a picnic, and Celia soon forgot her misgivings as they chatted comfortably. Johnno seemed a different man here away from the city. Casually dressed today, like her, in jeans and an open-necked shirt, he was neither the city slicker or the lycra-clad sportsman. He was just a man whose company she enjoyed, one who made her laugh, and whose touch made her long for more.

They whiled away the afternoon, and it was only when a cool breeze began to blow up and Celia began to shiver, that Johnno rose and held out a hand to help her up. 'We should be getting back.'

'Yes,' she said regretfully. She'd enjoyed her day out, a day which saw her forget all the challenges in her life and let her imagine life could always be like this.

Johnno threw an arm around her shoulders and gave her a squeeze. 'Cold?'

'A bit.' She shuddered, more from his touch than the temperature. It was the first time he'd held her. She fell easily into Johnno's arms, sensing his lips on her hair.

'My God, you're beautiful,' he murmured, as his lips moved from her hair to her forehead, her eyelids, her cheeks, her lips. Their lips met and clung for what seemed to be forever.

Celia shivered again, a hot flush of desire flooding through her. This wasn't supposed to happen. Not here. Not like this.

As if reading her mind, Johnno released her.

'I'll get everything together,' he said in a muffled voice, leaning down to collect the empty containers and the used plates and glasses. Soon they were all packed back into the basket and, taking her hand in a firm grip, Johnno led her back to the car.

Once there, he turned to give Celia a warm smile, then started up the engine. They drove back in a companionable silence, neither wanting to be the first to break the spell. But as they neared the city, it was Johnno who spoke first.

'Your place or mine?'

Celia swallowed. She'd known this was going to happen. It was as if there had been an unspoken agreement. Since that kiss. She touched her lips. She'd sensed his restraint, knew what they both wanted, needed. *Was she ready for all that it entailed? Ready to make love?*

That's what Johnno was asking. It wasn't a matter of if, but where. They both knew it.

'Mine,' she said faintly, unable to cope with the bachelor pad, to contemplate becoming one of the many women who'd slept there.

'Okay.' He smiled at her – a warm smile that sent tremors right down to her toes. He put a hand on her thigh, turning the spot he touched into a furnace. By the time they reached the North Shore, and Johnno drove the car into her unit's car park, Celia was a quivering jelly.

But once inside her apartment, Celia was beset with doubts. Bill was the only man she'd slept with in the past twenty-five years. What if, once he saw her naked, Johnno was repulsed. He was used to seeing the supple bodies of twenty-year-olds. She was twice their age and had borne two children. Maybe this wasn't such a good idea.

But Johnno didn't give her time for second thoughts. They were no sooner inside than he gathered her in his arms and, heedless of Bindi who appeared to rub herself against their legs, picked her up. 'Bedroom?' he asked in a voice thick with desire.

Celia pointed, delighting in the feeling of his strong body against hers, in the sensuous touch of his hands on her thighs as he carried her in and carefully laid her on the bed, immediately joining her and holding her close.

'Mmm. I love the way you smell,' he muttered stroking her forehead and eyelids. Celia stretched up to push back a lock of Johnno's hair – just as she'd often wanted to do in the past, but never dared.

Follow your heart, Heather had told her. Was that what she was doing now? It wasn't Celia's heart that had led her into this situation. It was something a lot more primitive. A sudden flare of yearning struck her, and she pulled Johnno closer.

She felt his hands unbutton her shirt, then reach round to unclasp her bra.

'Let me,' she said, sitting up and removing her upper garments then, with a cheeky grin, her jeans and pants – just as Johnno removed his.

'You're beautiful,' he said, dispelling her worst fears.

Even…' she began, only to feel a finger on her lips, as his mouth took hers again, and his body covered hers.

Twenty-three

Celia floated through the morning in a euphoric haze. When Johnno had left at the crack of dawn, planting a kiss on her forehead, he muttered something about having to get to the office and calling later. She'd barely heard him, groaning, turning over, and falling back to sleep.

Since then, there had been two text messages with smiling emojis and an invitation to dinner. Celia felt like a teenager again. She hugged herself in delight.

'Someone's looking happy today,' Val said, as the door closed behind another satisfied customer. 'Had a good day yesterday?'

'Yes.' Celia smiled. She intended to keep the change in her relationship with Johnno to herself. It was no one's business but hers. She was looking forward to seeing him again, but tonight? They'd barely had a wink of sleep. It had been close to dawn before they'd fallen asleep, and this morning she felt exhausted, though pleasantly so.

Celia wasn't as young as she used to be and a night like that, while wonderful, wasn't something she wanted to repeat – not just yet anyway.

In her mind, Celia relived the night of passion – the sort of night she'd thought she'd never experience again. Since she'd left Bill – and for some time before that – making love had been far from her thoughts. If she'd considered it at all, it was to imagine that side of her life was in the past.

She'd never expected to meet a man she could feel affection for, never mind a hunk like Johnno who seemed to return that affection tenfold.

He was a practiced lover, much more expert and patient than her husband, and Celia had thrilled to his touch as he brought her to a peak of pleasure she'd never experienced before. Whereas Bill had been rough and demanding, Johnno was gentle, tender and considerate, moving at her pace and understanding her needs.

'You're in your own little world.' Val's voice brought her down to earth with a thump.

'Sorry. Did you say something?'

'Lunch. I asked if you wanted to take first lunch, or you wanted me to get you anything.'

'Oh. No, you go. I'll head out later. I need a few things from the deli.'

Once Val had gone, Celia once again fell into a daydream, one in which Johnno played a major part. When her phone rang she was so lost in her thoughts, she assumed it would be him.

It was a surprise to hear Bob's voice instead, and Celia remembered she'd planned to call her solicitor to let him know about Bill's call two days earlier. She'd been so wrapped up in her new-found love she'd completely forgotten.

Bob's words were a shock.

'I had a communication from Julian Clarke.'

Celia's heart sank. All of the pleasure from the previous night disappeared. Heart in her mouth she asked, 'Wh…what did it say?'

'It's not good. As you anticipated, Bill wants to challenge the conditions. He says…'

'He doesn't think I deserve to get half?'

'That's it in a nutshell. I need to take your advice on this, but I'd strongly suggest…' Bob paused, presumably to allow Celia to adjust her thinking.

Her immediate reaction was that Bill could have what he wanted – anything to be rid of him. But on reflection, she found her opinion changed. It was exactly what Bill would expect – that she'd allow herself to be browbeaten, just as she always had.

Maybe last night with Johnno had coloured her views, maybe she'd just found some inner strength. But, whatever the reason, Celia now knew she wanted to get what she deserved from the divorce, and Bob had said she deserved half. 'Do you still stand by what's in the document – in terms of the division of assets?'

'I do. As I said, it's perfectly fair.'

Celia remembered Johnno's comment that many women got more than half – sixty percent even. And she'd managed the household, brought up their two daughters – daughters Bill had since disowned. If she held out for the full amount, she could give some to her girls. That idea energised her.

'I don't want to give in.'

'Good.'

But Bob sounded surprised. As well he might. The worm had turned. A flash of anger exploded somewhere inside Celia. The vulnerable, easily manipulated Celia had gone, replaced by one who was determined to fight for her daughters' rights. It was easier to think that way – to imagine it was for the girls rather than just for herself.

Though it would mean she'd be better off afterwards – a lot better off. The settlement would enable her to finalise the payment for the shop to Bel, pay off the mortgage on her apartment – or buy somewhere else should she choose. It would also ensure the future of her children and grandchildren. She could put together a trust fund for the little ones to take care of their schooling and university studies.

Bob was talking again. 'I'll draw up a reply, but you do realise this means it may have to go to court?'

Celia felt her throat tighten at the thought, but she was resolute. 'Whatever it takes.'

'Right. I'll get that off today. The book seems to be doing well,' he said in a different tone. 'I see it's up for some award or other and it was featured again in today's paper.'

Celia gave a grim smile. Although it was to her long-term benefit financially that the book sold well, she couldn't help but wish it had been a flop. It was full of lies – lies and inuendo.

'So I'll wait to hear from you?'

'I'll get back to you as soon as I can. But I have to warn you to be prepared for a legal battle.'

Celia flinched at the tone in Bob's voice and sighed. She really didn't want a protracted court challenge, but was determined not to allow Bill to get all his own way.

She was still seething when Val returned and, although she tried to put on a positive expression, Val guessed something was up.

'It's beautiful outside,' Val said with a smile, then frowned. 'What's up?'

Celia wondered whether she should share Bob's call, then decided her friend deserved to know why her mood had changed. 'I had a call from Bob.'

'Oh?' Val raised an eyebrow. 'Bad news?'

'I guess.' Celia sighed again. 'Bill's going to fight me over the settlement.'

'I hope you're not going to give in.'

'No, I'm not. But it may mean a long delay – and a court case.'

'Oh, I'm sorry.' Val moved to give Celia a hug, but she shrugged it off. 'Are you okay?'

'Yes. Now, I am. It wasn't completely unexpected. Bill's never liked to be thwarted and he'd hate to give up any of what he sees as his hard-earned cash to me. But it was something Johnno said that made me think.'

'Well, sounds as if he's done you some good then. Besides…' Val grinned knowingly, and Celia couldn't help but join her.

The next call *was* from Johnno, and they arranged to have dinner the following evening then go rowing together on Sunday morning. As she hung up, it occurred to Celia that, if she intended to make a habit of this rowing thing, she should get herself properly kitted out, and made a spur-of-the-moment decision to check out the local sports store in her lunch break.

By the time she returned to Isabella, she was the proud owner of a pair of tights in a nylon and lycra fabric and a special vest with a waterproof back. She'd eschewed the crop tops and singlets as being too revealing and unsuitable for someone of her age.

'You've been busy,' was Val's comment when she saw the bag. 'Sports gear, eh?'

'I'm going rowing again on Sunday – with Johnno and his friends – so I thought I'd better gear up.'

'Sounds like you're fitting this man into your life – or you into his,' Val commented sagely, making Celia hesitate.

Yes, she realised, that's exactly what she was doing. On the basis of a few dates and one night together, she was preparing to turn her life around. *Was she being foolish? Would it all be a flash-in-the-pan and would she regret setting herself up for failure?*

What the hell. Heather was right. She wasn't a young chicken anymore and this might be her last chance at love. She was determined to make the most of the opportunity, and if it all ended in disaster, then at least she'd have had fun while it lasted. She was sick of being cautious.

And it was only a rowing outfit. She remembered what Anna had said.

'I really enjoyed the rowing last weekend. And if this thing with Johnno doesn't work out, I can join a rowing club.'

'It seems you're taking my advice to heart,' Val laughed, 'but don't go overboard.'

Celia smiled at the unintended pun. Val's suggestions of a book club, choir or pilates had fallen on deaf ears. What she intended would be much more fun.

*

On Sunday morning, Celia awoke before dawn and snuggled into Johnno. She could get used to this. His arms felt so warm and comfortable. She had a sense of belonging which was stupid given it was only the second time they'd slept together. But she couldn't deny the way she felt, and last night their lovemaking had been, if anything, even better than the first time.

'Time to get up.' Johnno unwound his arms from Celia and slipped out of the bed.

Celia rubbed her eyes, wondering why on earth she'd agreed to go rowing when she'd much rather curl up here again and replay last night's passion. She must be mad.

But Johnno was already in the shower. She could hear the water running, the sound of his deep voice warbling some song she didn't recognise, then the shower door opened and closed. There was nothing else for it. With a groan, she rose to join him and, showered and dressed and a quick glass of orange juice later, the pair were in his car heading for the rowing club.

Johnno's pleased look of surprise when he'd seen Celia's outfit was nothing to Anna's loud whoop of delight.

'You've certainly taken this to heart,' she said, as Celia and Johnno stepped out of the car. Even Jonathon gave a hoot of glee.

'You'll have to look out now, Mum,' he yelled, his eyes raking Celia's trim figure. She was immediately glad she'd chosen the more conservative of the garments on offer, but still felt naked and wished she could get into the scull without anyone seeing her.

'With me again, Celia?' Anna asked.

'Yes please, if...' She glanced towards Johnno, but he was walking towards the shed, engrossed in something Marcus was saying.

'They're too busy talking tactics,' Anna dismissed the men, 'and Jon's keen to get into a single scull. Means he doesn't have to wait for us and can set his own pace.'

'Right.' Celia was amused at Anna's quick summation of the scene and strolled with her towards the water where the men were already launching the sculls.

'You two seem to be getting on well,' Anna said, when they were out on the water and rowing steadily. 'It hasn't taken you long.'

Celia blushed. 'We do get on well. And he's...'

'I know, sex on a stick and charming with it.'

Celia turned even redder.

'It's okay,' Anna said. 'I know the effect he can have on women. I just don't want you to get your hopes up then...'

'I think I can take care of myself,' Celia said, wondering if it was true, and wondering if she was just yet another of the *women* Anna referred to.

*

After Anna's inquisition, it was almost a relief to get into the car alongside Johnno for the trip to breakfast. The warmth of his hand on her thigh was a reminder of what they shared, and it was easy to dismiss the hint of uneasiness Anna's comments had raised.

'Everything okay?' he asked, as if sensing her unease.

'Very okay.'

'Was Anna giving you a hard time?' Johnno threw a glance in her direction, one so filled with love, Celia's heart turned over.

'Not really. Just warning me against you – reminding me how attractive women find you. As if I hadn't already worked that out for myself.' Celia relaxed with a grin.

'You're the one with me now. The only one I want to be with. You do know that, don't you? What else can I do to prove to you that…'

Celia interrupted him. 'I know. You don't have to do any more, but I think your friends may not be entirely convinced the leopard has changed his spots.'

She saw Johnno's lips tighten.

'Well it's time they did. What more do I have to do to prove to them that I'm no longer the person I used to be – the crazy bachelor who partied all night?'

'You don't have to prove anything to me. I know who you are.' Celia pictured the Johnno she knew – the one who was happy to spend an evening curled up with her in front of the television, her cat Bindi on his lap, a glass of wine in his hand. That was the real Johnno, the one she'd come to know and maybe even be on the way to falling in love with. The other was one who was playing a part – the part of the astute businessman, the inveterate party-goer, the member of Sydney's social scene and the consummate bachelor and man-about-town.

They'd arrived at the café by this time, and Johnno helped Celia out of the low-slung car, taking a moment to hug her and, after pushing a strand of hair out of her eyes, place a kiss on top of her head. 'Ready for the fray?'

As soon as they entered, they caught sight of Anna, Marcus and Jon sitting by the window and joined them. Marcus was reading a Sunday paper he must have picked up on the way. He was frowning as he flicked through the pages, then his eyes widened.

'You need to see this, Celia,' he said, passing it across the table.

'Oh, not again!' Celia stared at the headline in dismay as Johnno put an arm around her shoulder and read the page on which her eyes were riveted.

More allegations against footy legend

'What is it?' Anna asked, turning around and trying to see.

Celia closed the paper and looked up. 'It's Bill. More women have come forward with allegations against him.' She hid her face in her hands. 'This is going to kill him. Even if they're lying, it's become a top news item and...'

'Will it affect you?' Marcus asked, a frown appearing between his eyes. 'Surely not.'

'Last time, the reporters wanted statements from Celia,' Johnno said quietly. 'Celia, do you want to leave?' He began to rise, but Celia signalled for him to resume his seat.

'Let's just have breakfast and try to forget all about it,' she said. Although she knew *she* wouldn't forget it. While one allegation could perhaps be swept away, considered to be a case of a woman spurned, these new ones made it all much more real.

'Can I have a glass of water?' she asked, suddenly feeling her knees go weak.

Anna tried to change the subject. 'Have you all received your forms for the postal survey?' she asked, adding when Celia and Johnno nodded, 'Bob and Chris are quietly excited about it. I suppose your daughters are too?' she asked Celia.

Relieved at the change of topic, Celia agreed. 'They certainly are. They're sure the result will be positive. So much so, they're planning a wedding on Valentine's day. At least Ingrid is. Ingrid's my daughter Hannah's partner,' she explained to Johnno, not sure if she'd mentioned her to him before.

'It's about time,' Marcus chimed in. Then they all turned to look at Jonathon who asked, 'Will Uncle Bob and Uncle Chris get married too?'

'I don't know, honey. They haven't said anything. I guess they might.'

'My guess is there'll be a mass of weddings if the vote is yes,' said Marcus with a smile. 'Good news for all the wedding industries.'

'Mmm.' Celia was still distracted. The mention of her daughters had reminded her how vulnerable they were to the machinations of the media now Bill was in the news again.

'I'd like to go as soon as we've eaten,' she whispered to Johnno while the others were studying the menus. Johnno joined the other males in ordering the big breakfast, while Anna chose the eggs benedict. But Celia had lost her appetite, so ordered smashed avocado on toast, hoping she could manage to wash it down with several cups of tea.

'Coffee, everyone?' Marcus asked, when the waitress arrived to take their orders.

'Can I have tea – peppermint if you have it?' Celia asked with a smile. Jon opted for a banana smoothie while the others ordered coffee.

'Are you okay?' Anna whispered to Celia, when Marcus took possession of the paper again and began to debate the latest political news with Johnno, and Jonathon, taking advantage of the others' pre-occupation, began to check his phone.

'Almost,' Celia whispered back. 'I still can't believe it of Bill. He always tried it on, and I knew he had a few affairs over the years. There were always women, but I didn't imagine anything like this. It's the girls I'm concerned about. They got enough publicity from the march. They don't deserve to be put through any more angst just because Bill's their dad. He hasn't even seen or spoken to them since they left home,' she added bitterly, conveniently forgetting the scene with Hannah and Bill in Isabella.

By the time breakfast was over, Celia was anxious to see her daughters. Once in the car, she couldn't wait to get home, showered and drive over to their house. Johnno did his best to calm her, but Celia could feel her tension mounting. Despite the sun streaming through the windscreen, she felt chilled.

The shower was big enough for two, and Celia did feel a little calmer as Johnno soaped her body and rubbed himself against her in the shower. But the thought of the article in the paper wasn't far from her mind, so she pulled away.

'Sorry,' she said as they stepped out, and he began to pat her dry with a large bath towel. 'I can't...'

'It's okay,' he said soothingly. 'I understand. I'll be out of here in two ticks.'

They dressed together hurriedly and, after ensuring Bindi's food and water bowls were full, made their way down to the car park. Johnno released the lock in his car first, and left Celia with a quick hug and kiss. 'I'll ring later,' he called, as she opened her car door.

Celia slid into her little red mini with relief and turned the key. There was a harsh grinding sound. She tried again with the same result, then beat the steering wheel with her fists, close to tears. *What was she to do?*

'Having trouble?' The voice came from outside her open window.

She looked up to see Johnno. 'I thought you'd gone.'

'Not quite. I was just starting up when I heard your engine give out. Want a lift?'

Celia felt lightheaded with relief. 'Yes please.' She could get a cab back, or one of the girls could drive her. 'I'll direct you. I don't know what I'd have done if ...'

'But I'm here. And I have no doubt you'd have managed perfectly well, but you don't need to. Now, where are we going?'

Celia barely spoke on the ten-minute drive, hoping and fearing the girls had already seen the paper and on tenterhooks lest the journalists had staked them out.

To her relief the street was empty apart from a few parked cars and a couple clearly out for a Sunday morning stroll.

'Thanks,' she muttered, then a thought occurred to her. 'Would you like to come in with me?'

Johnno appeared surprised. 'You want me to meet your daughters?'

'Why not?' Celia felt that so much had already happened this morning, a meeting between Johnno and her girls couldn't hurt. And he had to meet them sometime. Maybe it was better to do it like this rather than make a big thing of it. 'I'm sure they'd be delighted to meet you and...'

'It'll take the heat off the article about their dad?' Johnno guessed.

'That too.'

'Mum,' Hannah greeted her at the door, then, seeing the figure behind Celia, '... and?'

'This is Johnno – a friend.'

'Welcome, Johnno. You'll find us in a bit of a mess this morning. We've just got back from the markets, and Chloe and Owen have taken Mia and Si to the park. We're unpacking, then we were going to brew some coffee. Come through.' She turned and led the way through the house to the large sun-filled kitchen where Ingrid was unloading a couple of cardboard boxes of fruit and vegetables and organising them into the fridge.

The Sunday paper lay, unopened, on the table.

Twenty-four

'It's nice to meet you, Johnno,' Hannah said, giving her mother an unfathomable look. 'Have you two known each other long?'

'Not long,' Celia replied. 'We met through Anna King – Jan and Bob's sister,' she lied, hoping Johnno wouldn't let her down.

'I know who Anna is.'

'We all went rowing together this morning,' Celia added, hoping that adding a modicum of truth would confirm her story.

'Rowing?'

'On Middle Harbour. It's lovely there in the early morning.'

'I'm sure,' Hannah said. 'But rowing? You?'

The four were sitting in the courtyard drinking coffee and eating slices of banana bread the girls had bought at the markets. The sun was throwing shafts of light across the paving stones giving them a warm glow. The only sounds were the faint chime of church bells in the distance and the strumming of a guitar from the house across the back fence.

'You should have seen your mother in her gear,' Johnno said.

There was silence, and Celia intercepted a knowing look pass between the girls. *Had they guessed? Of course they had.* She felt her ears turn red.

'Was there a particular reason you dropped in today?' Hannah asked, her words breaking into the awkward silence.

'There's… today's paper… your dad…'

'What's he been up to now?' Hannah asked, while Ingrid said, 'I'll fetch it,' and dashed into the house, returning with the paper.

'Page four,' Celia murmured, as if by speaking quietly, she could lessen the shock.

'Let me see!' Hannah leant over Ingrid's shoulder as the pair read the article. 'Well,' she said, when she'd finished. 'That's no surprise, is it? Where there's smoke… It would have been stupid to imagine there was only one of them. Did you really have no idea, Mum?'

'No, not this. There *were* women. They followed the footy players around like flies around a honey-pot. But as far as I knew, they were there of their own volition. They wanted whatever it was they got. They weren't…' Her voice dried up. 'Do you think they – those women – are only out for what they can get? With all the publicity from his book, do you think they just want to capitalise on that?'

'It's possible,' Ingrid said slowly. 'What do *you* think, Han? You know your dad.'

'I could believe him capable of anything. He's a slimy bastard. But I tend to agree with Mum. There were a lot of women who followed Dad around hoping to get a bit of the action – if you'll pardon the expression,' she said to Johnno with a grin. 'I was only young, but I can remember them.'

'Then there were the others he pursued – many of them friends of mine,' Celia grimaced. 'But he always seemed to find women to go along with him. I never thought he had any need to force himself on them.'

'Times change,' Johnno said. 'Maybe some of those who were willing back then can now see there's capital to be made from his recent publicity.'

'Anyway, it's nothing to do with us,' Hannah said, folding the paper. 'Why did you think we'd be interested in anything affecting him?'

'It may affect you too,' Celia said. 'The media linked you to him when you were photographed at the march. They may think it'll make a good story…' Her voice trailed off. *Was she the only one worried about this?*

'Han's right,' Ingrid said. 'Han's only link to Bill Ramsay is through an accident of birth. That's what we'll tell any journalists who dare to show their faces. But I don't think they will. I'm pretty sure they don't know where we live, and we're not important enough in the scheme of things for them to spend time ferreting out our address.'

'You may be right.' Celia wondered if she'd been worrying needlessly. The young were so resilient. She guessed Hannah and Ingrid had had to be.

As if reading her mind, Hannah said. 'It'll soon be over, Mum. Voting starts next week. By mid-November we should know the result.'

Celia saw her daughter's hand grip Ingrid's tightly. Hannah had more to worry about than her dad's peccadillos, real or manufactured. Her whole future was at stake.

'I hear you two plan to marry,' Johnno said.

'Ingrid does,' Hannah replied. 'I plan to wait and see.'

'We're getting married, babe,' Ingrid said in a husky voice. 'And you're invited, Johnno.'

'Will you stay to lunch?' Hannah asked. 'The others should be back soon. Then you can meet the rest of the family,' she said craftily to Johnno.

'No, I think not,' Celia said quickly, feeling she'd exposed Johnno to enough of her family for one day and beginning to regret her impulse to invite him to join them.

'If you're sure?'

'Things to do, people to see,' Johnno said lightly as they both rose to take their leave.

'Things to do, people to see? Really!' Celia laughed, when they were back in Johnno's car. 'Was that the best you could do?'

'Well, I could see you were stuck for an excuse.' He grinned back. 'Now, where *shall* we lunch?'

Ten minutes later, they were turning into the car park for Frenchy's café, nestled in the heritage landscape of Headland Park in Mosman. Celia sighed with pleasure. She loved it here, surrounded as it was by artist studios and ocean views, and only a bushwalk away from Balmoral, Chowder Bay and Taronga Zoo. She'd been introduced to the licensed outdoor café – complete with French-speaking staff – when she'd renewed her relationship with Hannah and Ingrid and, before Mia's birth, had often accompanied them there on Sundays such as this. Ingrid enjoyed practicing her French with the staff, complaining she'd forget it completely if she didn't use it.

Johnno helped Celia out of the car and grasped her hand as they made their way towards the café, pausing only to admire the agility of a little girl who was manouvering her billy-cart backwards and forwards across the road and down into the entrance of one of the galleries, oblivious of the pedestrians forced to move out of her path.

Celia felt her mood change. For the first time since she'd seen the paper that morning, there was a lightness in her chest and a sensation of being at ease with the world. If Johnno could make her feel this way just by holding her hand and taking her to lunch…

'Okay?' he asked as they reached the café.

She nodded, too full of joy to speak. Hannah was right. What did it matter what Bill did or didn't do, had done or hadn't? Celia had her own life to live. It was the weekend. She was with a man who appeared to think the world of her. She was falling in love. She really was!

She almost skipped into the café, barely able to stand still while they looked for a free table, finally finding one with a large shading umbrella close to the serving hatch.

'You've been here before?' Johnno asked.

'Yes. With the girls. But not recently.' She looked around. 'It doesn't appear to have changed much. I love it. It's so very… French.'

They laughed.

'You know this place has an amazing history from the eighteen-hundreds through to recent times. Did you see the mural as we came in?'

'I think so.'

'The café is on the site of the old All Ranks Club and the mural was painted by one of the soldiers – or so they say.'

'It's a lovely story anyway, and the whole place reeks of history.'

Johnno picked up a menu. 'I recommend the French Onion Soup then *Tarte Tatin* to follow – all washed down with a nice bottle of Sauvignon Blanc.'

How could Celia argue with that?

When lunch was over, they took a gentle walk along a bush track to admire the view of the harbour from North to South Head. The water sparkled in the sunlight and was dotted with the white sails of Sunday sailors. For an instant, Celia wondered if Bill was out there among them – he and Julian had often gone sailing together on Sundays, leaving her home alone – but she quickly suppressed the thought. She wasn't going to allow him to spoil this perfect afternoon.

'Ready to go home?' Johnno's arm tightened around Celia's shoulder and he kissed her forehead, almost as if he'd guessed her thoughts and wanted to impress his presence on her.

'Yes.'

The sun was weakening, and the day cooling. It would be good to get back, and Bindi would need to be fed. They'd had such an early start. But Celia didn't want the day to end.

'Would you…? I could…' *Would it be too forward to offer to cook dinner?* They'd already spent the entire day together – *and* last night. Celia hesitated.

Johnno seemed to understand her dilemma.

'I was hoping you might invite me back to dinner,' he said with a smile which lit up his face. 'But if…'

'No, I mean yes. Dinner. But I don't know…'

'We can order a takeaway. I already know you're a brilliant cook, no need to try to impress. And I don't want you slaving away in the kitchen when you can be with me.'

'Oh!'

They arrived back at Celia's apartment to a loud greeting from Bindi. Celia filled her bowls, returning to the living area to discover Johnno had loaded a CD of romantic music and that there was a glass of wine waiting for her.

'How lovely!' she said, joining him on the sofa.

Johnno's arm immediately snaked around to pull her close. 'I've been wanting to do this all day,' he murmured into her hair. 'Ever since you appeared in that sexy outfit. I almost took you back to bed right then.'

Celia returned his embrace, raining kisses on whichever bits of him she could reach, part of her wishing he'd done just that, and she'd been left in ignorance of the latest news about Bill. But soon, Bill and everything connected with him faded into insignificance as she became lost in the sensations Johnno's hands and mouth evoked.

Wine forgotten, the pair clung together, heedless of the beauty of the setting sun, the loud mewing of the cat, and the silence which signalled the end of the music CD.

Twenty-five

'I think you'll find Bill will withdraw his objection,' Bob said, peering over his glasses. 'I hear he's given Julian instructions to pay those women off. He can't afford any more bad publicity at this stage. I'd be very surprised if he continued to oppose the terms of the divorce settlement.'

'Really?' Celia couldn't contain her relief. But pay them off? Did that mean Bill was admitting he was guilty?

It was over a week since the most recent revelations and, so far, she and the girls had managed to evade the press. The same couldn't be said for Bill. His photo had appeared in the gutter press almost every day, as he was caught going about his business which included several more book signings. Celia was glad she'd managed to avoid any more of those. Though it seemed as if the publicity wasn't doing the book sales any harm, if Bob was to be believed.

'What do we do now?' she asked.

'We wait.'

'Wait?' Celia's head began to ache. Hadn't she waited long enough? But, after two years what was a few more ... days, weeks? 'How long?'

'Difficult to say. It depends how well your husband takes his solicitor's advice.'

Celia knew Bill was never one to take advice, but maybe this time? And he and Julian went back a fair way. They'd been best mates since their schooldays. If Bill was going to listen to anyone, it would be Julian Clarke. 'Okay,' she sighed. Then she remembered. 'There's something else I wanted to ask you.'

Bob looked curious. He removed his glasses and picked up a pencil, tapping his teeth with it.

'I don't want to have his name anymore. I want to go back to my maiden name. How do I arrange that? What do I need to do?' Celia's stomach churned, and she felt dizzy.

Bob gave her a worried look. 'Would you like a glass of water?'

'Yes please.'

While he fetched it, Celia had trouble sitting still, shifting in the chair and fingering the necklace she'd worn that morning.

'Thanks,' she said when he returned, and took a gulp from the paper cup.

'Now, you want to change back to your maiden name. Not a bad idea, and it can be done quite easily.'

Celia felt an unexpected release of tension and let out a huge breath. She sipped more of the water.

'I'm presuming you merely assumed your husband's name on your marriage?'

Celia looked at him blankly.

'What I mean is, you didn't take steps to legally change your name to Ramsay.'

'No.' *Did anyone do that?*

'Then all you need to do is arrange to change it on all the documentation which refers to you as Celia Ramsay. That would include your driver's licence, bank accounts, passport and so forth.'

'That's it?' If Celia had known it was so simple, she'd have done it long ago.

'They'll need you to produce supporting documents – usually your birth certificate and marriage certificate. You have copies of both of those?'

Celia tried to picture the papers she'd retrieved from the family home when she left. 'I know I have my birth certificate and passport, but...' She bit her lip. 'I'm not sure about my marriage certificate. Bill might still have it. Does that matter? Will I have to get it from him?' She shrank at the thought of facing him with such a request.

'No. That won't be necessary. You can contact the Registry of Births, Deaths and Marriages and request a copy – you can even do it online. Those documents should satisfy most authorities.' He smiled gently.

'And I can alter my own documentation right now. So, no more Celia Ramsay. You are now?'

'Celia Lang.' It sounded good, as if she'd got her identity back, been reborn. 'I'm Celia Lang,' she said more firmly.

'Celia Lang,' Bob repeated. 'I'll change the divorce papers to reflect that.'

Celia's mood suddenly changed. A cold shiver ran up her back settling somewhere at the back of her head like a lump of ice. *Bill would find out. How would he react?*

'But Bill...' *Had she said it aloud?*

'Yes, but he'll have to find out sometime, and you have every right to change your name. Does it worry you?'

Celia almost said, *Yes*, then her head jerked up as she realised she didn't care. She didn't care any more what Bill Ramsay thought. She was no longer Celia Ramsay. She may not be divorced from him yet, but it was only a matter of time.

Leaving Bob's office, Celia felt she was walking on air. She wanted to tell someone, to celebrate. But first, there was one more thing to take care of. Her usual hairdresser was on the other side of the harbour, but she knew of one right here in the city. It would be expensive, but it was worth it to finally shed the old Celia, to change the hairstyle that Bill had loved and insisted she keep.

An hour later, and feeling light-headed with her new hairstyle – a short, spiky cap that made her feel years younger – Celia left the up-market salon. Now it was done, she regretted not having taken this step before now. She finally felt free from all of Bill's restrictions.

Taking out her phone, she pressed Johnno's number, bemused at how natural it seemed he was her first port of call. It went to voicemail. She hesitated, unsure whether to leave a message, as to what she would say if she did, then closed the phone with regret. No, she'd wait till she saw him, tell him then.

She hopped on the bus that would take her back to Mosman. It seemed the city, the harbour, and the bridge were all bathed in a wonderful glow.

'Wow, you look amazing. I guess it must have gone well,' Val said when she pushed open the door and breezed into the shop.

'Mmm.' Celia placed her bag on the counter and leant on its surface, her chin in her hands. 'Guess what? You're now looking at Celia Lang. No more Celia Ramsay. She's gone!' She raised her head and brushed the palms of her hands together as if to get rid of the offensive name, then pirouetted to show off her new hairdo. 'What do you think?'

'Wonderful! I love it,' Val said. 'And will Celia Lang be returning to the catwalk?'

'Not a chance.'

The two women laughed.

*

Johnno made himself coffee and settled down to read the weekend paper, Bindi purring contentedly in his lap. He could get used to this, he thought with a satisfied sigh. In the past few weeks, his life and Celia's seemed to have blended seamlessly so that they spent more time together than apart when they weren't working.

This morning, he'd ducked out to fetch the paper, while she cooked him a slap-up breakfast before leaving for her shop. Now he had the place to himself, apart from the furry creature on his lap, and he was in no hurry to leave. The sun was shining in through the window, sending a wide band of light across the carpet, and both he and Bindi were enjoying its warmth.

Opening the paper, he shook his head as he browsed the political news before moving swiftly to the Arts pages. He planned to take Celia somewhere special that evening to celebrate her returning to her maiden name, and wanted to check reviews for the two plays currently being performed by the Sydney Theatre Company. Johnno automatically renewed his subscription – two seats to every play – each year, and had been in the habit of taking along his current lady – not that many of his previous women had appreciated the performances. But they'd enjoyed being seen on his arm, and he'd been secretly amused at their comments.

Celia was a different kettle of fish altogether, and he couldn't imagine why he hadn't thought to take her to the theatre before now.

Johnno spread out the paper, irritating Bindi who gave a loud meow and leapt from his lap to find her usual spot by the window in the sun. Both the Wharf and the Drama Theatre had plays which sounded possible. He scrolled down the descriptions and reviews. The one playing at the Wharf was interesting in that it heralded the return to the stage of John Bell, a favourite of Johnno's, in *The Father*, billed as 'a touching and deeply unsettling story' and written by Florian Zeller who'd been the recipient of a Molière award. Unsure, he pursed his lips, his eyes moving down to the review where he read, 'As sharp and surprising a play as you'll see all year'. *Promising.*

He then perused the offering at the Drama Theatre, which was the theatre he preferred, located as it was in the Opera House precinct on Circular Quay. *Dinner*, he read, was a black satire on middle-class assumptions. That sounded even more promising. And the review convinced him, noting that the play provided 'a delicious feast of comedy at its most heartless and macabre'. *That was the one.*

Johnno was folding the paper and considering whether to brew another coffee or go for a walk, when his mobile rang. Glancing at the screen, his mother's face looked up at him and with a trace of guilt, he accepted the call.

'Mum!'

'Johnnie. Are you well?'

Johnno's guilt heightened. *When had he last spoken to his parents? When had he been the one to call* them?

'I'm good, Mum. Sorry I haven't been in touch, I've been…'

'Busy. I know. Too busy to call your parents.' His mother's acerbic tone caught him unawares.

Shit! He should have realised. He knew what was coming before he heard her next words.

'Your brother is busy too – and he has two children – but he always manages to find time to call us, to keep us up to date with his life.'

It was all there – in these few words. The disappointment his parents felt that he'd left home, made a life for himself they neither understood nor approved of – and that he had failed to provide them with grandchildren.

'Dan's a good guy. I'm the reprobate,' he said, knowing his words only damned him further.

'That's as may be. But it's been too long since you've been up here. You need to… I'm… We had a bit of a scare with your dad,' she said finally, her voice betraying a slight tremor.

'Dad? Is he…?'Johnno could hear his voice rising, the paper falling from his lap.

'He's fine now. And before you ask why I didn't call before, we didn't want to worry you.'

Johnno cursed at this additional sign of his own lack of communication. If, like Dan, he'd called them on a regular basis, he'd be up to date with all the ins and outs of their life. Maybe that's why he didn't. He preferred to think of them as he last saw them – a fit and healthy couple who were aging well. Maybe if he was privy to the minutiae of their everyday lives, he'd be forced to acknowledge they were both close to eighty and couldn't go on forever.

He did know how old they were. Only last week Dan and he had discussed how they planned to send the pair on a cruise for Dad's eightieth the following year. He had a sudden thought. *Did Dan know about this recent scare? If so, why hadn't he told Johnno?*

His questions were answered by his mother's next words. 'It happened a couple of nights ago. We didn't want to worry you boys. Your dad got up to fetch a glass of water in the middle of the night – the old fool didn't turn on the light and he tripped over Bluey. You know how he likes to sleep outside our door?'

Johnno didn't. But he did know how attached his parents were to the old black Labrador they'd had for years. They'd even managed to get special permission to have him in the retirement village with them – when the regulations stated, *small dogs only.* The dog must be on his last legs now, and Johnno could well imagine his dad falling over the large form in the dark.

'Is he injured? Dad,' he added, in case his mother thought he was referring to the dog.

'Bluey was a bit shaken up, and your dad went down like a stone. For a minute I thought he was gone.' Her voice broke. 'I heard the thud and there he was, lying still, one leg caught on old Bluey. They took him into emergency and gave him a lot of tests. But, as your dad says, it'll take more than that to kill him.'

Johnno blew air through his lips. It had been a close call, then. Maybe closer than either of them realised.

'We're not getting any younger,' his mother continued, 'and we'd love to see you. Dan tells us you have a new friend, and it's looking serious this time?' The question mark in her voice was unmistakable, and Johnno cursed silently again – this time his brother the focus of his annoyance. He'd only mentioned Celia to him in passing, after his nephews told their parents a melodramatic tale of their meeting at the zoo.

Johnno sighed. 'Yes. I have met someone. Her name's Celia, she's around my age and she's been married before.' Hell, the last time he'd taken a girl home it had been Karen Littlejohn who'd lived two streets away in Brisbane and who he'd taken to his Year Twelve formal.

'Most people your age have been.'

Did he detect a note of reproof? It wouldn't be anything new. Johnno had been the bane of his parents' life since he was a boy, always in trouble, never repentant. It had been a relief to all concerned when he'd left home to go to university – and he'd rarely been home since, preferring to make his own life overseas, then interstate. It had seldom, if ever, occurred to him his parents might miss him – not until now.

Was it the usual note of censure, or something more caring?

On impulse, and with the knowledge that everything at work was going smoothly, and they could easily continue without him for a few days, he said, 'As a matter of fact I was thinking of bringing her up to meet you.'

There was no reply.

'I'll let you know once I have our flight booked,' he continued, ignoring the shocked silence, amused he could still surprise his mother.

'Good, good. I'll tell your dad. He'll be pleased.'

There didn't seem to be any more to say, and his mother soon ended the call leaving Johnno wondering if he'd made a huge mistake. *What if Celia refused to go with him? What if she considered it too soon in their relationship?*

No more coffee, he decided, choosing instead to go for a brisk walk to give himself time to consider the full implications of his promise.

Twenty-six

Wearing a thigh-length striped towelling robe, Johnno was filling the reservoir of the coffee machine when the buzzer sounded. Celia was early. He grimaced at his attire, buzzing her up without a word. His hand was on the door, opening it and he was about to open his mouth to greet Celia with a comment about her early arrival, when a vision in red sailed in, long black hair flying.

'Thank God you're home, Johnno! I didn't know where else to go. I've left him.'

Hello to you too, Johnno thought, catching a tumbling Siri with both arms, as he wondered how on earth he was going to explain her presence to Celia. But maybe he wouldn't have to. Maybe he could get rid of her before Celia arrived. She wasn't due for another – he took a quick glance at the clock – thirty minutes. Hell!

'Steady on, Siri. What do you mean you've left him? And why are you here?'

'Julian. I've left Julian Clarke. He's a beast. He's as bad as that mate of his – Bill Ramsay – the one who assaulted those women. Don't believe all his denials. They're two of a kind. Look!' She pulled down her top to display bruises on her neck, bruises which looked like the marks from fingers. 'That's what happened when I accused him of making advances to some of the Ramsay fan squad.' She widened her eyes and pouted in a way Johnno had once found attractive, but now repelled him. 'Can I stay here? I've nowhere else to go.'

Siri continued to itemise Julian's failings as a husband, not leaving out his and Bill Ramsay's sexual proclivities which were firmly focussed on the young women who found their money and power attractive. According to Siri, it had all come to a head when the allegations against Ramsay hit the headlines, and she decided she'd had enough.

How could he ever have imagined Celia was like Siri? Celia was warmer, softer, altogether more feminine than his former lover who was now becoming angry at his lack of response.

'Johnno!' she demanded. 'What...?'

'You can't stay here,' he said, uncoiling the arms which had wrapped themselves around his neck. 'I have to leave soon. I'm...'

There was the sound of the buzzer, a pause, then the hum of the elevator and a knock on the door.

In a daze, Johnno moved to open it. *How could he explain Siri's presence – and his own déshabillè?*

'There was someone leaving so I came on up. Oh!' Celia's voice faded away and her mouth fell open as her eyes focussed on something or someone behind him.

Johnno turned to a vision of Siri – a very different Siri, now wearing only a scanty bra and brief pants – lounging against the open bedroom door. *How on earth had she managed to get undressed so quickly, and what would Celia think?* Unable to come up with a believable explanation, Johnno held out both hands in entreaty. *Surely Celia couldn't imagine?*

But it appeared she did. Her face frozen, she uttered another, 'Oh!', turned, and left, disappearing into the elevator, the door closing before Johnno had time to remonstrate, to explain, to entreat her to stay.

Johnno gazed at the closed door of the elevator and cursed loudly. Celia's face had been full of disgust and perhaps a tinge of sadness before she'd vanished from his sight. Furious, he turned back into the apartment where Siri was still lounging against the bedroom door, smirking.

'Get your clothes on!' Johnno picked up the garments she'd hastily removed and threw them at her. 'And get your ass out of here. There's nothing for you here.'

Siri hugged the garments to her chest and moved toward him, pouting. 'Oh, Johnno, don't be like that. Where else could I go? I can't go back home, and Julian would never dream of looking for me here. He thinks... Oh,' she said, as if it had suddenly dawned on her. 'That was her, wasn't it? The Ramsay woman? You can't really be serious about her. She's…'

'Don't you dare say a word against her. She's twice the woman you'll ever be. And, yes, I *am* serious about her.' It was the first time Johnno had admitted it out loud, although he'd implied it to his mother. Now, he wondered if his chances with Celia were completely screwed up, if he could ever explain how an old girlfriend was in his apartment scantily clad at this time in the morning. And – he looked down at his towelling robe and bare feet – he appeared to have just got out of bed too.

He drew a hand through his already tousled hair, and said in a calmer voice, 'You really can't be here, Siri. I have to fly up the coast today to see my parents. Wouldn't a hotel be a better option? Now, be a good girl and put on those clothes, then you need to go.'

After this debacle, Johnno really needed his caffeine hit. As Siri disappeared into the bedroom to – he hoped – don her clothes, Johnno returned to the coffee maker which had been gurgling and hissing in the background. By the time she returned, still pouting, but clearly ready to leave, he'd already downed a large coffee.

Shunting a still irate Siri out the door, and still in his towelling robe, he wondered where Celia had gone, trying to second guess her. Remembering she had her own ticket for the flight, he considered it was just possible she'd decide to take the trip anyway. Maybe he could still make the flight and take the opportunity to explain and plead forgiveness. Forgiveness for something he hadn't done? Johnno didn't care, he just knew he'd do anything to see the light return to Celia's eyes.

Picking up his phone, he called her number, but it went straight to voicemail. 'Sorry, Celia, he said. 'Please let me explain. It's not what you think. Call me!'

*

Celia almost fell into the elevator, her eyes filled with tears. *How could he?* She'd trusted him, believed his protestations of love. Why, he'd even invited her to meet his parents. They were due to fly out that very morning. And to find him practically in *flagrante delicto* with that, that… She took a deep breath reliving the image which had met her in Johnno's flat. That had been Siri Lake, standing there with a satisfied smile on her face – the same Siri Lake who'd introduced herself as Julian Clarke's new wife, the same Siri Lake who rumour had it, had once been Johnno's favourite companion – the one he'd told Celia he was no longer interested in – never had been.

The elevator stopped at the car park level, though Celia had no memory of pushing the button. *What was she to do now? Go home?* She'd already made arrangements for the shop to be manned for the next week, for Bindi to be taken care of. If she returned now, everyone would know.

She reached into her bag for a tissue and the car keys, her hand brushing against a folder containing… her plane ticket. She took it out and gazed at it, remembering how Johnno had been annoyed she'd insisted on purchasing her own. *Could she still use it? Could she go alone?*

Celia had no idea what Johnno's plans had been for their week on the Sunshine Coast, apart from a visit to his parents. He'd made all the bookings for accommodation somewhere in Noosa. It was to have been a surprise. Well, she'd certainly had that.

Before she knew what she was doing, Celia was in her car on the way to the airport, certain Johnno would be too occupied with *Siri* to even think of following her, even though a tiny part of her wished he would.

At the airport, Celia moved as if in a trance. She parked and, trundling her small suitcase, made her way to the Jetstar check-in. She had an hour to kill before the flight left at nine-thirty, so made her way to the nearest coffee outlet. She was still in shock and a caffeine hit might help calm her frayed nerves.

Two cups of coffee later, Celia boarded the plane, conscious of the empty seat beside her. Trying to ignore it and how it signified the end of her dreams, she began to consider what to do when she reached her destination. She'd need to find somewhere to stay. She thought longingly of the surprise accommodation Johnno had booked – it would now remain empty too. She had no idea what he'd chosen. Giving herself a shake, she reminded herself of his betrayal. There was no way she wanted to stay in a place he'd booked, even if she did know where it was.

Sure she'd find somewhere with a vacancy, Celia decided to hire a car at the Sunshine Coast airport. That way, she'd be able to move around more easily. She tried to remember her holidays here when the girls were little and seemed to recall a nice family motel on the canal a couple of streets back from Gympie Terrace. Strange how it all came back to her as she drove up the highway.

She found the motel she remembered without much difficulty, and they had vacancies. Relieved, she unpacked in one of the small upstairs bedrooms and set out to find somewhere to have lunch. Celia was glad she'd chosen to stay in this part of the popular resort town, rather than the more touristy Hastings Street which was where she suspected Johnno had made a booking in one of the luxury hotels facing the beach.

If he decided to bring Siri up here, there'd be less likelihood of bumping into them. She flinched at the thought of that exotic, over-made-up tart taking her place – but she'd looked very much at home in Johnno's apartment. Had he been seeing her all the time he and Celia had been dating?

If she'd taken time to consider it properly, she'd have realised that couldn't possibly be the case given the amount of time she and Johnno had spent together, but Celia was far from being rational. All she knew was that the woman who'd married Bill's best friend seemed to be very much at home in Johnno's apartment on the very morning he'd made arrangements to spend a week away with Celia.

None of it made sense, but Celia was beyond trying to make sense of what a man could get up to. *If she couldn't trust Johnno, what hope had she of ever trusting a man – or her own judgement – again?*

*

Celia spent the day wandering along the river, wondering if she'd made a huge mistake coming here on her own. Everywhere she looked there were couples or small families. It seemed that everyone but her was happy. Maybe she should have gone home, holed up there for the week and pretended she was here.

She sat on a bench facing the river, closed her eyes, and turned her face up to the sun, letting its warmth seep into her bones. Gradually, she began to relax. She could hear the footsteps of passing pedestrians, the barking of dogs, the sounds of cars on the road behind her, and the roar of jet skis in the distance.

'Are you all right?' Celia was jerked into awareness by the soft voice and a shadow falling over her. Opening her eyes, she found herself gazing into a smiling face surrounded by a cloud of red hair. 'Are you all right?' the woman repeated. 'You looked as if you might be sick.'

'No, I'm fine.' Celia roused herself. 'Thanks for your concern.' The woman gave her a smile and walked on, a golden cocker spaniel at her heels. Celia gave a sigh of relief. She was in no frame of mind to have a conversation with a stranger. She wondered what Johnno was doing. Had he taken Siri out to lunch? Had they retired to his bedroom? She tried to suppress the image that conjured up. Finding it impossible, and seeing a tapas bar across the road, she decided it was time to drown her sorrows in a glass of wine.

Twenty-seven

Once he was alone again, Johnno showered and dressed, then took stock. He gazed around the apartment, recognising it as somewhere he no longer felt comfortable. The glass and black leather of this bachelor pad were so far removed from the comfort of Celia's soft blue and cream furnishings, from the gentle ambiance she'd developed, that he hung his head in shame.

No wonder she'd been quick to draw the conclusion she had. Siri had been standing there for all the world as if she belonged, as if – at the very least – she'd spent the night. It wasn't so long ago it'd have been true.

What was he to do now?

One part of him wanted to rush across the bridge to check if Celia had gone home. But another cautioned him to be sensible. There had been no reply to his phone message – or to the texts with which he'd followed it. He was probably the last person Celia wanted to see right now. He scratched his head and took yet another coffee out onto the balcony. But even the magnificent view failed to comfort him.

Leaning on the balcony railing Johnno made a sudden decision. He would drive across the bridge. There was no doubt in his mind that Celia would have gone home. He had to see her, try to make her understand. He couldn't bear to have her think he'd been with Siri. Damn the woman! She couldn't have chosen a worse time to turn up – and to strip off like that! Impeccable timing on her part if she wanted to ruin his life.

Arriving at Celia's unit block, he pushed the intercom. No answer. He was taking out his phone again when a young man cycled up and opened the door, giving Johnno a puzzled look.

'Thanks, mate. Forgot my key,' Johnno muttered as he joined him in the lift and rode up to Celia's floor, thinking that this was exactly what Celia had done at his place. But when he reached her door and knocked there was no answer, no welcoming meowing from Bindi. She wasn't here.

He stood for a moment, then checked his watch. The flight to the Sunshine Coast was due to leave in thirty-five minutes. It would already have boarded. Even if he could have reached the airport in time, there was no way he'd be allowed to board. He cursed under his breath, feeling as if his life was about to disintegrate. Maybe he should just go home and get drunk, try to forget that scene in his flat, forget the look in Celia's eyes, forget his hopes for the future.

But, once home, he remembered his mother's words, her anxiety for his dad, and calculated how long it had been since he'd seen them. They'd be expecting him this weekend. Maybe it wasn't too late to arrange another flight. And he had accommodation already booked, though the thought of being alone in the ocean-front room he'd planned to stay with Celia gave him no pleasure.

He picked up the phone.

Three hours later, Johnno was disembarking from the plane at the Sunshine Coast airport. The air, softer and warmer than he'd left behind in Sydney, was balm to his troubled soul. Hiring a little Getz, he took the road south to Caloundra, wondering how to explain Celia's absence to his parents and unsure where he intended to spend the night.

'Johnnie! We didn't expect you today.' His mum gave him a hug and looked over his shoulder. 'Isn't...? Your friend?'

'Celia couldn't make it after all. You'll have to make do with just me. Dad home?'

'Son!' Johnno's dad appeared from the living room, a cup in his hand. 'You're just in time for afternoon smoko. You haven't brought your girlfriend with you, then?'

'He's a bit old for a girlfriend,' Cath said. 'What is it you call them these days – partner, significant other?'

'Rubbish,' his dad replied. 'Nothing wrong with the good old term that I can see. So she's not with you?'

'No. She wasn't able to get away,' Johnno said, hoping that would help him duck any more questions. 'She has a shop to run,' he added, not sure why he felt obligated to provide that piece of information.

'Well, as Dad says, we're having our afternoon tea. There's plenty in the pot and I made a nice lemon sponge this morning. Have you eaten?'

Johnno realised he hadn't eaten since a quick sausage roll at the airport, and hunger pangs were beginning to make themselves felt but, 'I'm fine,' he said, not wanting to admit it. 'Tea and a slice of your lemon sponge will be good.'

Settled in a chintz armchair in the crowded living room, Johnno felt awkward. Although smaller, the room was a replica of the one he'd grown up in, down to the old-fashioned standard lamp in one corner and the china cabinet in another. The three-piece suite, which he knew had been purchased new for the villa, was oddly reminiscent of the one in their old home. Through the window, he could see the tidy backyard with its narrow stretch of grass bordered by a line of orange hibiscus.

He felt claustrophobic already.

'The place is looking good,' he said, to hide his discomfort.

'Your mum does her best. She keeps me in order,' Walter said with a grin.

'When he's not at bowls or lost in his shed,' Cath retorted.

Some things never changed. Johnno remembered why he'd left home in the first place and why he rarely came to visit. He couldn't stand the monotony of their lives. But they seemed happy, he loved them, and they *were* getting older. He owed it to them to visit more often, to make an attempt to share his life with them and to profess a genuine interest in theirs.

'Where's Bluey?' he asked, to change the subject.

'He's at the vet's,' Cath replied. 'Not content with tripping up your dad, the old fellow managed to get his paw caught in a pile of wire that *someone*' – she glared at her husband – 'left lying in the back yard.'

'It's nothing serious,' Walter said. 'But, like me, he's no spring chicken, so they've kept him in for a couple of days to keep an eye on him. He'll be right. We couldn't do without our Bluey.'

But some day, they'd have to. Dogs didn't live forever, and Bluey must be close to his allotted span. Johnno made no comment.

'So, tell us about this Celia of yours who couldn't make it,' Cath said, when Johnno had drunk two cups of tea and managed to scoff a couple of slices of the lemon sponge. The sponge brought back memories of his childhood, of days filled with sunshine, picnics on the beach, of surfing and sand-castles and holidays which seemed to never end.

'Not much to tell,' he lied, finding it impossible to describe the woman who he now knew had stolen his heart and who he might never see again.

The conversation then moved to his brother and nephews, and he was able to sound appropriately interested in their achievements. Dan had always been a favourite son, even when they were children. Johnno could remember his parents' pride in Dan's sporting prowess while his own more academic triumphs had received scant attention.

'Won't you stay the night?' his mother asked, when Johnno rose to go. 'If you're on your own, we can make up a bed for you in the study.'

For a moment, Johnno hesitated, then he shook his head. 'No, I've accommodation booked in Noosa. It would be crazy to waste it.'

'Noosa,' his father said with a grimace. 'That would cost you a pretty penny. Not short of a bob or two, then?'

Johnno didn't reply, not sure if it was a question, a compliment or an insult. With his dad, he'd never been certain of his meaning. Silence was his best option.

'I'll be up here for a few days,' he said. 'Why don't I take you out to dinner one evening?'

'We don't go out much at nights,' his dad said, closely followed by Cath saying, 'That'd be lovely, Johnnie. But it would have to be an early dinner. They do a nice one at the club.'

Dinner at the local club wasn't exactly what Johnno had in mind, but he was willing to defer to their choice. 'Right, I'll give you a call.'

'Mind you do.' His father's words were a reminder to Johnno that he'd been less than caring to his parents lately and of his recent vow to change that.

'I will,' he promised.

*

By the time Johnno checked into the luxury resort, he was ready for a drink. He'd found the visit with his parents stressful, stirring up his feelings of guilt. He dropped his case on the bed and headed out.

Once in the street, he was surrounded by happy tourists, all intent on making the most of their time here. Hastings Street, a mecca for holidaymakers with its many clothing boutiques, giftshops, cafes and restaurants stretched as far as the eye could see and hid the beach from the naked eye.

As he strolled along in search of a bar, he was buffeted by partially-dressed tourists chatting in groups, joggers in exercise gear and what seemed to be endless hordes of young children, all of them yelling at the top of their voices. Maybe this hadn't been such a good idea after all.

Finally, he spied what he was looking for. A half-empty bar opening off the street which boasted several low tables and comfortable chairs. Here was somewhere he'd be able to enjoy a quiet glass of wine and watch the passing parade rather than be part of it.

As he sipped a glass of a choice Merlot, Johnno reflected on how everything had suddenly changed.

He'd awoken happy, anticipating a week away with Celia, a week in which they'd get to know each other better away from his job, her shop, her children, and the challenges with her husband. Then Siri had shown up and... He rubbed his chin. Why on earth had Siri chosen to inflict herself on him? They hadn't been an item for years. She was newly married. That led him to her husband – Julian Clarke. Not one of Johnno's favourite people – not one of Celia's either, it seemed.

From what he could make out, Clarke had been far from the doting husband he'd appeared to be the single time Johnno had seen them together. But could he believe Siri? She'd proven to be unreliable in the past, prone to turn a situation to her advantage, even to lie.

Could they be in this together? Maybe with Ramsay's blessing, even connivance? No, surely that was going too far. But it had certainly put paid to his plans for a romantic getaway.

Enough!

Johnno ordered another glass of wine and, noticing the Real Estate insert from the local paper lying on the table, picked it up. He'd concentrate on one of his earlier notions to look for a property up here

– a retreat from the city, maybe an apartment overlooking the river. He flicked through the pages. There were a few properties that caught his eye. All had open houses next day. Taking out his phone, he noted down the addresses and times, then decided it was time to unpack and make plans for dinner.

His belongings took up hardly any space in the large room, another cruel reminder that he had never planned to be here alone. Walking out onto the balcony, Johnno saw more of the holidaymakers he'd noticed earlier. Some were by the resort pool, packing up their belongings, while others were sauntering along the boardwalk after a day on the beach.

If he closed his eyes, he could imagine he was down there among them, Celia at his side. They stopped. She looked up into his eyes. One hand on her shoulder, he swept back a strand of hair and bent to kiss her... He opened his eyes with a start. There was no sense in dreaming about what might have been.

Dinner. Johnno remembered a favourite restaurant from a previous trip and wondered if it was still there. Season was set on the boardwalk, right on the beachfront and, to his delight, it was exactly where he remembered. Shown to a corner table facing the beach, he settled to examine the menu, ordering a bottle of wine. He wasn't driving tonight, and more wine was a sure cure for the disappointment that flooded him as he sat there on his own.

'Enjoy your meal,' the waitress smiled as she set down the grilled barramundi and mash, served with confit garlic and local tomatoes he'd ordered, and now had little appetite for. Johnno gazed out at the dark and now deserted beach and wondered if he could last out the week.

*

Celia hadn't slept well. She'd tossed and turned most of the night, only falling into a light sleep as the sky began to lighten. Now it was half-eight and the whole day stretched before her. Maybe coming here really had been a mistake.

She showered and dressed in a pair of tailored jeans and a fitted pink tee-shirt before going downstairs. She'd meant to buy in some supplies the day before, but had forgotten, and didn't feel up to having breakfast in one of the many restaurants by the river. Instead, she decided to take a brisk walk to the shops she remembered and buy a few staples.

Carrying them back to the motel, Celia poured herself a bowl of muesli, topped it with yoghurt and, carrying the takeaway coffee she'd also purchased, took a seat on the deck facing the canal. From here she was protected from the elements and could watch the comings and goings of the other residents.

The neighbouring room appeared to be inhabited by a family of two children and their parents. The children, who must have been around seven or eight, were intent on fishing, using what looked like home-made rods, and became very excited when they thought they'd hooked a fish.

It reminded her of her own children. They'd been little when they'd stayed here. Bill had quickly become impatient and had retreated to the hotel bar, leaving Celia and the girls to enjoy the tranquillity. There were both good and bad memories of those times, and Celia preferred to remember the good. She and the girls had enjoyed paddling by the river, playing in the sand and in the playground. When they were older, they'd gone paddle boarding together, none of them interested in the jet skis that attracted Bill, with their speed and hint of danger.

At a loss as to how to spend the day, Celia set off along the street, heading for the river where she thought she remembered there were several boutiques similar to Isabella. It might be a good idea to check them out, maybe get a few ideas for her own shop.

She was right. A couple of hours later, Celia had visited at least five different stores, spending several minutes in each, examining the range and chatting with the assistants and owners. Checking her watch, she found it was almost time for lunch. She hated eating alone and wished she'd thought to bring along a book. Somehow a single woman with a book looked less noticeable than one without. And a book would help while away the hours.

Celia was regretting her decision to come to Noosa.

Walking aimlessly back in the direction of her hotel, Celia noticed a bookshop. The Book Nook, she read above the window. It looked fairly new and had an attractive window display showing recent releases of two of her favourite authors. Pushing open the door, she found herself in what at first appeared to be a maze. On closer inspection, Celia could see that the bookshelves had been cunningly placed to give that impression, with comfortable chairs dotted around to encourage the customers to linger.

'Good morning.' A smiling woman around Celia's age with a mop of wild dark curls approached. 'Can I help you or are you happy to browse? Just let me know if you need anything.' She disappeared again, leaving Celia wondering if she'd imagined her.

Celia enjoyed browsing the shelves. When she finally carried her purchases to the counter, the same woman greeted her with another smile. 'You found something then?'

Celia handed her the two books she'd chosen.

'Oh, you'll enjoy these. My taste, too. Are you up here on holiday?' she asked, as she dropped the books into a bag and processed Celia's credit card.

'Yes. Sort of. I… I'm not sure how long I'll be here. I do like your shop, and I love your chairs and those cushions.' Celia pointed to the tropical patterns on the cushions which lay invitingly on each chair. They'd look good on the sofa in her apartment.

The shopkeeper beamed. 'They're great, aren't they? They're designed by a local woman and she sells through a shop nearby – at Acres. There's a café and garden centre there too, plus a spa – everything you need to relax,' she laughed.

'New since I was last here,' Celia said, 'but that was years ago, when my girls were little. They're all grown up now.' She felt she was babbling. *Did she look as stressed as she felt?* Was that why the woman was telling her about a spa? Though a relaxing massage wasn't a bad idea, and she could perhaps have lunch there too, then go back for a lazy afternoon with one of her new books. That would at least take care of today.

'Drop in again if you run out of reading matter – or just want a chat. I'm Rosa.'

'Celia. Thanks. I may do that.'

Celia picked up her package and left the shop with the odd feeling she'd made a new friend.

*

Johnno spent the morning inspecting the four apartments he'd picked out from the multitude of offerings in the paper. While he loved the aspect, overlooking the Noosa River, he was disappointed to discover they were all very small. He'd expected some reduction in size from his Pyrmont home, but those felt claustrophobic. Also, while the view of the river was amazing, when he stepped out onto the balconies the traffic noise from the street below was annoying.

About to give up in disgust and head to somewhere for lunch, he remembered one of the agents mentioning a town house for sale. It was located on a canal a few streets back from the river. Checking that he still had time to make the viewing, he went back to the car and fed the address into the GPS.

Turning into a quiet street, Johnno was struck by the ambiance. This seemed far from the touristy part of the town, while still being within walking distance of the river with its assortment of restaurants, shops and cafes. The townhouse was located right at the end of the cul-de-sac, giving it a sense of privacy. Once inside, he admired its proportions, the wide deck and extensive balcony. The complex boasted a lap pool, not as luxurious as the indoor and outdoor pool facility, the steam room, gym and tennis courts he enjoyed in Sydney, but sufficient to provide him with daily exercise.

Standing on the balcony of the generous bedroom, looking across the canal to other luxury homes – what the realtor's pamphlet had described as a *long water view* – Johnno experienced an adrenalin rush. He'd found what he was searching for.

'What do you think?'

Johnno turned at the realtor's question. He was standing on the deck, lost in contemplation of how he would come here to relax from his busy life. In his imagination, he'd already furnished the townhouse, not in the black leather he'd favoured in Sydney, but in softer tones more appropriate to this coastal neighbourhood, more like… a picture of Celia's warm home appeared in his mind's eye. The only thing missing was Celia herself.

'I like it,' he said decisively. 'Can I come into your office with a deposit on Monday?' He calculated he'd have to juggle some funds around to come up with the required amount, but should be able to arrange that easily.

The woman, in her smart black pants teamed with a bright red blouse and heels which, although high, only brought her up to his shoulder, seemed surprised. Flicking back her blonde hair, she took a note of his name and number.

'I'll be there by ten. Don't sell it to anyone else,' he joked, and left.

Driving back towards the river and trying to decide whether to eat here or closer to his accommodation on Hastings Street, Johnno caught sight of a garden centre on the corner and noticed that there was also a café. All within easy walking distance from what he already thought of as his Noosa weekender.

He decided to try it out.

Twenty-eight

Celia found the garden centre complex quite easily. It was on the way back to her hotel. Surprised she hadn't noticed it when she'd walked to Gympie Terrace that morning, she decided she must have taken an earlier street down to the river.

As she walked through the car park, she experienced a strange sensation, a feeling that something was about to happen. The skin on the back of her neck prickled.

Seeing more of the cushions she'd admired, Celia stopped to inspect them. It would be impossible to carry the several she wanted on the plane, but she was able to arrange for them to be mailed to her. Moving on, she skirted the café and was heading toward the spa to book a massage when, out of the corner of her eye, a blond head at one of the tables caught her attention. It couldn't be – but it was. Johnno Henderson!

He looked up at the same moment and their eyes met, a gleam of surprise and pleasure appearing in his.

Celia glanced around wildly. Siri must be somewhere close. But there was no one else in sight and Johnno was… No! He was rising and coming towards her. There was nowhere for her to hide.

'You came,' he said.

'I… I had the ticket.' Celia felt her heart thudding. How was she going to handle this? She drew herself up to her full height which, since she was wearing flat shoes, barely brought her up to Johnno's shoulders. She felt at a distinct disadvantage. 'I don't think we have anything to say to each other.'

'I think we do. I owe you an explanation.'

'No need.' Celia looked around again. Was Siri in the ladies? Or perhaps she was having a massage or treatment in the very spa Celia was headed for. She drew in a deep breath.

'Look, we need to talk. Let me at least buy you a coffee.' Johnno gestured to the shaded alcove where he'd been seated.

Celia was tempted. Coffee sounded attractive, and Johnno was at his most charming with his lopsided smile and hair falling over one eye. Today he was dressed casually in jeans and a cream cotton shirt which emphasised his hazel eyes and clung to his body – almost as revealing as his rowing outfit.

Before she knew what was happening, Johnno had taken Celia by the elbow, hustled her over to where he'd been sitting, sat her down and ordered her favourite skinny cappuccino.

She perched uneasily on the green seating. 'Where's your friend?'

'That's what I need to tell you. She's not... my friend, that is. Hell, Celia. When you arrived, Siri had just turned up out of the blue. I thought it was you at the door when I let her in. She spun some cock-and-bull story about leaving Clarke, about him being as bad as your Bill, and having nowhere else to go.'

'It didn't look that way to me.' Celia sat primly, ankles crossed, hands clasped in her lap, and refusing to make eye contact with Johnno.

Her coffee arrived, and she spooned up the chocolate topping, concentrating on the task as if her life depended on it. Meantime her mind was going around in circles. *Could he be telling the truth?* She saw again the half-naked woman leaning in the doorway.

'I swear it's the truth. I was as surprised as you when I turned around and saw her undressed.' He pushed back his hair. 'What can I do to make you believe me?'

Celia wondered that, too. She stirred her coffee then, cradling the cup in both hands, took a cautious sip. It was good. As the warm liquid coursed through her, she considered Johnno's explanation. Maybe he *was* telling the truth. Maybe she'd over-reacted. But that woman had been standing there as if she belonged, as if she and Johnno... Celia tried unsuccessfully to dismiss the image of Siri and Johnno in bed together which immediately followed.

'Where is she now?' she asked.

'Damned if I know.' He dragged a hand through his hair again. 'Back with Clarke for all I care. I threw her out as soon as you left. I had no idea where you'd gone. I dashed across the harbour to your house, even though I knew you'd be too angry to see me. But you weren't there. So I came up here, visited my parents, checked into the accommodation I'd booked. That was a mistake. I kept seeing you everywhere. In fact, when you walked in here I thought you were a mirage.'

A faint smile began to play around Celia's lips, and she raised her eyes to his, meeting such a look of anguish her heart began to melt. She remembered their hours of passion, his kindness, his gentleness, his tender touch, his…

'Can you forgive me?'

Celia wanted to – so very much. But she hesitated. Her experiences with Bill made her wary. It was easy for Johnno to say it had all been a mistake, that Siri and he weren't… had never… But Celia knew what she'd seen. *Had it really all been an act on Siri's part? Could she believe Johnno?*

'How about some lunch while you decide?'

Celia was about to refuse, when she realised she was hungry, and they were in a café, and it wouldn't kill her to have lunch with him. She had to eat somewhere after all.

They ordered pear and macadamia salads and, while they were eating, Celia darted glances towards Johnno wondering if she could trust him again. Her thoughts raced, caught between wanting nothing more than to forgive him, to be in his arms again, and wanting nothing more to do with him – a form of self-protection. She'd learned to her cost what it was like to be involved with – to live with – an inveterate liar. And Johnno didn't have a good track record.

But, something was telling her he was being truthful. It could even be that the whole Siri thing was a set-up – a way of Bill getting back at her. Could he be that devious? Yes, with the connivance of his shady solicitor, Celia believed he could. He and Julian Clarke had managed to set up a few ruses in the past. This would be child's play to them. And from what she knew of Siri, it wouldn't have taken much to persuade her to go along with them, not if it meant the opportunity to spend time with Johnno.

'This may sound farfetched,' she said, when they'd finished eating and were on their second cups of coffee. 'But did it occur to you that Bill and Julian might have been behind this?' She swallowed, afraid she'd been too blunt.

'It did, then I dismissed the idea as being too implausible. Surely even those two wouldn't have been so devious as to send Siri to break us up? And how would they have known you'd turn up when you did.' He shook his head. 'Then again, it was odd the way she appeared out of the blue – and stripped off when you arrived.'

'In record time if what you say is true. Although,' Celia tilted her head to one side, considering, 'as models we all had to change in record time, so it would have been easy for her.'

'So you believe me?' There was a lightness in Johnno's voice that hadn't been there before.

'Maybe. It's beginning to make some sort of sense. But don't think you're getting off that lightly. I still need to make sure I can trust you.' She glanced up from beneath her brows.

'That's good enough for a start.' Johnno exhaled loudly as if he'd been worried she was going to walk out on him again. 'Now, what have you been doing since you arrived here?'

'Not a lot.' She wasn't going to tell him how miserable she'd been, admit how she'd regretted her decision to come by herself, reveal how much she'd missed him. 'Relaxed, walked around. Oh, and I found this cute bookshop.'

Johnno didn't seem impressed. 'Where are you staying?'

'Just up the road at a motel on the canal. It's nice.' *And very lonely.* 'You?'

Johnno hesitated. 'In Hastings Street.' He pushed a hand through his hair. 'It's the place I booked for us. The room overlooks the beach. It…'

Celia could picture it, imagine how it would have been to be there with Johnno, maybe drinking champagne on a balcony watching the sunset. She trembled, understanding what might have been, what could perhaps still happen if she…

'I'm buying a townhouse.'

Jolted out of her imaginings, Celia stared at Johnno. 'A townhouse?' She vaguely recalled his talk of looking for a weekender in Noosa. 'Here?'

'Just around the corner. Feel like a walk? I can show you the outside, but the open house will be over by now.'

'Sure.' Having seen Johnno's city apartment in a block designed for single professionals, complete with gymnasium, pools and tennis courts, Celia was curious to see what had caught his eye here in Noosa. It would be good to get a change of environment too. Their conversation seemed to have run its course, and she still hadn't decided what to believe about Siri.

They walked briskly along, careful not to touch each other. As they turned into the cul-de-sac, Johnno pointed out the well-appointed homes, the council park with its bench facing the water and finally, when they reached the end, he said, 'This is it. What do you think?'

Celia gazed at the small gated complex, the tall white townhouses rising up from the paved courtyard, the long glass windows overlooking the canal. It appeared to be an exclusive enclave affording unexpected privacy to its residents. She glanced at the man beside her who was contemplating the complex with affection.

'Which one?'

'The one on the far end. It's more private than the others and has direct access to a council park on the other side. There's a pool too – a lap pool.' He was so enthusiastic, he reminded Celia of a dog eager to please his master or, in this case, mistress.

Celia smiled. 'It looks lovely. I'd love to see inside. The view from the balcony must be spectacular,' she said without thinking.

'Long water views they're called. I can probably arrange that once I pay the deposit on Monday.'

Monday – that was two days away. *Would she still be here? Had she decided to stay? Had she made up her mind to accept Johnno's explanation?* Celia's mind raced, searching for a decision, but she was still unsure, reluctant to give her trust again, unwilling to make any sort of commitment.

As if reading her mind, Johnno said, 'I suppose it's no use inviting you back to my hotel? To admire the view?' His lips turned up in the hint of a smile. She fought back the urge to kiss them.

'No. I need to…' But there was nothing she needed to do. All that awaited her back in her motel room were the books she'd bought, books she knew she wouldn't be able to concentrate on – not now she knew Johnno was in the same town, that he'd come alone, that…

'I thought not.' While they'd been talking, Johnno and Celia had been walking back toward the café. Now they stood awkwardly on the kerbside, Celia with arms folded, Johnno's hands in his pockets. He shuffled his feet. 'Well, what about dinner? Are you willing to risk coming over to Hastings Street? I could book a table at Season.'

It was a restaurant which, for Celia, held fond memories – memories of breakfasts with the girls, followed by lazy days on the beach, reading books, swimming, surfing... 'That would be nice,' she said without thinking, then the significance of her acceptance hit home. 'I mean I...' But the sight of Johnno's delighted expression, stifled the denial which sprang to her lips.

'Good. I'll make a booking for seven then? Can you get yourself over there or...?'

'I have a car.'

'Right. Well.' Johnno seemed loath to leave, and Celia didn't want to turn her back on him. The pair stood looking at each other till a tour bus stopped beside them to unload a group of elderly ladies, clearly intent on entering the garden-café environment.

'I'll be off, then,' Johnno said, as the group threatened to push them apart. 'Seven.'

'Seven, 'Celia agreed, before walking off in the opposite direction.

Twenty-nine

Celia dressed carefully for her dinner date, not quite sure if she'd been wise to accept, but excited nevertheless at the prospect of spending the evening with Johnno. As she donned the turquoise dress with the handkerchief hem and slipped her feet into a pair of high-heeled cream sling backs, Celia remembered her excitement choosing the outfit from the summer range at Isabella. When she'd packed for this trip, it had been with the anticipation of spending a whole week with the man she... loved was too strong a word, but close.

Now, she reflected, everything had changed. Celia had no idea where she stood. Johnno appeared to want them back on the same footing, but did she? Could she forget what she'd seen, ignore Siri's implicit sense of belonging in Johnno's apartment, and go on as before?

But, despite her head warning her to be cautious, to protect herself from the risk of being hurt, she couldn't dismiss the spark of hope that flared up when she remembered Johnno's abject apology, and Heather's advice to follow her heart.

Unlocking the car and starting the engine, Celia decided to dismiss her misgivings and enjoy the evening ahead. By the time she reached the tourist strip which housed Season, along with lots of other restaurants and clothes shops, she'd almost decided to believe Johnno's explanation. She remembered stories she'd heard about Siri Lake. The woman had entered the modelling circuit several years after Celia had left it, but it was a close-knit community and gossip abounded.

From what she could recall, Siri hadn't been well-liked, and had been accused of doing whatever it took to get her own way. Sure, it was a cut-throat profession, but it appeared Siri took it to extremes, managing to offend many of her peers in her efforts to reach the top. That, combined with the machinations of Julian and Bill, might well be what led her to Johnno's – and to the speedy way she'd divested herself of her clothes when Celia arrived.

Having settled that to her satisfaction, Celia drove slowly along the street, keeping a lookout for a free parking spot. There was none to be had, so she kept going to the end of the street and into Noosa Woods where she knew there would be some free spots at this time of night.

To her surprise, Celia found herself overcome with nerves as she walked up the street. There was an empty feeling in the pit of her stomach that had nothing to do with hunger, and she was biting the inside of her cheek. Her hand strayed to her stomach as if that would calm her. She was eager to see Johnno again – she wanted to flee.

Celia was still undecided when she reached the laneway leading up to the restaurant which was situated right on the beachfront. Suddenly Johnno was standing in front of her, his eyes twinkling with delight, a warm smile on his face, his hand reaching out to take hers, and all her doubts disappeared.

'Champagne, I think?' He raised one eyebrow.

Celia nodded.

They were seated at a corner table, so close to each other that the slightest movement meant their thighs touched. Outside, the waves roared onto the beach and a few brave surfers dared the darkness to ride them to shore.

Celia barely tasted the delicious seared scallops or the pumpkin, ricotta and sage cannelloni which followed, while Johnno enjoyed a spanner crab, then eye fillet. Her entire being was suffused with the sensation of being with him again and the champagne they were drinking only served to heighten her emotions.

Afterwards, as they wandered along the boardwalk, Johnno's arm carelessly thrown across her shoulders, Celia admired the large pools and the resort hotels rising up on her right-hand side. So this was where he was staying?

'I'm up there.' Johnno pointed to a high balcony in one of the most luxurious of the resorts, and Celia felt a blaze of desire at the thought of being there with him.

He stopped, turned her towards him and, heedless of any passers-by, pulled her into an embrace. Celia felt the heat from Johnno's body through the light material of her dress. He tipped up her chin with one finger, and their lips met in a kiss that made Celia feel as if she was floating on air.

'Will you…?'

Celia nodded, unable to speak.

*

The hotel room was enormous, the focal point the large king-sized bed, carefully turned down ready for use. Scarcely letting go of her, Johnno led Celia towards it and dropped her carefully onto the taut surface, taking time only to slip off his shoes before joining her.

'Mmm, I've missed you so much,' he murmured as he pushed the flimsy dress down from her shoulders and his hands found her breasts.

Celia moaned with pleasure and wriggled to free herself from the rest of her clothes, Johnno's mouth on her nipples sending shockwaves of pleasure through her body and making her cry out for more. She felt her heart would burst with joy as her body responded to his demands. They lay entwined, each bent on satisfying the other's needs, till both were replete and, unable to make love any further, they lay back panting with exhaustion.

'Wow!' Johnno's comment was heartfelt and echoed Celia's sentiments exactly.

They lay without speaking. Then Johnno leant up on one elbow and gazed down at Celia. 'I guess this means I'm forgiven?'

'I guess so,' she replied lazily, reaching up to trace a finger around his lips. He drew the digit into his mouth and sucked on it, almost bringing her to orgasm again. *How could she ever have doubted him?*

*

Johnno stretched languidly and shaded his eyes from the bright sunlight streaming in through the floor-length glass windows. His eyes fell on the woman lying beside him and he shuddered at how close he'd come to losing her. He stroked her short hair gently. Her eyes opened.

'Johnno?'

'Good morning, sweetheart.'

Celia smiled, but he could see a hint of doubt in her eyes.

'Everything's going to be all right now.' He enfolded her in an embrace, revelling in the familiar feeling of her soft skin against his, the delicate fragrance that was hers alone. *My God*, he thought, *I love this woman. I want to spend the rest of my life with her, to wake up with her every morning, to be the one she turns to, relies on. How can I be worthy of her?*

Sensing that, despite their night of renewed passion, Celia was still unsure of both him and her feelings, he remained silent, vowing to do everything within his power to win her respect and her love.

'What would you like to do today?' he asked, gently stroking her eyebrow with one finger. It was like stroking a feather. *When had he become so lyrical?*

'Mmm.' Celia stretched. 'I'm not sure. Any ideas?'

'We could stay here.'

She laughed and wound her legs around his, but he could tell she had no intention of remaining in bed all day.

'Or we could do the touristy thing – visit the Ginger Factory, take a trip to Fraser Island, cruise the Everglades…'

'Sounds good, but maybe not today. I feel lazy. And I need to fetch some clean clothes from the motel.'

'About that. It's crazy for us to be staying at opposite ends of town. Why don't you check out at your place and move in here?' Johnno held his breath waiting for her reply.

He could see her considering before her face broke into a wide smile. 'It would make more sense,' she agreed. 'And this room is a bit big for one.'

'And lonely. There's no fun in keeping all this luxury to myself. Now, why don't we shower, and I'll take you out to breakfast?'

After a breakfast of almond croissants and two cups of coffee in a café on Hastings Street, Johnno and Celia drove over to Noosaville to fetch Celia's belongings. Her car was still parked where she'd left it the previous night. It was madness to have two cars, now that they were together again. One more matter he needed to raise with Celia, or perhaps he'd let it wait till she mentioned it. He intended to be super-cautious from now on and do nothing to risk driving her away again.

'Did you see your parents yet?' Celia asked, when they were driving back towards the beach and his hotel.

'Yes. I called by when I arrived. Dad seems okay, but they look a lot older than last time I saw them. They wanted to know where you were.'

'What did you tell them?'

Johnno could see she was amused at the thought of him having to make excuses. 'You'd been held up.'

'And I'm not held up any longer?' she grinned.

'I've promised to take them to dinner this week sometime. Do you mean you'd still be willing to meet them? It won't be much fun,' he apologised. 'They want an early dinner at the club. I presume it'll be the Power Boat Club. They live at Golden Beach, and it's the closest. I think Dad's always fancied himself owning a power boat, and it's a good club as those clubs go.'

'Just not your usual type of haunt?'

'No.' Australian sports clubs with their poker machines, gaming lounges, meat raffles and sports bars were as far from Johnno's usual dining spots as night from day.

'I think it's wonderful you're happy to go along with their choice.'

Johnno gave her a quick glance to gauge if she was mocking him, but Celia appeared to be perfectly serious.

'So you'd be willing to risk a meal with them?'

'Listen to yourself. If you still want to introduce me to them?'

'Of course.' Johnno knew it was a big step – his parents would be hearing wedding bells – but he was more sure of this than he'd been of anything else in his life. 'I'll call them as soon as we get back.'

The rest of the day was passed in a leisurely fashion, ending in another night of fervid lovemaking which almost convinced Johnno Celia returned his feelings. But he was still afraid to voice them for fear of her reaction. He didn't think he could face her rejection.

He'd arranged for them to have dinner with his parents the following evening, picking them up in time for the five-thirty dinner they'd requested. 'At least we can watch the sunset,' he told Celia. 'The club's right on the waterfront.'

'And maybe we can have our own sunset rendezvous the following evening,' she replied. 'I hear it's beautiful from the Boathouse on the Noosa River.'

Buoyed by this suggestion, it was with a light heart that Johnno helped Celia into the car for the drive down to meet his parents. His dad had insisted they meet at the club.

'Were not too decrepit to make our own way there, son,' he'd said when Johnno offered to pick them up.

They were waiting in the reception area ready to sign Johnno and Celia into the club, and Johnno was surprised in the change in his parents in the last few days. Dressed in what he assumed was their best – his mother in a smart pair of tailored navy pants with a loose white top, and his dad in grey slacks and a blue and white striped shirt, they seemed to have shed several years and to be more youthful than he remembered.

'So this is Celia,' his mother greeted them, kissing her on the cheek. 'I'm so pleased to meet you.'

'Where has our ne'er-do-well son been hiding you?' was his dad's greeting, but Johnno was pleased to see Celia warming to them, smiling and shaking their hands.

'I'm sorry I got held up in Sydney,' she said, glancing ruefully towards Johnno, 'but I'm here now, and I'm so glad to have the opportunity to meet you. Johnno's told me so much about you both.'

'Oh!' Cath preened, while Walter grunted.

The evening went well. After enjoying the sunset and dinner, the four parted with promises on Johnno's part to do it again soon, while his parents expressed the hope to meet Celia again 'before too long'.

'They're lovely,' Celia said as they drove back along the Sunshine Coast Highway. 'Exactly what I expected. A bit like my parents would have been if they were still alive. You're lucky.'

Taken by surprise, Johnno realised she was right. He was lucky his parents were still alive and well, despite his dad's recent mishap.

*

Next day, they did what Johnno referred to as the 'touristy thing', joining groups of holidaymakers, mostly from interstate like themselves or overseas, to cruise up into the Everglades where they admired the mirror-like surface of the water and the wildlife which inhabited those upper reaches of the river.

It was close to four-thirty when they returned.

As they passed the Boathouse, Johnno pointed to the top deck and said, 'If we hurry we can change and be back for those sunset drinks you mentioned.' He raised an eyebrow.

'A perfect end to a perfect day. Let's do it.'

Barely an hour later, the pair were perched on high stools overlooking the river drinking champagne, nibbling on a shared plate of cheese and lavosh, and watching the sky change from gold to rosy pink to red to blue.

'This is so romantic,' Celia breathed as the sun finally dropped below the horizon sending dark shadows over the water.

'Glad you came?'

Celia didn't reply, instead huddling closer to Johnno, her head on his shoulder. Did he mean glad she came to Noosa or glad she came to the Boathouse with him? Either way, it didn't matter. What did matter was they were here. Now. Together.

When the sky had turned completely dark, they rose to leave. Johnno pulled Celia towards him as if he never wanted to let her go, and she snuggled into his arms, relishing the secure feeling of his strong arms around her.

They were walking along the river towards the car when Johnno suddenly stopped, pulled Celia towards him again, and spoke softly.

'I love you, Celia Lang.'

A heartbeat.

'I... I love you, too. I...'

But Celia was silenced by Johnno's lips meeting hers and whatever she had been going to say was lost forever in the intensity of his kiss.

Thirty

Had she really told Johnno she loved him? Celia studied the still-sleeping figure in the bed beside her. He looked so youthful, so innocent lying there as if he hadn't a care in the world. She did love him. She, who had vowed never to give her heart again, who'd believed men were not to be trusted, had fallen in love with one-time philanderer Johnno Henderson. And the miracle was that he seemed to love her too. At least he said he did. And, despite some evidence to the contrary, Celia believed he was a man of his word.

She hugged herself with delight. Then Johnno's eyes opened, his arms encircled her, and blotted out all thoughts.

When they emerged again, it was later than they'd intended but, as Johnno reminded her, they were on holiday, and time didn't matter.

'Would you like to take a look inside my new townhouse today?' he asked, when they were eating breakfast.

'Can we?'

'I don't see why not. I arranged for the deposit to be transferred on Monday, so I'm sure I can sweet-talk the agent into letting us have another look. It's vacant, so we won't disturb anyone.'

'Sounds good,' Celia said between sips of coffee. She felt Johnno was quite capable of sweet-talking anyone into anything, and it gave her a glow of satisfaction to know his allegiance was to her.

A brief call, and it was arranged. Ten minutes later, they were parked outside the complex Johnno had pointed out to Celia a few days earlier. So much had changed in those few days.

The agent's car drew up, and she handed Johnno the keys saying, 'I'll wait for you here, I'm sure you'd prefer to wander around on your own,' before focussing her attention on her mobile phone.

'This is it.' Johnno opened the door and stood aside to allow Celia to enter.

'Wow, I love it!' Celia moved swiftly across to the tall window and stood gazing out across the water before turning back to Johnno. 'It's perfect.'

'Wait till you see the rest.'

He led her upstairs to examine the bedroom with its ensuite and the room he'd designated as a study, before the two returned downstairs to the kitchen, laundry and living/dining areas.

'I hope you don't plan to decorate it in black leather like your Sydney pad,' Celia said with a smile.

'Not at all. I see it furnished in a softer style – more like your place. Soft, comfortable chairs and sofa, a low table, maybe wooden, and in terms of colour… I'll be guided by you there. As you've seen, I'm not much of an expert at interior design.'

'I'd love to help.' Celia's eyes gleamed at the prospect of selecting furnishings for the townhouse. 'But…' she frowned, 'what if you're not satisfied with my taste?'

'I will be.' Johnno sounded so sure, Celia thought it best not to question him further, but decided to ensure she consulted him every step of the way. It would be fun to decorate a place like this from scratch with, no doubt, a larger budget than she'd had setting up her own small apartment in Sydney.

'Then I'd love to.' Celia hugged him, slipping a finger between the buttons of his shirt to touch the skin on his chest, and they stood close for a few moments enjoying the warmth of each other's bodies.

'I guess we'd better go or the realtor will come looking for us. Otherwise, we could christen the place.'

Celia saw the twinkle in his eyes, but she looked at the tiled floor with a shudder. 'I think I'd prefer to wait till we had something soft to lie on, tempting though the prospect is,' she laughed.

'Spoilsport.'

But Celia knew he didn't mean it. A hard floor was not the most conducive surface on which to make love, no matter how appealing the idea might be.

'Well, guess we'll have to wait till our next trip.' He grinned and taking her hand, swung it as they walked back to the car.

'Coffee?' Johnno asked when they were back in the car. 'How about somewhere by the river?'

'Sounds good. I remember seeing a nice spot near the ferry wharf.'

They drove down to the river and found a parking spot without any trouble. The crowds from the weekend seemed to have disappeared, and the footpath along the river was almost deserted.

They located the café Celia remembered and ordered takeaway coffees, preferring to choose one of the many wooden benches to sitting in the café proper.

'That looks like fun,' Johnno said, pointing to a couple guiding their stand-up paddle boards along the smooth water. 'Maybe we should try it?'

Celia was considering her response when her phone buzzed. She slipped it out of her pocket, wishing she'd turned it off. She was enjoying this respite from the rest of her life. Being here with Johnno in this beautiful spot, she'd been able to relax, to forget for a while all the anxieties that still awaited her back home.

She was about to decline the call, when she saw Hannah's number and, worried that something might have happened to the children, pressed *Accept*.

'Han?'

'Mum, have you looked at Facebook this week?' Hannah had an odd note in her voice.

'Oh, darling. You know I don't bother much with that. I've more interesting things in my life. And I'm on holiday. What do you mean?' she added, wondering why Hannah had called her to discuss Facebook.

'It's this *MeToo* campaign – the one women in the States set up to share their experiences of being sexually harassed. It's gone viral, and I know some of the local women who've been posting. They're parents of my old friends – women you and Dad used to socialise with. You don't think…?'

Celia sighed. *Was this never going to end?*

She knew exactly what her daughter meant. 'No! He wouldn't – would he?' Celia remembered Bill's flirting with her friends. It was one of the things she'd hated about their dinner parties. But harassment?

Sexual assault? If she believed the women who'd already come forward to accuse Bill, why should ones they knew be any different? *But they're my friends*, she wanted to yell.

'You never guessed?'

'No!' But had she? Had that been another thing she'd chosen to ignore – the possibility that… If she'd thought anything, it was that they were willing to play along with the popular footy player, perhaps stopping short at a full-blown affair. At least he'd kept his affairs separate from people in their social circle – as far as she knew.

'The women, did they…?' Celia took a deep breath, her heart beating madly. 'Did they name him?'

'No. They don't name names – they just hashtag *MeToo* and sometimes cite the incident.'

Celia breathed a sigh of relief.

'It's all over the news too,' Hannah continued. 'And there's a Hollywood producer been named. It's big.'

But not Bill this time.

She'd read something about the campaign in one of the newspapers they'd flicked through waiting for their table for breakfast the previous morning. It seemed that masses of women were taking to social media to recount their stories of being sexually harassed – verbally abused, groped, molested, and even raped by bosses, teachers and friends, after an actress called on Twitter users to share their experiences using the *MeToo* hashtag.

But that had been in the US. This was Australia.

'What's up?' Johnno mouthed.

Celia shook her head.

'What do you want me to do? There's nothing… Do you need me to…?' But even as she asked, Celia knew there was no point in cutting her trip short.

They chatted for a few more minutes, Celia getting caught up on family news, then she hung up, her hand gripping the phone tightly. She was trembling.

'Bad news?' Johnno put a hand on her shoulder.

'No, not really. Just… Han wanted me to know that this *MeToo* thing has reached Australia and some people we know have posted on Facebook.'

'And Hannah thinks they're referring to Bill?'

'That's about it. It doesn't mean he's done anything – anything more than he's already been accused of. But Han… Oh, shit, Johnno. When is it all going to stop?'

'Do you want to go home?'

'No. There's no point. I don't want to spoil our time together.' But Celia knew it was already spoilt. The spectre of Bill Ramsay had managed to reach out to her even here and threatened to force itself between Celia and her new-found happiness.

Thirty-one

'What's the matter?'

Celia walked into the living area to see Johnno sitting deathly still, his iPad in one hand, his face ashen.

They'd been back from Noosa for a week, and it had been one of pure delight.

Celia had met with Bob Frazer and discovered that, to her surprise, Bill had decided to take his solicitor's advice and agree to all the conditions of the divorce. She couldn't quite believe it. It seemed that, after all this time, everything was going her way.

'What's the matter?' she repeated, leaning over Johnno's shoulder. Had he read something that troubled him? Had someone died?

Johnno held up the iPad so she could see the screen. It showed a breaking news item stating that a Sydney developer, previously thought to be of good character, had been found to be corrupt. The company was in receivership.

'What?' Then it struck her. 'Vernon Wright. Isn't that the company...?'

'It is.' Johnno's lips tightened. He dropped the iPad into his lap and dragged a hand through his hair. 'The bastard!'

'Is there anything I can do?' Celia asked helplessly. What could she do, apart from be there to comfort him? She reached out a hand to touch his shoulder, but he shrugged it off.

'I need to go,' he said, rising and looking around in a daze. 'I need to go into the office.'

'But it's Sunday.'

Johnno didn't appear to hear. He was intent on putting on his shoes, collecting his phone and car keys. As he reached the door, he turned as if suddenly realising she was there. 'I'll call you.' And he disappeared, the door banging shut behind him.

Left alone, Celia wandered around, unsure what she was going to do. As if sensing her distress, Bindi began mewing at her ankles. She picked the cat up and hugged her. 'Oh Bindi, I wish I could do something to help. Maybe…' *I'll make a special meal,* she decided. *For when he gets back. And I'll keep busy today. That'll make the time go faster.*

As if on cue, her phone rang. Hoping it was Johnno, Celia opened it quickly, without taking time to check who was calling. 'Hello,' she said eagerly.

'Mum? What's up with you this morning?'

'Oh! Han. I thought it was Johnno.' Celia wilted.

'Isn't he there? We wanted to invite you both over to lunch. Chloe and Owen will be here too.' Hannah's voice was filled with excitement due, Celia thought, to the approaching closure of the postal vote. They'd soon know the result. 'But *you'll* come, won't you?'

'Of course I will. Johnno had to go into the office. There are some problems.' There was no need to bother Hannah with Johnno's worries. Celia hoped he'd manage to fix things – and soon. She had no idea of the consequences to him of his developer going bust, but knew it would be a massive headache.

Celia promised to take some dessert as her contribution to lunch. Making her signature apple cake would fill her morning nicely, and maybe Johnno would call before she had to leave.

He didn't.

Things must be really bad. Since returning from Noosa, they'd been in constant touch when apart, whether it be a phone call or a simple text – maybe even a heart emoji. Johnno had quite a romantic side, she'd discovered, much to her delight. And he loved to surprise her with little gestures – flowers, texts, hugs and kisses when they passed each other in the kitchen. It was a new world for Celia who'd become accustomed to being treated like a lesser being during her marriage.

Telling herself she'd hear from him soon, Celia slid into her car and drove the ten minutes it took to reach Hannah and Ingrid's home.

Chloe, Owen and Simon were already there, and the little boy rushed to greet her, a wide grin on his face.

'We're all here now,' Hannah said with satisfaction. 'Thanks, Mum.' She took the apple cake from Celia and put it on the kitchen bench. 'Chloe has some news.'

Ingrid handed around glasses of champagne, while Celia stared at Chloe who was beaming up at Owen. *Were they...?* 'Chloe?'

Chloe blushed. Her right hand grasped Owen's, and she clutched Simon with the other. 'I... we... Owen and I are having a baby – a little brother or sister for Si.'

At the sound of his name, Simon tried to wriggle free, and they all laughed.

Celia gasped.

'And,' Owen added, 'we're getting married.'

Cclia gasped again. 'When?'

'Just a small affair. In a park we thought – maybe in December.' Chloe threw a glance at Owen. 'I don't want to be waddling down the aisle, or to have a fancy big wedding. Sorry, Ingrid,' she added, as if suddenly realising Ingrid would be eight months pregnant if she and Hannah got married in February as planned.

'No worries,' Ingrid said. 'I don't care if I'm as big as a house. I just want to marry this woman.' She gripped Hannah's hand firmly.

Celia suddenly felt isolated. This was her family. These were her daughters. She was happy for them, and with the news of another grandchild. But they were all so happy with their loved ones. She wanted Johnno to be here to share it with her, to hold her hand, to... Did *she* want to be getting married again? She wasn't free to marry, so it was a moot point.

She suppressed the thought and raised her glass. 'To Chloe and Owen.'

'Me, too, Grandma!' Si yelled.

'And to Simon.'

The group burst into laughter.

'Now, lunch,' Ingrid declared, and they all took their places around the table while Hannah and Ingrid set out platters of cold meats and salads.

Lunch was a cheerful affair, only Celia becoming lost in her own thoughts from time to time and surreptitiously checking her phone for messages. *What on earth was happening with Johnno?* She ached to hear from him, but knew she had to let him contact her in his own time.

*

Johnno was tearing his hair out. Papers were spread everywhere. He'd called Allan on his way into the city, and his faithful offsider had met him at the office, not unduly concerned at the loss of his own Sunday with the family.

'This is a disaster,' Johnno told him. 'But maybe we can save the day. We just need to find another developer who's willing to step in. We can't let the project die. There's too much at stake.' There was the reputation of the firm, Johnno's own reputation, not to mention the vast sums of money involved and – Johnno realised – his own purchase in Noosa which had been dependent on his profit. And his colleague, Ross, would have a ball. He'd always envied what he referred to as Johnno's luck and had been opposed to this project from the start, labelling it as too ambitious.

'I can't see how we can do it,' Allan said at last, when it appeared they'd investigated all avenues. 'We've been here all day and we're no further forward.'

Johnno looked up from the computer screen he'd been peering at for hours and saw it was getting dark outside. For a fleeting moment, he wondered what Celia must be thinking. But, if he couldn't find a solution to this, he'd have nothing to offer her. If only Guy were still here.

Even as he thought it, Allan said, 'If Guy were here…'

That's it, Johnno thought. *He'd contact the old man. His old friend and mentor would be able to advise him.*

'You go home, Allan,' he said, waving his colleague away. 'You have a family who must be wondering where you are. I'll handle this. I'll contact Guy.' But even as he said it, he wondered if Guy was in the country. He'd mentioned an overseas trip. What if he was somewhere on the other side of the world swilling pina coladas or some such thing, Sydney the farthest thing from his mind.

Well, it wouldn't do any harm to try, and he needed some fresh air. Instead of calling to check if his old mate was home, Johnno took his car and, with the top down to blow away the cobwebs of his muddled thinking, took the route to the eastern suburbs, to Rose Bay where he knew Guy and his wife lived.

If there was no one home he'd try phoning, and failing that, give up and consider the alternative future that awaited him – his reputation would be shot over this disaster for sure.

Johnno had never visited Guy at home before and was impressed by the large pale pink stucco structure which greeted him as he drew up outside the address. He wasn't sure exactly what he hoped the older man would do – could do – to help, but he'd helped Johnno out of a few scrapes in the early days of his career, as well as providing a willing ear when required.

Johnno took a deep breath and headed for the door. There was a light behind the fanlight window – a good sign. He pressed the bell.

'Johnno! What brings you here?'

'You're home. Thank God!' Johnno felt his knees buckle and he had trouble finding the words. 'I really need to speak to you. I'm up the proverbial shit creek and I'm hoping you may have a paddle.'

'Come in, lad. You're in luck. We just got back a couple of days ago. Had to cut our trip short as the wife's mother took ill. Marie's having an early night after a day at her mother's side in the hospital. You look like you need a stiff drink.'

Guy led Johnno into a comfortable study. A large wooden desk filled the oriel window and two well-worn leather armchairs sat either side of an empty fireplace in front of which stood an embroidered screen. It was like a room from another era.

'Get this down you.'

Johnno grasped the glass he was offered and took a gulp, the fiery liquid going straight to his head. It was only then he realised he hadn't eaten all day. He shook his head in an attempt to clear it.

'Now, what's up that has you driving all the way out here on a Sunday night? Couldn't it wait till Monday, or wouldn't a phone call have done?'

'No. I need… Hell, Guy. I don't know if I can get out of this one. Did you see the news today?'

'No. I've made a vow to avoid all news on weekends. Works pretty well, too.' He leant back in his chair, lifting his glass to his lips and asking before he took a sip, 'What's happened to get you into this state?'

Johnno tried to relax and gather his thoughts. He must look like a madman – he certainly felt like one. Was it only this morning he'd been in bed with Celia without a care in the world, his only concern where they'd go for lunch? Celia! He'd barely given her a thought since… But Guy was waiting for his response.

'It's Vernon Wright – the guy I lined up for the new town project. He's gone bust.'

Guy slowly lowered his glass. 'That's a bummer!'

'To put it mildly.'

'And the money's already been allocated?'

'All signed and sealed. The first instalment went into his bank last week. There was a delay in his signing, I should have anticipated some problems, but he assured me all was well. I believed him.' Johnno raked a hand through his hair, and took another gulp of the whisky, this second gulp hitting his stomach like the kick of a mule. 'The investors will be after my hide if I can't find a solution.'

'Hmm. Have you eaten?' Guy asked, as if suddenly aware of Johnno's reaction to the spirits.

'Not since this morning. I've been flat out all day trying to come up with a solution. Allan helped, but I sent him home before I headed over here.'

'Let me make you a sandwich. Come on through. Bring your drink. We may be in for a long night.' Guy rose and, with his glass in one hand, the whisky bottle in the other, gestured to Johnno to follow.

'No, I can't put you to that trouble.'

'It's no trouble, and I can't have you collapsing in front of me. I have a few ideas I want to run past you, but you'll need something in your stomach to allow you to process them properly.'

Johnno sighed and followed his companion through a wide hall and into a large kitchen. It reminded him of the kitchen in his parents' house, the house he'd grown up in. Central to the room was a large wooden table, clearly used both for family meals and for a number of other pursuits. Guy pushed aside a partly finished model ship and a bundle of knitting, before drawing out a chair for Johnno.

'Won't be a tick,' he said, foraging in the fridge before emerging with a loaf and a block of cheese. 'Lucky Marie did a shop and got a few basics. She's spent most of her time at the hospital since we got back. But you don't want to hear about that.'

After a thick cheese sandwich had filled the hollow in Johnno's stomach, the pair worked through the night. As daylight began to filter through the window, Johnno listened as Guy outlined the possible solutions.

'You think this South Australian firm is the shot?'

'They'd be my choice. But if I were you, I'd go down there to meet them. Frank Jenkins is the CEO. I can give you an introduction, but you'll have to take it from there. I don't have the credibility now I'm a superannuated gentleman.' Guy chuckled. 'But I'm sure he'll remember me. I knew his father well too, back in the day.'

'Adelaide?' Despite being up all night, Johnno was wide awake, maybe the result of the whisky. 'Thanks, Guy, I knew you'd come up with the goods. I'll get back to the office now, book a flight and do my due diligence on Jenkins' company.'

'You're not out of the woods yet. There's no guarantee he'll be able to help. But I read an article about him recently in the *Financial Review*, and your project sounds just the sort of thing to interest him.'

'Thanks again.' Johnno rose, and the two men shook hands.

Johnno couldn't wait to get back to the office. The fresh air cleared his head as he drove through the deserted streets on the way back to the city. He wanted to call Celia but it was too early. She'd still be asleep. He'd call later – or when he'd something positive to report; he was sure she'd understand.

He had no need for sleep himself. The adrenalin rush he always experienced at the start of a new project would carry him through. He had a good feeling about this. It was going to work. It had to.

Thirty-two

Celia was sitting in front of the television with a glass of wine and a Chinese takeaway. She hadn't heard from Johnno since he left in such a rush on Sunday. It was now Wednesday, and she was worried sick. She'd lasted out till yesterday before trying to call, had only reached his voicemail and been too proud to leave a message. He'd call when he was ready – but when would that be? And what was he doing in the meantime? Where was he? The phone in his apartment didn't answer either. She hadn't called his office, but maybe she should.

She was so stressed she almost missed the news item until, catching sight of some vision showing her and Bill at his book launch, Celia turned up the volume.

What she heard shook her to the core. She felt the sobs build up and found she was trembling. The announcer's voice continued:

As more allegations from young women emerge, footy legend Bill Ramsay has been found in his car in what is rumoured to be an attempted suicide. It is believed his wife of over twenty-five years is currently seeking a divorce. Speculation is rife as to what prompted this desperate act – was it the break-up of his marriage or the many allegations of sexual misconduct which are predicted to lead to a court case? This is Andrew Wilson of Channel Six News.

There followed several shots of Bill in his younger days holding up various trophies, one of their wedding day, one of a flashy young woman – maybe one of his accusers? Then the announcer moved on to another news item.

Celia shook her head in disbelief. *Bill? Suicide? Surely not? He wasn't the type. But was there a type?* The glass in her hand tipped over, spilling wine on the carpet. Bindi leapt out of the way.

The phone rang, and Celia saw her daughter's face on the screen.

'Mum, are you watching the news? Did you see?'

'Your dad. Yes. But,' she bit the inside of her cheek, 'it may not be true. We should…'

'It's on every channel. He's really done it this time. One even showed the shots of us taken at the march. I've been getting texts from all my friends to ask if it's true, if he's my dad. It's so humiliating. Chloe's been on the phone too. She didn't see it, but Owen's mum did and wanted to know if it's true, too. Are you okay? Do you want me to come over?'

Celia realised it must have been on the earlier news bulletins – and probably the internet. 'Han, I don't know any more than you do. I just saw it a few minutes ago. It's not something I ever expected your dad would do. And, no. I'll be fine. But thanks for the offer.'

'Do you think he did it to get attention – a publicity stunt? They said his car was parked outside his solicitor's house – in the driveway. Did he want to be found, do you think?'

'Honey, I don't know. Julian Clarke's house? I could call him, I suppose.'

Celia was having difficulty understanding why Hannah was so upset. Bill had behaved appallingly to her for years. But he *was* her dad.

'Will you? And let us know?'

'Okay.'

Celia picked up the phone, looked at it for a moment, then reluctantly dialled Julian Clarke's number.

'Clarke here.'

Celia drew in her breath before speaking. 'Julian, it's Celia. I saw the news. Is it true? How is Bill?'

'Not good. You know there were more accusations? A group of the women had got together and were going to sue. I think with the impending court case it all got too much for him.' He coughed. 'It all got out of hand. They were around him like flies around a honey pot – around me too – but then some saw a way to exploit old Bill and others jumped on the bandwagon.'

Celia heard him exhale heavily.

'I didn't get off unscathed either. You know Siri – my wife – has left me? This business has affected all of us. But Bill more so.'

Celia could imagine his expression, his pursed lips, his piggy eyes, and was glad she was on the other end of the phone and couldn't see him. 'But, Julian, did he really mean to…' Celia couldn't bring herself to utter the word.

'Difficult to say. He's still in a coma so I haven't been able to ask him. They say there may be brain damage. Does it really matter?' Julian sounded unlike himself, as if the usually bluff, confident man had been crushed by this turn of events. 'You'll be glad to know he signed the divorce papers yesterday,' he said bitterly.

'Did he…' Celia swallowed. 'Did he leave a note?'

'The police haven't said. There was no sign of one when I found him. He's in St Vincent's. Would you like to visit him?'

'No. Thanks, Julian, but no.'

Celia hung up, feeling no better than before the call. But she'd done it. What now?

Relief warred with despair and sadness that Bill had considered this his only option. She felt churlish refusing to visit him, recalling a conversation with her old friend, Bel. Bel had provided succour to her ex-husband during his terminal illness and, at the time, Celia had wondered how she'd feel if put in the same position. Now she knew. She felt nothing for the man she'd married, was still married to – but not for much longer. She had no desire to see him again.

Celia looked at the now empty wine glass – most of it had gone onto the carpet – and was making for the kitchen to refill it when her phone buzzed. Expecting it to be Hannah again, she didn't check the caller. 'Hi,' she said tiredly.

'Celia, I just saw the news item about Bill. Are you okay?'

'Johnno!' Celia sank into the nearest chair and clutched the phone as if it was a lifeline. 'Where are you? I've been worried sick.'

'I haven't been home for three days, apart from a quick shower and change of clothes. I had to fly to Adelaide.'

Adelaide? What was he doing there?

'You could have contacted me.'

'I know, I know. I'm begging your forgiveness yet again. Seems to be becoming a habit.'

Celia could hear the weariness in his voice, could imagine the lines around his eyes, the lock of hair falling over his forehead, his lopsided smile, and her heart missed a beat. She wanted to comfort him, to pat his shoulder, to hug him.

'But Bill – is it true? Did he try to commit suicide? How is he?'

'He'll live.' Celia knew she sounded callous, but she had difficulty feeling sympathy for the man.

'I'm sorry. I know it must make things hard for you. I should be there to help you cope with it. But I'm stuck here for another day. Can you manage till then?'

Celia started to say, 'Of course I can', but found her eyes filling with tears. She wanted him here with her right now, wanted his arms around her, wanted his comforting presence.

'My poor baby. I wish…'

'You couldn't have known this was going to happen, but you could have called to let me know where you were. Why are you in Adelaide?'

'It's a long story, but what it comes down to is that I had to line up another developer and the only one available is this South Australian guy. We're just finalising the contracts and I'll be on a plane back to Sydney. I'll call you as soon as I arrive.'

When Celia hung up, she saw she'd missed a call from Hannah, so called her back to fill her in on what she'd gleaned from Julian and was shocked by Hannah's bitter comment that she wished he'd managed it. Her daughter really did have a love-hate relationship with her father, but Celia knew she didn't mean her spiteful words.

Thirty-three

Wearing a fixed smile, Celia pushed through the crowd of media outside Isabella. The TV cameras must have set up at dawn. The thought that they'd frighten away customers passed through her mind as she fitted her key into the door, then closed it firmly behind her with a sigh of relief.

She needn't have worried. The customers arrived in what seemed to be droves, obviously either eager to be featured on the television news, or taking a ghoulish interest in the fact the owner's husband had tried to commit suicide. They stood around the shop whispering, and Celia took refuge in the back of the shop while Val took charge and managed to ensure most of them left with at least one purchase.

Bob rang mid-morning to check how she was coping and suggested making a press statement. He said he'd draw one up and email it through, but Celia knew *she'd* have to find the courage to walk outside and face the cameras.

She'd handle it just like one of the television ads she'd done as a model, she decided. Although she'd ended up a top model, that hadn't always been the case. In the early years, those advertising gigs had helped pay the bills.

She'd treat Bob's prepared statement like a script, she told herself, as she refreshed her make-up and tidied her hair, glad she'd chosen to wear her white linen suit and red blouse this morning. Though choice had little to do with it. Dreading facing the media she knew would pursue her, she'd been so flustered she'd grabbed the first thing that came to hand. The suit and blouse were garments she'd recently picked up from the dry cleaners and, still in their plastic bags, they'd been hanging on the back of the bedroom door.

Celia read through Bob's words again, took a deep breath and opened the shop door, hoping the crowd might have diminished. But, to her jaundiced eyes, there seemed to be just as many as there had been when she arrived a few hours earlier. They started to rush her then, obviously seeing the paper in her hand, fell back and stopped talking.

Clearing her throat, Celia began to speak, her modulated voice sounding much calmer than she felt.

When she finished there were a flurry of questions.

'Have you seen Bill?'

'Do you think your divorce contributed to his suicide attempt?'

'Is there any truth in the allegations?'

'Is it true his accusers have been paid off?'

'Will the proposed court case still go ahead?'

'How have your daughters taken the news?'

While Celia had expected some questions, the substance of them and the way they were asked left her breathless, and she felt a sudden coldness steal through her. She put up both hands to ward off any further questions.

'I have no more to say.'

She turned and went back into the shop, closing the door determinedly behind her and standing with her back against it, her breath coming in gasps.

'I don't think I can do this,' she said to Val, her voice trembling. 'Maybe we should close up for the rest of the day.'

'And let them think they've won? That doesn't sound like the Celia I know. Look,' she peered past Celia into the roadway, 'they're beginning to pack up. They got what they came for and they're off to meet their deadlines.'

Celia turned warily and peered out too. Sure enough, they were beginning to disperse. The street was clearing, and all who remained seemed to be genuine shoppers. She breathed another sigh of relief.

*

Unable to face her empty apartment, Celia drove to Hannah and Ingrid's home after work, relieved to be able to share her concerns with her daughter.

'Saw you on telly. You were on the early news,' Hannah greeted her. 'You looked elegant, like someone totally in control of the situation. But you weren't, were you? I detected a slight tremor at the corner of one eye. A dead giveaway.'

'I just read what Bob prepared, then turned and fled.' Celia gave a shaky laugh. 'It was the questions that floored me.'

'They didn't show those, but they surmised various scenarios as to what caused Dad to take this step – the divorce, Ingrid and me, his accusers. I guess that's what they asked you about?'

'More or less. But enough about me,' Celia said, when all three were seated with a glass of wine, and Mia was happily playing with her blocks on the floor at their feet. 'What have you girls been up to? How are the wedding plans going?'

Hannah looked across at Ingrid.

'Well, Han doesn't want to make too many plans till the results are in, but I keep telling her it's a foregone conclusion,' Ingrid said.

Hannah grimaced. 'Just over a week to go, then you can plan all you like. More important are Chloe and Owen's plans, Mum. They've decided on the date and venue. Didn't she call you?'

Celia realised how preoccupied she'd been for the past few days, worrying about what was happening with Johnno. She'd ignored a couple of texts from her younger daughter, assuming they were about Bill. She'd planned to call her later, but hadn't done so yet.

'No. I planned to call later tonight, when Si was asleep. Tell me.'

'It's to be December nineteenth – a Tuesday – at Headland Park with a small lunch afterward at Frenchy's.'

'How lovely.' Celia could picture the scene. It reminded her of the day she and Johnno had spent there, soon after she'd realised how much he meant to her. 'I will ring later.'

'No need. They just decided today, and they'll be over for dinner. We'd planned to call you to come too. She's dying to tell you all about it. She wants to have you included in the ceremony. I think she wants you to take what would have been Dad's place and give her away.'

Mention of Bill silenced the three again.

'I called Julian,' Celia told the girls, 'and Bill's still in a coma. I expect he'll let me know when that changes.'

'If you don't hear it on the news first,' Hannah put in.

'Right.' Bill was now big news. If his suicide attempt had done nothing else, it had brought him back into the limelight, and word was his book was flying off the shelves again.

'Will he recover, do you think?' Hannah asked. 'Did he really mean to kill himself? It doesn't sound like the sort of thing Dad would do.'

The questions took Celia by surprise, though it was what they were all wondering. 'I don't know, honey. It may have been a publicity stunt that went wrong. Your dad was always good at those. But Julian didn't seem to know either. Though to do it outside Julian's house...'

'That makes me think he wanted to be found, 'Ingrid said. 'Don't people usually do it in their own garage if they're serious about it – somewhere they're not going to be discovered till it's too late? That's what I'd do if...'

'Don't even mention it,' Hannah said, looking at her partner with frightened eyes. 'I couldn't live without you.'

'Don't worry, I've got too much to live for,' Ingrid assured her.

But their words made Celia wonder yet again what had prompted Bill to take his own life – if indeed it had been a serious attempt. Was the thought of a court case too horrific to contemplate? Was the resultant loss of his reputation too alarming a prospect? She supposed she'd never know. Even if Bill recovered fully – and Celia hoped he did – he was unlikely to reveal anything about his innermost thoughts to her or anyone else, except perhaps Julian Clarke, and he'd keep it to himself.

They were interrupted by a knock at the front door, the sound of voices and the pitter-patter of little feet, followed by Simon bursting into the room.

'We're having a wedding!' he shouted, his voice high with excitement. 'And Mummy's getting a new dress, and I'm going to be the... the...'

'The ring-bearer,' Chloe finished for him, entering with Owen and laughing at her son's antics. 'I guess you've heard the news, Mum? Save the date.'

Celia hugged all three. 'It's good to get some good news. We've been talking about your dad.'

Chloe's expression changed. Her face fell. 'I've been trying not to think of him. Is there any news?'

'No.'

'Well, then. There's nothing we can do, is there?'

'Chloe,' Owen remonstrated. 'He's your father.'

'I know, and I'm sorry he did this.' She hesitated, her eyes misting. 'But he didn't think that when he heard about this little one.' She looked fondly at Si who was trying to leap into Celia's lap.

Celia's phone buzzed and, seeing Johnno's face, she said to Si, 'Not now, sweetheart. I need to take this. Excuse me,' she said to the others, before pressing to accept the call and moving into the hallway, the blood rushing to her face.

'Johnno!'

'My darling. It's so wonderful to hear your voice. I plan to have things tied up here by lunchtime tomorrow; I'll be on the Qantas flight that gets in around four. Can I come straight to you?'

Celia felt her knees go weak. Only one more day. 'Of course. I can't wait.'

'Me neither. I saw you on the news tonight. That was a tough call for you. I wish I could have been there.'

'So do I. But I coped. I'm with the girls now.'

'Good. I'm glad you're not on your own. This damnable business has taken too long. I wish…' But the call ended abruptly, and Celia was left looking at a silent phone. Either he'd gone out of range or his battery had died. But the important thing was he'd be here this time tomorrow.

'Johnno?' Hannah guessed, when Celia returned beaming.

She nodded. 'He'll be back tomorrow.'

*

Next day the hours passed slowly for Celia who was filled with anticipation at the prospect of Johnno's return, and afraid something would happen to screw things up yet again. She seemed to have been living on a knife's edge for the past few weeks and just wanted everything to settle down.

Closing time came not a moment too soon. Celia had been counting the minutes and her heart skipped a beat when she received a text to tell her Johnno's plane had landed. Leaving Val to count the day's takings and lock up, she drove home, her heart singing.

Once in her apartment, she ignored Bindi's demands for attention, more concerned with making sure the champagne was chilled, along with a couple of glasses which she popped into the freezer. Then she set out a tray of cheese, olives, and some special fig and almond crackers and headed to the bedroom to check her hair and make-up, wondering if she had time to change.

She was still dithering, when the intercom buzzed. Taking a deep breath, Celia pressed the release button and made for the door. She had barely opened it when Johnno burst out of the elevator and took her in his arms smothering her with kisses. It was as if time stood still.

'Champagne?' Celia murmured, after what seemed like hours.

Johnno's clasp on her tightened. 'It's not champagne I need, it's you.'

Celia fleetingly thought of the champagne cooling, the glasses chilling, the tray of nibbles she'd set out so carefully, and allowed herself to be carried to the bedroom.

Thirty-four

'Shall we watch the news?' Johnno asked as he poured two glasses of Celia's favourite Chardonnay. He'd been back from his Adelaide trip for two weeks and had spent hardly any time in his harbourside apartment, claiming that Celia's home was much more comfortable.

'If you want.' Celia emerged from the bedroom having changed into a more casual outfit, but even in jeans and a tee shirt, she looked immaculate and elegant. *How did she do it? Most women of her age had run to fat or, at least, showed signs of aging. Celia still looked like the model she'd been over twenty years ago.*

'What are you looking at?' she asked, reddening. 'Is there something wrong?'

'Just admiring you and marvelling at my luck in finding you.'

She rose on her toes to kiss him, the wine forgotten for a moment.

When they drew apart, Johnno handed her a glass and went to turn on the television at the same time as Celia's phone rang.

'Leave it,' he said, but saw Celia glance at the screen with a frown.

'It's Julian Clarke,' she said nervously. 'What does he want?'

She answered the call just as the television screen came into focus showing a full-face shot of Bill Ramsay. Celia's cry of anguish came at the same time as the breaking news banner appeared at the foot of the picture: *Footy Legend Bill Ramsay loses his fight for life.*

Johnno hit the off switch and raced to Celia's side. She dropped the phone, her hands covering her face. Johnno picked it up.

'It's Henderson here, Clarke. I presume you're calling about Ramsay? Just saw it on the news. I'm sorry he didn't make it.'

Julian Clarke's normally strident voice was almost breaking. 'We thought he was going to pull through. He's lasted this long, and the doctors...' There was a pause, then he continued, 'They're telling me it was for the best. He'd never have been able to function fully, even if he'd managed to survive.'

Johnno heard the other man groan.

'We were best mates – from our first day at school. We did everything together. I don't know how...' He sighed. 'Tell Celia I'll be in touch.' Then, with a touch of the old Julian he added, 'I suppose she'll be pleased now.'

'No, she...' Johnno began, but Julian had ended the call.

Johnno dropped the phone and pulled a tearful Celia into his arms. He stroked her head as she wept for the man she'd once loved.

'I'm sorry, Johnno,' she sobbed. 'I hated how he treated me and the girls, but I loved him once. He was such a hero as a young man. I must tell the girls before...' She disentangled herself.

'They may already have seen it on the news,' Johnno said, but relinquished his hold on her and handed her the phone. While she made the calls, he hunted for the Scotch, he knew Celia kept for emergencies, knowing she'd need something stronger than white wine. She was suffering from shock, and he could do with a shot of whisky himself, suddenly realising that with Bill Ramsay's death, Celia was a free woman, free to do as she pleased, free to marry again.

'How did they take it?'

'Mixed reactions,' Celia said. 'Chloe is very soft-hearted and had a little cry, but Hannah is only sorry he didn't survive to see same-sex marriage come into law, and to see her and Ingrid married. She still wants revenge. Her lasting memory of him is him raging and calling her a butch bitch who was no daughter of his.'

'Did Julian say anything about the funeral?' Celia asked some time later when, after a couple of glasses of scotch, they were curled up together on the sofa. At Celia's urging, they'd turned on the television again and had been treated to a review of the life of the former football star.

'No. He said he'd be in touch. That's likely what he meant. You'll go?'

'Yes.' Celia picked at an invisible thread on her jeans and sighed heavily. 'I suppose I'll need to play the grieving widow. That sounds strange. I don't feel like a widow, I feel...' she thought for a moment – at least Johnno presumed she was thinking – before adding, '...as if a weight's been lifted. But it's the one last thing I can do for him.'

*

Eyes downcast, Celia, leaning on Johnno for much-needed support, followed the funeral procession into Waverley cemetery after a moving tribute to Bill at St Andrew's Cathedral in the centre of Sydney. The cathedral had been packed with friends, former players, and a few politicians, along with crowds of fans who'd come to pay their last respects, and, of course, the usual mob from the media.

It had brought back memories – she and Bill had been married in the cathedral all those years ago. That had been a happy day, a day filled with a sense of laughter and jubilation, of joy she'd thought would last forever.

Today the atmosphere was very different.

She'd be glad when it was over. It had taken a week for Julian to arrange the funeral, to contact all the necessary luminaries, and arrange a venue he considered suitable for a man of Bill's stature. Celia had snorted silently when he'd told her how he knew Bill would want to be sent off with a flourish, but she knew he was right. Her late husband – the phrase still felt odd – would have loved all the pomp and ceremony of the flash service in Sydney's premier cathedral and the many plaudits from his former colleagues.

Celia remained dry-eyed through the eulogies, but when Chloe's hand reached into hers as the soloist's voice rose in a soulful rendition of *Ave Maria*, the tears began to slide down her cheeks.

Chloe and Owen had accompanied them to the service, but had chosen not to go to the graveside, while Hannah and Ingrid refused to have anything to do with it. Celia was sad about their decision, but understood their determination not to be hypocritical. *Was that what she was being by attending, a hypocrite?* She didn't think so, and Johnno had agreed it was only fitting she should attend.

Johnno. She was glad he'd agreed to come with her today. She'd leant on him so much over the past week, as she tried to evade the media and come to grips with the fact there was now no need for the divorce for which she'd waited so long and fought so hard to obtain. She was free at last, but this wasn't how she'd wanted it to happen. Despite all Bill was and all he'd done to her and the girls, he didn't deserve to have died like this.

She stood at the graveside, shivering despite the warmth of the day, and moved forward automatically when asked to throw a handful of earth into the grave.

It was a relief when the ceremony was finally over, and Johnno led her back to the car. But, just as they were about to drive off, Julian Clarke knocked on the window.

'I'll expect you at the reading of the will. Monday, my office, eleven o'clock.'

He left without another word.

*

'Are you sure you don't want me to come with you?' Johnno asked, as they dressed on Monday morning. 'I can duck out of the office for a bit.' He radiated concern.

Celia was grateful for the offer, but said, 'No thanks, honey. This is something I have to do myself. I'll be all right. Julian said Bill had signed the divorce settlement. I guess this is just to confirm I'll get the share we agreed to.'

'Do you know how sexy you look today?' Johnno murmured, holding Celia close. For a moment, she drew strength from his nearness before pulling away.

Celia checked herself in the mirror, seeing only her usual workday persona, dressed today in a black business suit with a royal blue blouse, her feet encased in black high-heeled shoes. It was nice to be appreciated – one of the many things she loved about this man – especially today, with the reading of Bill's will hanging over her. Regardless of what she'd told Johnno, there was a niggling worry that things might not be as straightforward as she imagined. Maybe she should let him come with her – or have asked Bob?

She dismissed the apprehension that threatened to engulf her. No, everything would be fine. Surely Julian would have contacted Bob himself, if there had been anything controversial?

'Well, if you're determined to do this on your own, at least agree to meet me afterwards for lunch,' Johnno said, when they were both ready to leave.

'Okay.' Celia submitted to his hug and kiss, but her mind was elsewhere. She felt Johnno wince at her uncharacteristic lack of response. 'Sorry.'

'It's okay. It's a big day for you. Call me when you're through.'

*

'Mr Clarke's expecting you. He won't be a moment.' The svelte blonde receptionist gestured to a seat, and Celia took it, her hands playing nervously with the clasp of her bag, her foot tapping on the wooden floor.

In an attempt to calm herself, she fixed her gaze on a painting of a beach scene on the far wall, only to start with surprise at the sound of her name.

'Celia? Come through.'

Julian led her into a light-filled office where a large glass-topped desk took up most of the space. He seated himself behind it gesturing to Celia to take her place on the opposite side. Celia looked around in surprise. This was obviously Julian's office. Somehow, she'd expected the meeting to take place in a boardroom, around a large table, with others present. Julian and she were alone in the room.

Julian cleared his throat. 'I have here the last will and testament of Bill Ramsay, who was your husband at the time of his death.'

Celia flinched at the formality of his words.

'You have to understand that he was in the process of making another will, one which took into account the arrangements signified by the proposed divorce. Unfortunately, he passed away prior to that will being signed.'

Why so formal? It's as if he doesn't like what he's about to say. Maybe I get nothing. It might be better if Bill had left everything to charity –

or to his beloved football club. She didn't really care for herself, but it would mean she wouldn't be able to help the girls.

'As it stands,' Julian continued, glaring at her across the desk, 'as his wife when he died, you are his sole beneficiary.'

Julian continued to outline all the assets Bob had uncovered during the divorce proceedings, but Celia had ceased to listen. Sole beneficiary – that meant she got everything. Now she knew for sure Bill hadn't really intended to kill himself. He'd never have done that knowing everything he owned would go to her.

'You do understand?' Julian asked.

Celia nodded, unable to speak. Bill must be turning in his grave at the thought of Celia inheriting everything he'd spent his life accumulating. She got the distinct feeling Julian would take Bill's view and would have loved to alter the will.

Somehow, she made it out of the office and called Johnno.

'I'll be right there,' he said. 'Was it as bad as you expected?'

'Surprising. I'll tell you when I see you.'

Once they were seated in a café under Town Hall station, Johnno ordered coffees and sandwiches and took Celia's hands across the table.

'Now?' He raised an eyebrow. 'Ready to tell me what happened?'

'He left me everything,' she said, still finding it difficult to believe. 'He can't have meant it, Johnno. He wouldn't have wanted it this way. His death – it must have been an accident. He didn't mean to die.' Her eyes filled with tears.

'Hey, none of that. Whether he intended it or not, he took a calculated risk, and the result is you're going to be a rich woman.'

'But I can't accept it all. I know it wouldn't have been what he wanted.' She was silent, trying to work out exactly how she felt. 'I mean, we were to have an agreement – half was to be my share, not all of it.'

'It's yours, and you can decide what to do with it – give it all away if that's how you feel, but...' Johnno picked up her hands and kissed the knuckles of one, then the other, '...hadn't you decided to give some to the girls?'

'Yes, and there were other... Oh, I don't know what to do.'

'Well, there's no need to decide right now. It'll take a while for probate to be granted. You'll have time to think about it, talk to the girls, talk with your solicitor.'

'You're right.' Celia smiled a watery smile. 'What would I do without you?' But it wasn't really a question. Celia knew she'd be lost without Johnno in her life, without this man who'd given her a new reason to live.

Thirty-five

It was a glorious day for a wedding. And today was the big day.

Celia awoke in Johnno's arms, thrilled at the thought that, two months after the Australian Government had passed the same-sex marriage bill, her daughter was finally about to marry the woman she loved, and who loved her in return.

'Happy?'

'Mmm.' Celia snuggled up to her own hero. It had been a tough year for her, at the beginning of which she'd never have guessed this day would come. And the past few months hadn't been easy either. But now things had been settled to her satisfaction.

With Bob's help, and some judicial input from Johnno, she'd made the decision to use much of Bill's legacy to set up one scholarship for young players with his old team, and another at his old school. She'd set an amount aside in trust for their grandchildren, allocated appropriate sums to both Hannah and Chloe to enable them to purchase homes either now or in the future, and only retained for herself the amount she'd have received from the divorce settlement. With the remainder of her inheritance, she'd set up another trust to be managed by Bob and her daughters to be used for any suitable purpose which might emerge in the future.

She hadn't seen or heard from Julian Clarke since the morning in his office, all negotiations having been carried out through her solicitor. But she'd heard on the grapevine he was a broken man. Like her, he'd realised Bill's will sent a clear message the suicide attempt had been just that. Julian had been meant to find him earlier. But Bill's best mate, the man who was to have been his saviour, had been out drowning his own sorrows that evening, and had arrived too late to save Bill. It was almost poetic justice for the man who'd always wanted to be in the spotlight.

And now there was Johnno in her life. She'd been accepted into his family, and Cath and Walter had joined them all for lunch on Boxing Day, along with Johnno's brother and his family. The group had picnicked on Balmoral Beach where Simon had renewed his acquaintance with Johnno's nephews. Celia had enjoyed the sensation of being part of a large family and had found she had a lot in common with Johnno's sister-in-law. They all planned another get-together at Easter – on the Sunshine Coast this time.

'Penny for them?'

'Not worth even that. We should get up.'

'We should.'

But it was so soothing to lie there in Johnno's arms, that it was several more minutes before either of them made a move. Finally, it was Johnno who extricated himself first. He rose and opened the blinds to reveal a glorious day.

'Beat you to the shower,' he shouted, leaving Celia to move into the warm space he'd vacated, knowing she'd have to get up soon too.

When they were both dressed in their wedding finery – a pink linen suit for Celia and a grey one for Johnno – they enjoyed a breakfast of pancakes with strawberries and yoghurt, before setting out for the wedding venue.

Celia remembered Chloe and Owen's wedding only two months earlier.

'They were lucky to be able to make a booking,' Celia said as they drove along Military Road. 'The park can be booked out twelve months ahead. I think it was a cancellation.'

The car park already held a number of cars when they arrived, and Celia could see the rest of her family in the distance – a group on the grass near several white chairs and a table covered with a white tablecloth.

Celia and Johnno made their way over to the group which comprised Ingrid, Owen and his parents, the grandchildren, Jan with Graham and Andy, and several friends of both Chloe and Owen. It was a small gathering, just as Chloe had said she wanted. Celia's eyes misted over at the scene – the stunning Sydney Harbour in the background, the stage set for a beautiful wedding.

The ceremony was short and beautiful. Chloe and Owen both read their vows – words they had planned together – in ringing voices as Simon looked on in awe, for once stunned into silence.

'I now pronounce you man and wife. You may kiss the bride,' the celebrant said the familiar words. Owen and Chloe gazed at each other, their eyes filled with love. Owen brought his hand up to cup Chloe's face, his lips moving toward hers as she leaned into him in their first kiss as a married couple.

Celia, who'd managed to remain dry-eyed throughout the short ceremony, now felt the tears run down her cheeks. Her baby girl was married.

Beaming with happiness, the couple turned to face the group and raised their clasped hands to show off the rings, while Simon, clearly relieved the formal part of the day was over, ran across the grass to hug Celia.

Today was going to be a very different affair. Ingrid had booked a large wedding venue in Lane Cove and, according to Hannah, no expense was being spared.

'We're here!' Johnno's voice brought Celia back to the present as the car drew into the manicured grounds of the mansion where the wedding was to take place. The place was already busy with friends of both women, of Bob and Chris, and Ingrid's extended family.

As they walked towards the entrance, Celia saw Chloe and Owen standing there, and Simon ran towards them with a cry of, 'Grandma!'

'I thought I could avoid looking like a whale in a wedding party,' Chloe groaned, trying to smooth down the pale turquoise dress she was wearing as one of the witnesses at today's ceremony.

'You look beautiful,' Celia replied, kissing her on the brow. 'Where are the happy couple?'

'They have a room inside. Now you're here we can go in together.'

With a smile to Johnno and telling Simon she'd be back soon, Celia joined Chloe as they made their way inside the building and into a small flower-filled room where Hannah and Ingrid were drinking champagne and laughing.

'It's really happening, Mum,' Hannah declared, when she saw Celia at the door. 'Can you believe it?'

Celia hugged her daughter, then turned to Ingrid. 'Should you be drinking champagne?' she asked. 'You're...'

'I know. I'm eight months pregnant. But today's special. I don't think Robbie's going to mind too much.'

'Robbie?'

'Didn't Han tell you. It's a boy and...'

'He's to be called after me,' Bob said, suddenly appearing behind them. 'As a witness to the wedding of these lovely ladies and the father of their two children, I think it's only right, don't you?' he said with a smile.

'Of course.' Celia accepted the glass which Ingrid was now offering her. 'But we don't all want to be drunk before the ceremony.'

'I hope not. I'm sticking to orange juice,' Chloe said.

'Don't you two look amazing?' Celia said to Hannah and Ingrid as she suddenly noticed their matching outfits. Both were dressed in white V-necked ankle-length dresses with flower garlands filling the necklines. They'd clearly chosen the full-skirted dresses in an attempt to hide Ingrid's burgeoning baby bulge, and both were to carry the posies of freesias and rosebuds that were currently sitting on the table and filling the room with their fragrance.

'Are you ready, ladies?' The cheerful and elegantly dressed wedding celebrant joined the group. 'It's time.'

'I'll go.' Celia slipped out. Hannah and Ingrid were breaking with tradition, arguing that neither of them needed to be *given away*. They were giving themselves to each other.

Joining the others in the front row of chairs covered in white and sporting wide pink bows, Celia was grateful for Johnno's hand which immediately grasped hers. Her emotions today were quite different from they had been at Chloe's wedding. There would be no tears today, unless they were tears of joy. She was thrilled that Hannah and Ingrid were finally able to make this public commitment of their love for each other. It had taken so long for them to get to this day, and she couldn't be happier for them.

The crowd grew silent as a trio in the corner began to play *Only You* and, despite herself, Celia felt her eyes mist, as Hannah and Ingrid entered the room where the wedding guests were waiting, necks craned to get their first glimpse of the brides. They were followed by

Chloe and Bob and all four walked slowly between the two rows of chairs towards the celebrant.

Celia barely heard the words of the ceremony which was over all too soon, and the trio joyfully started up again, this time with the well-known Abba tune *I do, I do, I do*. The ceremony, for which they'd waited so long, was over.

They all gathered outside, and a friend of Bob and Chris lined everyone up for the mandatory wedding photos, then Hannah held her flowers up in the air.

As she fixed her gaze on her mother and threw the bouquet, Celia's hands rose as if of their own volition to catch the posy of freesias and pink rosebuds. Her daughters cheered as she blushed.

'Guess we'll have to make it legal now, too,' she said.

'Is that a proposal?' Johnno's grin was infectious.

'I will if you will."

Heedless of their audience, Johnno drew Celia close, the flowers crushed between them, their heady fragrance rising to envelop them with the promise of a rich future together.

The End

Read a Preview of Band of Gold

One

'I don't want to be married anymore.'

The band of gold, symbol of our twenty-five years of marriage lies on the table between us. I am stupefied, unable to speak. Tears prick my eyes as my first coffee of the day grows cold beside me. The sun is shining brightly through the kitchen window. The turkey is sitting on the kitchen bench waiting to be cooked. My parents, daughter, brother and sister, along with her husband and children are due to arrive in five hours' time. The house is redolent with the scent of pine needles and Christmas pudding. It's Christmas morning and my world has collapsed.

'What do you mean?' I finally utter, thinking this must be Sean's idea of a bad joke. My mouth goes dry. My head begins to spin. The bottom has dropped out of my world. I look over at the man I have loved for over twenty-five years, his bushy greying blonde hair, his ruddy cleanshaven cheeks. He looks no different from any other morning. He's wearing the bright yellow tee shirt we bought on our holiday in Bali last year. His steely blue eyes meet mine. This isn't happening.

'I can't do this anymore, Anna.' His waving arms take in the kitchen including me, 'All this; family, house, job. I need to get away.' He pushes his chair back from the table and strides out of the kitchen. I sit there in a daze, my mind going round in circles. *Is it too late to call off Christmas lunch? How can I even think of such a thing? Does Sean mean he's going to leave right now? How will I explain his absence? God, this is really going to be the Christmas from Hell.* But mean it he does. 'I'll be in touch.' His head peers around the door. I see his small backpack hanging from one shoulder and a weekend bag in his left hand.

'What?' The sight of him standing there looking so calm goads me into action. 'What the hell… Are you joking?' My voice rises as I jump up from the table, my feet slipping on the tiled floor. 'You're not serious. You can't do this.' I grab Sean's arm, forcing him to drop his bag. I begin punching him, my blows ineffective on his rugged body. 'You bastard! You shit! It's Christmas!' I yell. 'Everyone's coming. You can't do this to me!' I take a deep breath. 'Sit down!' I demand. 'We can talk this through.' I try to sound sane, though it's the last thing I feel. My stomach is churning. 'Maybe we…' I'm not sure what I'm saying.

Sean's hands grip my upper arms, and he holds me away from him. 'Don't make this harder, Anna. It's over.'

My heart drops. This is real and it looks like it's no sudden impulse. He smiles grimly and picks up his bag. He's off, making for the front door with me flying behind him, still yelling. I follow him to the car, pulling on his arm in an attempt stop him. 'Sean…' I'm wailing now. I stand there in the driveway in my summer nightie. 'You can't do this. Come back inside. We can sort this out. Think of Lissa. What…?' But it's too late. He's in the car. The door slams shut and he engages the central locking. I rush to the car window and hammer on it making one last ditch attempt but it's useless. The window slides down.

'Just leave, it, Anna.' And he drives off.

I stand there, immobile, gazing after him. I hear a scream and realise it's coming out of my mouth. The tears begin to run down my face, but I don't have the energy to wipe them away. I taste their saltiness on my tongue as I lick my lips. I don't know how long I remain there unable to think clearly. It's as if all this is happening to someone else; that it's a dream and I'll eventually wake up, describe it to Sean and we'll both have a good laugh about it. But it's no dream. Eventually the warmth of the sun reaches me and my body comes alive.

From somewhere I find a tough determination. Christmas lunch must go ahead. The turkey has to be cooked with all the trimmings and I have to make it through family questions and joyful gift giving before I can curl up into a ball of misery.

*

'What a pity Sean couldn't be with us.' My mother sighs for the hundredth time. 'Fancy his aunt demanding his presence at this time of year, and with so little notice too. He's a good man.' She smiles in my direction and I manage to smile back. I'm only relieved they bought my lie: an urgent trip back to Scotland at the behest of his aged aunt. I've noted the worried look in Lissa's eyes and know that my daughter hasn't been fooled. Time enough for her questions later. The worst is almost over.

'It's been lovely, Anna!' My sister Jan gives me a hug and I'm enveloped in a fog of her favourite scent, expensive. 'Hope Sean makes it back for New Year. Remember you're coming to us this time.'

I mutter something as my stomach plummets. I've forgotten the next family get-together is only a week away. *How long can I keep up the pretence? If they would just all go, go and leave me alone.*

'Are you sure everything's all right, Mum?' Lissa's eyes seem to bore right into me, threatening to reveal my innermost thoughts. 'I mean, Dad's trip, it was awfully sudden, wasn't it?'

'I'm fine.' I manage a wide smile. 'You enjoy the rest of Christmas. A party tonight you said? Anyone special?'

As I expect, the question diverts her from my own situation.

'Will. We met last week. It's early days but I think you'll like him.'

She spins out of my hug and stands in the doorway, an excited twenty-two year old with her life ahead of her. She tosses back her hair, thick and blonde, reminiscent of her father when we first met, and gives me a serious look. 'You would tell me. If anything was wrong, I mean.'

'I'm fine,' I repeat, and close the door before she can ask anything more. Alone at last, I turn and lean my back against the door, oblivious to the fact that, if she turns round, Lissa will see my slumped body against the frosted glass. I give a sigh of relief as I hear her car start up and drive off. I slide down to the floor, legs outstretched and arms hanging loose like a rag doll. I begin to sob uncontrollably.

Eventually I manage to push myself up and walk past the dining room where the table has been cleared of most of the remains of Christmas lunch. Only a few guttering candles and the remnants of hats and crackers lie abandoned on the white linen tablecloth. Peeking into the kitchen I note that, despite my protestations, the family have completed the washing up and piles of clean dishes and leftover food, tightly sealed in plastic wrap, are waiting for me to tidy away.

My hand reaches for the handrail on the stairs. My instinct is to call Gina, my best friend and yoga instructor, but she's told me she's spending Christmas with friends in Byron Bay. Otherwise I'd have invited her to join us despite Sean's derisive comments about aging hippies. But Sean isn't here. Another sob escapes me.

I push open the bedroom door seeing the empty space on Sean's side of the bed, usually cluttered with his current book, reading glasses, watch and other impedimenta waiting for his return. They are gone, like him.

Another sob wells up and I brush it away with the back of my hand. I catch sight of my running gear pushed to the side of the ensuite where I left it on Christmas Eve. *Was that only yesterday?* I debate calling Gina's mobile, and actually have my phone in my hand, but I think better of it and drop it back into my pocket. I'm not ready to talk to anyone yet.

*

I need fresh air. It's five o'clock on a glorious summer's afternoon. All over Australia everyone and his dog is celebrating Christmas, and I'm standing here relieved that my family has gone. I don my running gear and take out the car.

When I reach Manly beach I can see that most of the celebrating groups are winding up for the day. Parents are gathering up children, chairs and blankets. Fathers in shorts, their naked chests bronzed by the sun, are dumping the remains of Christmas lunch into the overflowing bins. Some are desultorily playing a game of beach cricket while others have succumbed to post prandial lethargy and are lying prone while squawking seagulls demolish the remains of their food.

I walk slowly to the edge of the water, my shoes making deep imprints in the packed wet sand. I look out at the vastness of the Pacific Ocean and stretch my arms up high. I wish I could sail away, away from having to explain to everyone and be the subject of their pity. I stand, oblivious to the waves lapping against my favourite running shoes, and gaze up at the buildings etched against the skyline on top of the cliff. Northern Beaches Girls Grammar School is where I spend every day during term time, teaching English to a combination of eager and reluctant young girls. It's going to become my lifeline now.

Turning, I begin to run. If I can run fast enough maybe I can forget, forget that my husband has abandoned me, that, at the ripe old age of forty-seven, I've become a statistic, an abandoned wife, a single mother.

By the time I stop, the beach has become deserted. It's too early for the evening parties and too late for the family gatherings. I gaze along the sand, deploring the debris my fellow humans have left behind and begin the run back. Halfway there, the memory of Sean's face at the breakfast table rears up again and I slow to a halt and drop to my knees in despair, tears once again streaming down my cheeks.

'Are you all right?' The voice comes from somewhere above my head. I look up into a pair of concerned brown eyes framed by black-rimmed spectacles. Floppy brown hair is falling over the lenses and, as I look, a hand pushes back an errant lock.

'Are you all right?' the voice repeats. 'Is there anything I can do?'

I rise slowly, gulping back the tears, embarrassed to have been caught in such a state. 'I'll be right, thanks.' I brush the sand from my knees and I wish I could brush away his presence as easily. 'Really,' I assure my prospective rescuer, and run on, feeling his eyes boring into my back as the distance between us lengthens.

To read more of Anna's story, you can purchase Band of Gold here:

http://maggiechristensenauthor.com/books/band-of-gold-2/

From the Author

Dear Reader,

First, I'd like to thank you for choosing to read A Model Wife. I hope you enjoyed Celia's story and, if you've already read Broken Threads and Isobel's Promise, I hope you enjoyed meeting Celia again. I really enjoyed writing her story in this book.

If you did enjoy it, I'd love it if you could write a review. It doesn't need to be long, just a few words, but it is the best way for me to help new readers discover my books.

If you'd like to stay up to date with my new releases and special offers you can sign up to my reader's group and you'll also get a FREE book.

You can sign up here:

https://mailchi.mp/f5cbde96a5e6/maggiechristensensreadersgroup

I'll never share your email address, and you can unsubscribe at any time. You can also contact me via Facebook Twitter or by email. I love hearing from my readers and will always reply.

Thanks again.

Acknowledgements

As always, this book could not have been written without the help and advice of a number of people.

Firstly, my husband Jim for listening to my plotlines without complaint, for his patience and insights as I discuss my characters and storyline with him and for being there when I need him.

John Hudspith, editor extraordinaire for his ideas, suggestions, encouragement and attention to detail.

Jane Dixon-Smith for her patience and for working her magic on my beautiful cover and interior.

My thanks also to early readers of this book –Helen and Louise, for their helpful comments and advice, and to Annie of *Annie's books at Peregian* for her ongoing support.

And all of my readers. Your support and comments make it all worthwhile.

About the Author

After a career in education, Maggie Christensen began writing contemporary women's fiction portraying mature women facing life-changing situations. Her travels inspire her writing, be it her frequent visits to family in Oregon, USA or her home on Queensland's beautiful Sunshine Coast. Maggie writes of mature heroines coming to terms with changes in their lives and the heroes worthy of them.

From her native Glasgow, Scotland, Maggie was lured by the call 'Come and teach in the sun' to Australia, where she worked as a primary school teacher, university lecturer and in educational management. Now living with her husband of over thirty years on Queensland's Sunshine Coast, she loves walking on the deserted beach in the early mornings and having coffee by the river on weekends. Her days are spent surrounded by books, either reading or writing them – her idea of heaven!

She continues her love of books as a volunteer with her local library where she selects and delivers books to the housebound.

A member of Queensland Writer's Centre, ALLIA, and a local writers group, Maggie enjoys meeting her readers at book signings and library talks. In 2014 she self-published *Band of Gold* and *The Sand Dollar, Book One of the Oregon Coast Series*, in 2015 *The Dreamcatcher, Book Two of the Oregon Coast Series* and *Broken Threads*, in 2016 *book Three of the Oregon Coast Series, Madeline House*, and in 2017 *Champagne or Breakfast*, set in Noosa on Australia's Sunshine Coast, in which characters from the Oregon Coast books make a reappearance. In 2017, she also published *The Good Sister* which follows the story of Bel who readers first met in *Broken Threads*, when she returns to her native Scotland to visit her terminally ill aunt, and in 2018, *Isobel's Promise* which continues the story of Bel and Matt from *The Good Sister*.

Maggie can be found on Facebook, Twitter, Goodreads, Instagram or on her website.

www.facebook.com/maggiechristensenauthor
www.twitter.com/MaggieChriste33
www.goodreads.com/author/show/8120020.Maggie_Christensen
www.instagram.com/maggiechriste33/
www.maggiechristensenauthor.com/

Also by Maggie Christensen

A relationship after a failed marriage. Can Anna love again? Does she dare?

Anna Hollis believes she has a happy marriage. A schoolteacher in Sydney, Anna juggles her busy life with a daughter in the throes of first love and increasingly demanding aging parents.

When Anna's husband of twenty-five years leaves her, on Christmas morning, without warning or explanation, her safe and secure world collapses.

Marcus King returns to Australia from the USA, leaving behind a broken marriage and a young son.

When he takes up the position of Headmaster at Anna's school, they form a fragile friendship through their mutual hurt and loneliness.

Can Anna leave the past behind and make a new life for herself, and does Marcus have a part to play in her future?

A story of loss, grief and the struggle to survive against adversity.

Jan Turnbull's life takes a sharp turn towards chaos the instant her eldest son, Simon takes a tumble in the surf and loses his life.

Blame competes with grief and Jan's husband turns against her. She finds herself ousted from the family home and separated from their remaining son, Andy.

As Jan tries to cope with her grief and prepares to build a new life, it soon becomes known that Simon has left behind a bombshell, and her younger son seeks ways of compensating for his loss, leading to further issues for her to deal with.

Can Jan hold it all together and save her marriage and her family?

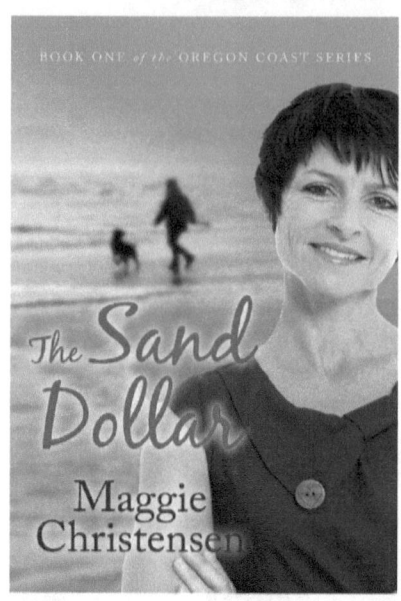

A well-kept secret and a magical sand dollar. Can Jenny unravel the puzzle of her past?

What if you discover everything you believed to be true about yourself has been a lie?

Stunned by news of an impending redundancy, and impelled by the magic of a long-forgotten sand dollar, Jenny retreats to her godmother in Oregon to consider her future.

What she doesn't bargain for is to uncover the secret of her adoption at birth and her Native American heritage. This revelation sees her embark on a journey of self-discovery such as she'd never envisaged.

Moving between Australia's Sunshine Coast and the Oregon Coast, *The Sand Dollar* is a story of new beginnings, of a woman whose life is suddenly turned upside down, and the reclusive man who helps her solve the puzzle of her past.

Dreamcatchers trap bad dreams – but sometimes nightmares escape.

Ellen Williams, a Native American with a gift for foretelling the future, is at a loss to explain her terrifying nightmares and the portentous feeling of dread that seems to hang over her like a shroud.

When Travis Petersen – an old friend of her brother's – appears in her bookshop *The Reading Nook*, Ellen can't shake the idea there's a strange connection between her nightmares and Travis' arrival.

Suffering from guilt of the car accident which took the lives of his wife and son, Travis is struggling to salvage his life, and believes he has nothing to offer a woman. But Ellen's nightmares come true when developers announce a fancy new build, which means pulling down *The Reading Nook* – and she needs Travis' help.

Can Ellen and Travis uncover the link between them and save her bookshop? And will it lead to happiness?

A tale of dreams, romance, and of doing the right thing, set on the beautiful Oregon coast.

She thought he couldn't hurt her anymore...

Madeline House

Maggie Christensen

She thought he couldn't hurt her anymore – she was wrong.

When Beth Carson flees her controlling husband, a Sydney surgeon, and travels to Florence, Oregon, she is unsure what her future holds. Although her only knowledge of Florence comes from a few postcards found in her late mother's effects, she immediately feels at home there and begins to put down roots.

But Beth's past returns to haunt her in ways she could never have imagined. Distraught over alarming reports from Australia and bewildered by revelations from the past, Beth turns to new friends to help her.

Tom Harrison, a local lawyer, has spent the past five years coming to terms with his wife's death, and building a solitary existence which he has come to enjoy. Adept at ignoring the overtures of local women and fending off his meddling daughter, he is intrigued by this feisty Australian and, almost against his will, finds himself drawn to her when she seeks his legal advice.

What forces are at work to bring the two together, and can Beth overcome her past and find a way forward?

Set on the beautiful Oregon Coast this is a tale of a woman who seeks to rise above the challenges life has thrown at her and establish a new life for herself.

Rosa Taylor is celebrating her fiftieth birthday with champagne. By the river. On her own.

After finishing her six-year long affair with her boss, Rosa is desperate to avoid him in the workplace and determined to forge a new life for herself.

Harry Kennedy has sailed away from a messy Sydney divorce and is resolute in kick-starting a new life on Queensland's Sunshine Coast.

Thrown together at work, Rosa and Harry discover a secret. One that their employer is desperate to keep hidden. To reveal it they must work together, but first they must learn to trust not only each other but their own rising attraction.

Are these two damaged people willing to risk their hard won independence for the promise of love again?

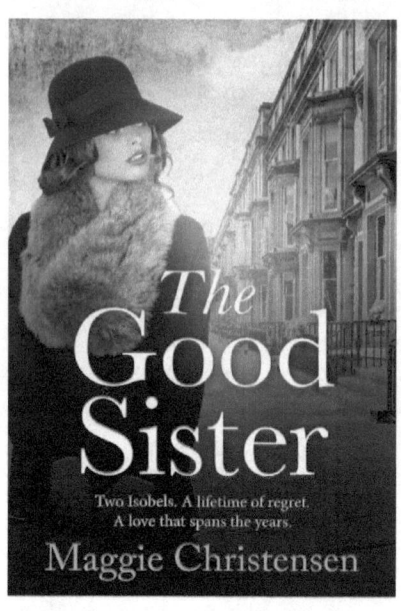

Two Isobels. A lifetime of regret. A love that spans the years

In 1938, as the world hurtled towards war, twenty-year-old Isobel MacDonald fell madly in love. But fate and her own actions conspired to deny her the happiness she yearned for. Many years later, plagued with regrets and with a shrill voice from the past ringing in her ears, she documents the events that shaped her life.

In 2015, sixty-five-year-old Bel Davison returns from Australia to her native Scotland to visit her terminally ill aunt. Reading Isobel's memoir, she is beset with memories of her own childhood and overcome with guilt. When she meets her aunt's solicitor, events seem to spiral out of control and, almost against her will, she finds herself drawn to this enigmatic Scotsman.

What is it that links these two women across the generations? Can the past influence the future?

A promise for the future. A threat from the past. Can Bel find happiness?

Back in Sydney after her aunt's death, sixty-five year-old Bel Davison is making plans to sell up her home and business and return to Scotland where she has promised to spend the rest of her life with the enigmatic Scotsman with whom she's found love.

But the reappearance of her ex-husband combined with other unexpected drawbacks turns her life into chaos, leading her to have doubts about the wisdom of her promise.

In Scotland, Matt Reid has no such doubts, and although facing challenges of his own, he longs for Bel's return.

But when an unexpected turn of events leads him to question Bel's sincerity, Matt decides to take a drastic step – the result of which he could never have foreseen.

Can this midlife couple find happiness in the face of the challenges life has thrown at them?